BAD WATER

N. M. Browne

kristell-ink.com

Hardback ISBN: 978-1-913562-13-7

Paperback ISBN: 978-1-913562-14-4

EPUB ISBN: 978-1-913562-15-1

Cover design by Ken Dawson

Typesetting by Book Polishers

Kristell Ink
An Imprint of Grimbold Books
5 St John's Way,
Hempton,
Oxfordshire,
OX15 0QR
United Kingdom
www.kristell-ink.com

For William, Morgan, Owen and Christa.

CHAPTER ONE

OLLU

THERE WAS GOING to be a storm sure enough. Ollu hadn't yet got her Ma's weather sense, but she knew this was going to be a Big One.

'It's getting proper choppy, Ma. What do you want me to do?' She had to shout. The wind ripped the words from her mouth, whipped stray strands of fair hair from under her billowing head scarf. She heard Ma curse, then yell from below deck, 'Your call, Ollu. What do **you** want to do?'

She heard the weariness in her voice. *Pox and piss.* This wasn't right.

Ollu wedged the tiller in place to keep them heading straight. Wisdom had it that this was Bad Water. Wisdom might be right. The sky darkened, hiding the sun so that the toxic solar cut out and the paddles that moved the Ark puttered to a halt. She didn't like the way the turby that powered the lights clicked and whirled, or the way it trembled on its mountings as the wind gusted. The river tide was flowing so strong, she couldn't fight it, even though it was sending them the wrong way, further into Bad Water.

She opened her mouth to yell down to Ma, then shut it. Ma would already know. Ma always knew where they were and where they were going. She must be toxic sick indeed to stay below with disaster looming. She hadn't been right since she'd had the twins. She was too old. All that feeding and fussing over them was wearing her out. Ma's state frightened Ollu as much as the storm.

She chewed the inside of her mouth, reckoning up their chances. The Ark was a civilised craft, fabricked to weather any ordinary storm. It had lasted for getting on four generations and wouldn't fail them. The trouble lay with the trail barges the Ark pulled behind. One time when Ma was a girl the Ark had nearly turned over when a Big One hit the stock barge, and Ma's sister died unhitching it to save them. Ollu felt sick at the thought.

If she unhitched the trail barges they lost everything that sustained them: the livestock, the goats – Marla, Blinky and Lalo, plus the six chickens, their crop barge, with its harvest of herbs and vegetables, their business, their trade stuff, the salvage. Ma had taken some crazy risks and gone further down-stream than was safe, but they'd got a haul all right – the best ever. They'd have bartered it easy, for new supplies, food, maybe even old tekk. If they lost it, they'd be on short rations for months. Maybe worse than short rations. Ollu tasted blood from her bitten cheek. What if she didn't unhitch the trail barges and the Ark was sunk? She was not up to this. This was Ma's call.

A wave slapped hard against the bow. The Great River was a powerful vengeful bitch when the mood was on her. She could batter the Ark to driftwood. Ollu glanced at the lowering black sky. There was worse to come. She had no choice.

She took a deep breath, the steadying kind. She leapt nimbly across the gap between the home barge and the stock barge, setting the whole platform rocking and the hens flapping in their coop. 'Hey, sweeties, come, come.' As the goats butted against her, investigating her pockets for treats, she untethered them as deftly as she could, so they would have a chance at swimming to safety. She was crying as she grappled with the latch to open the coops. She would have to cover the crop barge against the brackish water, just in case they ever found it again. Looking at the size of the waves, she knew the odds. Best bet was that they'd lose everything.

6

Her fingers moved stiffly as the first heavy drops of rain started to fall. The storm had brought the cold, enough to make her shiver in her thin cut-offs and smock. She gripped the wet deck with her toes and tried to rub some life back into her arms. There was still the crop-barge and the trade barge to decouple. The rain was getting heavier. There wasn't time to mess around. Better not to think about it. She eased herself over the side of the pitching stock-barge and slid into the icy, heaving water. 'Your permission, River' she mumbled. Ma said it was only superstition to think that the River was alive, but Ma couldn't hear her, down below.

It was colder even than she'd expected, cold enough to take her breath away. She felt the powerful current dragging at her, pulling her like one of the demons Ma didn't believe in. Ollu gripped the edge of the barge with both hands, closed her mouth against the poisons in the water and pulled herself hand over hand to the crop-barge. She fought to cover them with the plastic sheet, the one she and Ma had fabricated. The trail-barges which held the salvage were already tightly covered in tarpaulins, tied securely with ropes, like parcels at gift-giving time. Perhaps they would somehow be all right. Her fingers were so cold they hurt, but she tried not to think about anything but doing what had to be done. She needed to separate each trail barge from the others, so they might not sink. She dared not let go of the rough lip of the barge's side, or she might have been swept away.

First, she needed to separate the trade barges from the crop barge. Putrid Piss, but the rusty chains were hard to move. It was impossible with one hand, hers were still as small as a child's though she was old enough to be a woman. If she used both hands she risked being swept away, but it was a risk she had to take. She caught her right palm on the sharp edge of the hook, sharp pain making her sick for a moment. She couldn't give up. It took four goes and her hands were cramping by the time she somehow got the trick of it. She maneuvered the great hook that held the crop barge connected to the trade barge into the right position then, using both her feet, pushed with all the strength in her legs to release the coupling and set the trade-barges free.

It gave way all of a sudden and she was left gasping, clinging to the chain. She watched the trail barges that held the careful work of years bob out of sight, lurching and rocking in the high waves until they were swallowed up in the cavernous maw of darkness. Her whole body shook and she couldn't stop making a strange choking noise – a kind of sobbing. She'd saved the Ark and ruined them, all in the same moment.

The torrents of water pouring from the sky were more like the curtains in the Daso's manor than normal rain. It was getting harder to grip the side of the barge, but she had to move quickly. She'd found the knack of it now and even though her fingers were almost numb, it was still a little easier to uncouple the crop barge than it had been to shift the hook of the trade barges. That just left the livestock.

She was whimpering a little through her closed mouth by the time she got there. She was condemning Marla, Blinky and Lalo to death. If she'd been stronger she might have got them on board the home barge somehow, but she was slightly built, and scrawny with it. It took all her strength to pull herself out of the greedy water. The Great River took everything and was hungry for human souls. Ma said that was toxic superstition too, but Ollu believed it. She felt the river sucking at her, eager to swallow her up. She'd been blooded as a baby so that it would know her as a Barger, but even Bargers died of drowning or water fever. The Great River didn't care, whatever the cultists said. Her muscles were shaking and it took two goes to heave herself up and flop like a beached fish on the barge. Marla, hungry as only a goat could be, tried to eat her hair. She picked up one of the hens, Claudia, and tucked her under her arm, then jumped the gap between the bucking stock-barge and home. She threw the bird below, yelling a brief warning to her mother. Did she have time to fetch another? She took off her sodden scarf and with thick, unresponsive fingers tied it around Lalo's collar. She grabbed Chloe, who flapped wet wings in her face, and hauled

Lalo towards the Ark, gripping the ungrateful hen in her other hand. It was hard to stay upright now, in the driving rain and wind. The gap between the stock barge and the Ark was filled with churning water and her voice was stolen from her mouth as soon as she opened it.

'Jump!' She jumped, and the goat followed. When she looked back the stock-barge was wallowing alarmingly. There was no time to go back for the rest of the stock. She lay down flat on the deck of the Ark, so the wind could not knock her over, and fumbled with the final hook to set the stock barge free. She could not bear to watch it go.

Her hands lick with blood and rain, she pulled Lalo and Chloe with her into the dryness of below. She had done it.

It was shockingly silent when she managed to slam the door shut. The roaring in her ears stopped. Ma took one look at her and said calmly, 'Clean out that cut with sweet water and dry yourself. Is all secure up top?'

'I think so.' Ollu's teeth chattered, and her legs were all bumpy with the cold.

'You've lashed the tiller?'

'Yeah. I think I may need to steer, though,' she said.

'You've gone blue.' Her mother moved towards the hatch.

'You can't go. You'll be swept over.'

'There's a bit more of me than there is of you,' her Ma said, with a trace of humour. 'See to the babes. I'll tie myself on.' She unhooked the rope from its place by the door. 'The babes want changing,' she said over her shoulder, and hauled herself through the hatch. The roaring of the wind began again and rain poured into the cabin, making an enormous puddle on the floor in the brief moment the hatch door was open. Her mother banged it shut and Ollu rushed to secure it. One of the babes, the boy one, cried out and Ollu took him from his hammock, pressing him to her tightly.

'Hush, Ma'll be back soon,' she said, and hoped that it wasn't a lie. The girl babe slept soundly in her hammock, her tiny thumb in her mouth. The worrying rocking of the barge seemed only to help her sleep. Ollu peeled off her wet clothes with one hand, clutching the babe to her. He was warm, his head sticky with sweat from Ma's embrace, and he smelled sweetly of Ma and milk.

Ollu let her tears flow. They'd been doing all right. They'd managed everything between the two of them after Davey came of age and left them. Then Ma had got with the babes and everything had gone wrong.

She looked down at the squalling, skinny creature in her arms and tried very hard to hate him. His hand reached out to her and his touch was soft as moth wings. She wished he and his sister had never been born, but they had been born, and so she had to try and keep them alive. She hugged the boy fiercely, so that he cried his new-born mewling cry again.

The light in the cabin guttered and died, leaving her in semi-darkness. The wind-turby must have broken. Then she saw the lightning crack the sky and a moment later thunder rumbled overhead. 'Great River, keep us safe,' she murmured as the barge lurched and she patted and rocked her half-brother to calm.

CHAPTER TWO

BUZZ

BUZZ TRIED NOT to show that he was afraid. He didn't think he succeeded. Either way Pa was too busy wrestling with the controls of the small plane to notice. It wasn't hot in the cabin but, in the green light of the control panel, his Pa's anxious face glistened with sweat. The wind took them as if they were a paper plane, and the rain darkening the window was so heavy it was like trying to see through a waterfall. The *Queen B*, the comp they were seeking on the Isles of Briton, should be near now. They'd follow the coordinates of last contact. They couldn't be more than a few miles away. They'd so nearly made it.

'Buzz!' His father had to shout over the tumult. 'I can't land as planned. You know what to do?'

The tightening in Buzz's throat and chest made it difficult to get his words out.

'Sure, Pa. But you can land this!' Buzz wasn't sure that was true. The comp was dead and he had got nothing from it that made any sense for hours. They couldn't even see if they were over land or ocean and they had no data that might have told them. They'd been flying blind for what seemed like a lifetime and every muscle in his body ached with the tension and the strain of trying to see, of trying to help, when both he and Pa were helpless.

'We'll be fine, son.' Pa said, his calm voice barely audible above the noise of the wind and rain. Buzz tried to respond, but suddenly the ground, the hard, black shape of something large and solid, loomed up to meet them. There was a screeching, a shrieking, the sound of tearing, of metal scraping, of screaming, of jarring impact. The plane buckled and broke. His Pa cried out, and then there was silence.

*

Buzz had lost some time: hours maybe. His internal clock wasn't working properly. It was light and the sky was green. No. Delete that. He was hanging upside down and it was the ground that he saw beneath him, lush, verdant and almost within touching distance. 'Pa?' Buzz's voice still worked, which was a surprise. There was no reply. They should have still been in the plane, the plane he and Pa had built together; the plane the two of them had flown for so long across the open sea to this place somewhere on the Isles of Briton.

So, where was the plane?

He was no longer in it. Buzz carefully turned his head. He couldn't see much, and for a moment he panicked that there was something wrong with his eyes. Then he remembered. His crash helmet, the helmet that that restricted peripheral vision, and blocked his ears. They must have crashed. Nothing hurt, which was strange unless he were dead.

It came back to him then. He remembered the moment the ground had hurtled up to meet him, the moment everything had crumpled and splintered and shrieked as loudly as the storm. He didn't expect to be alive, but he was, wasn't he? Because dead men did not ask questions. Did they?

He was caught in a tree by his harness. Had they bailed out? He didn't remember bailing out, but then his memory was so confused it was hard to say what had happened. He didn't think they'd had time, so he wasn't caught by his parachute, but by his seat belt. Where was the rest of the plane? Where was Pa?

His guts churned. He had a bad feeling. It was time to show that he was made of the right stuff. Pa put a lot of store in being made of the right stuff. He shut his mouth and tried to make his brain work. Hanging upside down was disorienting. He needed to get himself the right way up.

The ground was not that far away. The fall wouldn't kill him. He wriggled his arms free of the restraints. He took a deep breath, released the catch on his belt, shut his eyes and let himself fall.

He landed on his feet, but as they had gone numb they collapsed under him so he fell backwards onto his back. Landing hurt. The grassy ground was harder than it looked. It was also wet. He felt the moisture on his neck. When he opened his eyes and looked up he could see the wreckage of the plane, and his father. Oh, Christ in Gaia! His father was hanging there right above him. His limbs were all splayed out and bent all wrong. Dried blood discoloured his face and his dead eyes were open, staring right down at Buzz, seeing nothing.

Buzz swallowed down the cry that was in his throat. He had to keep breathing, in and out; get control of himself. He was made of the right stuff. He was. He had to take control. He shut his eyes and counted to twenty, then thirty slowly.

When he opened them, his father was still in the tree and breathing was still much harder than it should have been. He must not cry. He must take control. He must think. What, for Gaia's wounds, did he do now?

He sat on the ground, rocking back and forwards to soothe himself. Then he started to imagine his father's voice shouting at him, telling him to be a man of civilization, a man of science and reason and courage. He knew it wasn't his father's voice. Of course he did; his father couldn't speak, would never speak again, but he did as he was told in any case because that's what a good son did.

First off, he should try to ascertain his location and his security status. All he could see was trees. As for his security status? How could he tell? The comp was as dead as his father. He hadn't heard the flow of its data stream rippling through his thoughts since before the crash. That empty space in his head bothered him like the empty socket of a lost tooth. It felt all wrong, and if he was in danger he had no way of knowing about it in advance. The thought made him shiver.

He should deal with the crash site. There were bits of wreckage on the ground, but most of the plane was up the tree with his father, who still very obviously dead and still staring at the ground as if there was something about it that he found puzzling. It looked like the engine and sealed compartments were still intact, if up the tree. It was the fuselage, nose and wings that had crumpled as if they had been made of paper. In fact, because weight had been an issue in the plane's construction, they had built it of metal that was deliberately thin as paper so that it could act as a glider where necessary, to save on fuel. Pa had even lost a few pounds before the trip.

Buzz thought about that for a minute. For all his efforts, Pa was still heavy, a big man. There was no way Buzz was going to be able to lift him down out of the tree. He was going to have to let him fall and then what? Pa would want to be buried, to give something back to the earth which had always sustained them. Buzz sat down heavily and finally removed his helmet.

It was a good job he was made of the right stuff or he wouldn't have been able to cope.

He had to overcome his squeamishness about touching his father's body. He did not know exactly when Pa had died, but he knew that if he did not move the body before the stiffness of death set in, his father would be stuck there, up that tree till his carcass rotted and the birds took his eyes. His father would have wanted all the goodness in his body given back to Gaia's good earth. It was what Buzz wanted too.

There was a parachute with the gear. He laid it on the ground so that he could wrap his father in it. Then he climbed the tree. The dead man's arm was caught in a mesh of branches and his seat belt had got so entangled Buzz had to use his knife to saw through wood then hack through the fabric of his father's belt. He removed everything that held his father in place and he still did not fall. Oh, Gaia's wounds! Buzz forced himself to put his hands to the corpse, to push him out of the tree, to let him fall. He blocked his ears so he would not have to hear the meaty thud of the landing. Then he scrambled down from the tree and threw the parachute over the body as fast as he could, so that he would not have to see the ruin of his father's face.

It wasn't a quiet operation, especially as Buzz could not keep from sobbing the whole time. Pa would not have been impressed.

Buzz removed his father's boots. He ought to have stripped him of his flying suit which had taken so much work to make, but he couldn't do it. He had used up all his courage just touching him. It was enough that Buzz would bury him and say the right words. He could not be expected to be perfect.

He dug until even his tough hands were blistered and he was as drenched with sweat as with rain water. When the hole was big enough he wrapped the corpse properly in the parachute. He argued with his father in his head about that. Yes, it was a fine thing that he ought to have kept for trade or to use as a shelter, but he was going to use it as a winding sheet, OK?

He could not be expected to be perfect.

It took all his strength to roll the body into the hole, which was probably too shallow.

He covered the silk shrouded form of his father with the wet earth. He was glad he did not have to see the corpse's unforgiving face. He found some stones to lay on top of the grave and scratched on the biggest of them the symbol of the cross in the circle – the symbol of Christ crucified for the purification of Gaia. Then, when he had caught his breath, he made another, smaller hole for all their precious gear. His fingers were bleeding by this time so his hasty burial of the wreckage would not have satisfied his father's exacting standards. But it would have to do. He buried all the fragments of Pa's great construction he could find: the engine, the corpse of the comp and the sealed equipment boxes. He could not carry them, so he would have to come back later when he'd found what they'd come for, if that was even possible.

They'd made no contact with their friends in the Isles for ten years. They'd tried every relay, every bandwidth, every trick they knew to patch a signal from their comp *The General* to *The Queen 'B'*, the one working comp they'd ever found in the vast degenerate, fallen lands outside their compound. Pa didn't know if the comp had failed or if his friends who used it had died. That's what they'd come to find out.

Standing by his father's grave, knowing he could never go home, Buzz wondered why they'd risked everything to find a comp. Pa was so keen to hold onto 'civilisation' and 'international communication' it was possible he was not entirely sane. Wherever Buzz was, it didn't feel much like civilization to him.

He covered the two graves with leaves and branches to disguise them and said his prayers by each in turn: the grave of his father and the grave of his goods, the plane he built and all the possessions that marked him as a man of Science, of Civilisation and a servant of Christ in Gaia.

He said all the words of the service of the dead that he could dredge from his memory and then he walked away. Pa was dead, and he was utterly alone.

CHAPTER THREE

OLLU

THE BABES WERE finally asleep. It had taken a while for them to stop screaming and now in the empty place in her head that their silence made, all she could hear was the roaring of the storm. It was bad. Ollu hastily tied the babes to their hammocks with a couple of her clean headscarves, careful to bind the scarves around their chests with their arms over the top so they could not wriggle and strangle themselves. It was not easy to do in the dark, and it was risky, but Ma had been out there too long and Ollu was afraid. What if Ma had fallen overboard? What if she had got sick? The rain still battered the thick glass of the port hole, but at least the storm was no longer overhead.

Ollu hauled on her bright yellow placky waterproofs, 'A' grade stash from before the Chaos and good as new. She struggled with the ancient, tekky fastenings, zippers, poppers and toggles. Those Preekers always overdid everything. She tied up the goat, stuck the chickens in a cupboard so they could not cause trouble, then opened the hatch and entered another world; a place of darkness and demons, wind and water.

She dropped to her knees and half crawled, half slithered her way across the surface of the barge. There was no point calling out to her mother. The wind was too loud; it filled her ears with a wild, insistent roaring. A breaker higher than the rest crashed over the barge and knocked the air out of her. She clung to the guide rope so she would not be swept away.

Oh, God have mercy, pray to Allah and the Great River that her mother had not died.

It was impossible to see anything for certain, but Ollu thought she could see a dark blur, her mother's bulk, a solid thing to aim for in the storm. At least Ma hadn't fallen overboard.

Ollu made it to the stern. She struggled to her feet, grabbing on to her mother for balance. Her mother did not move, or speak. Ollu felt her heart freeze. Was Ma dead?

'Ma!' She shook her mother hard, but nothing happened. She could not see her mother's face, could barely make out her outline, it was so dark. She seemed to be sprawled, kneeling, her hand still clasping the tiller. Somehow she was still steering them straight through the deepest water at the middle of the river. It was where the tide flowed fastest, but where they were least likely to get snagged by flotsam and jetsam or by the shore side trees. Ollu tried to prise her mother's hands off the tiller. Ma's grip was firm as rusted iron, and as unyielding.

She found her mother's face by touch alone. She was hot. At least she wasn't dead. Not yet. The dead were cold. She let out the breath she'd been holding in a kind of shaky sob. Ma wasn't dead, but she had a fever, that much was sure. If her mother had the water fever, the wet plague, they would all die, and quickly.

Ollu touched her mother's face again. There was no doubt. She was on fire with heat. Ollu screamed all the bad words her mother would never let her say into the wind, until her throat was raw. The wind whipped them away as if they'd never been said.

Ma always said if she got the fever Ollu was to leave her land-side and fend for herself. Ma had made her promise. It was wet-plague that did for the Preekers. The Bargers only made it through because they knew what to do and they did it. There was no mercy if there was plague. You could fire a boat if there was plague. There was no salvage if there was plague. Everything had to burn if there was plague. But was this plague? How could she tell?

There had been no cases for a long while. The word was that plague only lurked in Bad Water. Most times this would have made Ollu feel safer, but they were *in* Bad Water, had been since the birthing. Ma had risked everything for good salvage, enough to keep them going while she nursed the twins plus a bit extra to put by for the babes' Naming, should they survive their first year.

What had Ma done?

Ollu buried her own face against the sodden fabric of Ma's shirt. Even through the cloth her mother felt hot as a genny, hotter than the furnace on the Island of Spring. What was the right thing to do? If she left Ma to die, the twins would follow soon after.

'Ma, Ma! Wake up! Tell me what to do!'

Her mother groaned. 'Ma what's wrong? Is it plague?' Her Ma tried to get to her feet but the rope that tied her to the deck had got caught. Ollu worked at it with wet, clumsy hands. She was shaking with fear. 'Ma! Ma! Stay awake, please.' Her Ma didn't have much truck with weakness, but Ollu couldn't help her voice coming out in bursts, broken by sobs. She got the rope undone and her Ma's heavy body sagged against her so that Ollu nearly buckled. She braced herself but then a wave sent her stumbling, nearly knocking them both over the side. Ollu grabbed her Ma's bulk with one hand and the rope with the other. She had to be strong enough to hold on. She had no choice. Her Ma was heavy, a big woman still bloated with baby weight.

'Is it plague, Ma?'

Ma groaned and seemed to shake her head, though it was hard to tell in the dark. 'Babies,' she said.

'They're 'kay, Ma.'

Her mother's hand was on her neck now, trying to balance her own weight. Ollu got her shoulder underneath her mother's arm to offer what support she could. 'Baby... fever,' her Ma muttered. 'Can't catch it.' At least that's what Ollu thought she said. She would have been overwhelmed with relief had not another wave threatened to wash them both overboard. It wasn't the plague.

She wouldn't have to ditch Ma overboard. She thanked God, Allah and the Great River each in turn.

'Hold on, Ma,' Ollu said, securing the tiller with one hand to keep their course steady.

Ma was barely with it, but she understood the danger and tried to help as Ollu battled to support them both and get them to the cabin. The barge rocked and tilted dangerously with their joint weight, but somehow they held on. Ollu kicked the cabin door open and they both fell inside, waking the babies who began to howl. River water slopped in from the deck, pooling on the scrubbed wooden floor and Ollu had to put her whole weight against the hatch door to get it shut and secured. An army of machete men could not have pushed any harder. Her mother lay like a corpse on the floor and Ollu could do nothing but lie beside her, panting and sobbing and shivering, while the babies screamed with all the strength in their three-day-old lungs.

By the time Ollu was able to get back on her feet, the babes had screamed themselves to sleep. It was past dawn, but the surging grey water was running so high it all but covered the windows. She fumbled around to find the oil lamp they used in emergencies, fending off Lalo, who bleated hungrily. Once they'd had a lecky-torch, but there'd been no batteries for it for years. Her tinder box was safely secured and once she got the lamp lit, she felt better. The hens were making horrible noises, beating their wings against the cupboard door, so Ollu let them out. The hens were fine, the goat was fine, the babes were fine; her mother was not. She was lying where she'd fallen in the puddle of river water. She was still breathing, but raggedly, and she burned with fever. Ollu dragged Ma's dead weight away from the hatch and stripped off her wet clothes. She ripped Ma's shirt in the struggle. Ma opened her eyes briefly. 'Cassie,' she said, glassy-eyed.

Ollu could not lift her mother onto the narrow bunk bed; she did not have the strength and she didn't even try. She managed to roll Ma onto a mattress on the floor and get her comfortable. She made her drink a sip or two of sweet water. By the time she had done that the babes were awake and squalling. They were still so tiny she was afraid to handle them. She picked up the boy baby, feeling his fluttery heart beat under her fingers. It startled her so much she nearly dropped him. She put pillows under her mother's head and upper back so she could put the babies to each of her mother's breasts in turn. They made greedy sucking sounds, grunting and snuffling as they went about their business before falling into a milky sleep. Her mother only moaned. Ollu had to hope the fever hadn't made the milk bad: The babes were too young to thrive on goat's milk.

When that was done, she changed them while they slept, and milked the goat who was trying to eat the rope that tethered her. The smell in the cabin was rank. She let herself rest for a moment. They were still alive so far, and it was her job to keep them that way.

It was hard to make herself get back on her feet. Her legs felt wobbly and weak, but there was no one else. Whatever needed to be done, she would have to do it. Her mother was right – as ever. Ollu had to get her to Cassie's, shore-side. Cassie's was the nearest farmstead on their trade circuit, the closest to Bad Water. Cassie had birthed ten live children and half of them still lived. She would know what to do and, should her mother die on the way, Cassie might have the twins fostered on her estate. Ollu did not want to think about that, but Ma liked her to prepare for the worst, to be ready.

She forced herself to gulp down some goats' milk and eat the dried fish with biscuit that they kept for lean times. She even made herself eat some of the seaweed Ma said was good for her, though it always made her gag. She needed her strength. She had to steer the boat and do what repairs she could to get them safe.

She made the babies safe, then led Lalo and the hens out on deck where they could do less damage.

'Ma, I'm going out.' She whispered, but if her Ma could hear, she didn't respond. She looked ill, writhing around as if in pain. They'd used up all their birch leaf and willow bark some time back. Cassie had a trained healer on her estate. Maybe she would have the herbs Ma needed?

Up on deck, Ollu could see things were not as bad as they might have been. The turby that gave them lecky-light had sheared off, but they would be able to make another from salvage. She knew they had the stuff they needed on the trade barge.

It was a moment before she remembered that they'd lost everything on the trade barge.

The tide had turned and they were at least heading away from worse water. She would have to fix the tide-turby before it turned again. That meant going underwater. With no one to help her, she'd be done for if she got entangled in weeds or wreckage down below. Maybe the sun would come out and she could run on solar. Maybe Lalo would grow wings.

The Great River was wide here, as broad as a lake and she strained her eyes for any sign of the stock or the barges, but all she could see was the still raging water and the marshes of the distant banks. When the river was low you could see the ghosts of Preeker buildings, spires and scrapers marking dreg waters, salvage grounds and difficult steering, but the river was too high. This was a dangerous time. It was hard to know when you might be floating over barge-ripping debris. She tied her wild frizz of hair back off her face with her head scarf and peered at the river ahead. She refused to think about her mother and the babes below. Not yet. She could not cope with everything.

Chapter Four

Buzz

WALKING AWAY FROM his father's grave was probably the hardest thing Buzz had ever done. It was harder than crashing, harder even than burying him and that had been bad enough. Leaving him there in a hasty grave, dug in foreign soil, leaving him and every connection Buzz had with home; that was something else.

Buzz couldn't think of anything for a while. Pa would have hated the way he stumbled along. He tripped over a tree branch hidden in the high grass and fell, sprawling on his face. That shock brought him to his senses. He was on his own now. Pa was no longer there to yell at him and remind him of his blessings. He wasn't a neobarb, one of the fallen, but that rare thing, a gifted boy born to an educated father in a haven of civilization. He was a beacon of Gaia's light in a world grown dark. Pa always went on about that, as if he wasn't sure Buzz was worthy of his good luck.

He didn't want to think about Pa. All he could see was his dead face staring down at him, as if the only father he had ever known was that corpse with the blind eyes.

Anyone would be afraid in his position. He wasn't a coward. It was time to get his thoughts in order and make a mental list of his assets. It was what his father would have done.

First and foremost, he was alive and uninjured, apart from the cut on his palm and the heavy stone that had lodged in the hollow cavity of his chest where his heart had been. Second, well, he had managed to salvage his emergency kit in the small backpack he had rescued from the tree. In that he had a knife, a lighter, an automatic, a heat blanket, a purifier filled with good water, and one packet of emergency rations – enough for one day. Third, his father had trained him to be tough. He would need to be. He was wearing only his undershorts and over shirt and it wasn't enough.

The sound of nearby voices made him realise the cold and the wet were the least of his problems. The voices were loud, male and too close for comfort. Time to pull himself together.

Buzz picked the closest tree and shinned up it quicker than a wild cat, even though it was slick and slippery with rain. He had to get his loud and frightened breathing under control. He'd been in danger before. He knew what to do. The owners of the voices were close. He strained to listen. The accent was strange to him – so strange he wasn't even sure if they were speaking his own language. The men made no effort to be silent. A dog barked and he felt his panic rise. All dogs at home were bred to guard and he had once seen what his father's Rottridger had done to an intruder who'd broken into the compound. That memory had filled his nightmares ever since. Buzz was trembling, which wouldn't do. He didn't want to set the tree branch shaking. He tried to focus only on the voices, which were coming closer. They did not sound friendly.

A man with a deep voice was laughing.

'… you're not wrong. We don't need worry about the old bitch – we got the sons so she's over. But – once our machete-men are done with their boozing and binting – we need to rethink the defences. Especially along the river. The Dasos were laissez – lucky for us. I'm not going to get caught making the same mistake: a gaffer-man can only have what he can hold.' Even though the man's low voice was hard for even Buzz's keen ears to hear, the tone was clear. This man was frighteningly determined.

'It's a guzzling lot of land, Stitch, a massive holding and we'll need to use fighting men to tend it. We finished too many of the yokel drudges and as for the survivors...' The second, lighter voice, tailed off as if reluctant to spell out what must have been obvious.

'The rest will work for us or starve.' Deep-voice said shortly. 'They know Daso's done for so. Live or die – that's their choice...' his voice carried on but became little more than a drone as the men moved away.

Buzz couldn't see much from his position, high in the tree's crown: he hoped that meant he couldn't be seen. He only got a glimpse of the two figures from behind the patchwork curtain of foliage. They were dressed oddly, in old-timers' biker leathers and thin, plastic rain capes. The only bit of homespun he could see was in the strips of purple cloth they had tied round their heads. One man was dark skinned and black haired, the other fair: both were bearded. One carried an antique Kalashnikov slung over his brawny shoulder and the other held a spear. Buzz knew that his eye sight was exceptionally good – according to Pa anyway, but there were times when he questioned it. He was certain of one thing though, these men were the neobarbs Pa was so worried about, men of violence to be avoided. He thought about reaching for his own weapons, but he'd have to let go of the branch and his chances of making a noise or even falling were too high. He was not going to risk that. It was not cowardly to be cautious.

Buzz's stone-like heart was beating so fast it felt as if it might shatter. What if the men noticed the freshly dug graves? What if they spotted him?

He waited until the voices died away, until he could no longer hear the tramp of their feet as they strode through the wood, and tried to make sense of what he had heard. The two men were obviously the new owners of this land, won from someone else in a fight. He did not know what a yokel-drudge was, but he had gathered these men would be looking for more of them and he was pretty sure that was not the future his father had planned for him. He swung cautiously down from his high hiding place and sniffed the air, heavy with the acrid scent of a bone-fire, such as the neobarbs outside the compound used to burn their dead at home. The men had spoken of a river. A river meant traffic, boats, ships even. Maybe tekk and civilization, if there was such a thing still in the Isles.

He did not want to leave the grave behind, but he could not stay close by, not if it meant getting involved with the purple-banded men. He took his rations from his backpack and began to eat the nuts, dried fruit, and biltong slowly, trying to make it last. There wasn't nearly enough food. Eating slowly was supposed to make you less hungry, but it didn't work.

Pa had been so sure that they would be able to live off the land, or find allies, trade their knowledge for their keep. All his ideas now seemed to Buzz to be hopelessly optimistic. They had focused so much upon copying the journey of Pa's forbears, crossing the broad ocean, proving that civilised men could still roam the globe as they had before Gaia flooded the world, that they hadn't thought much about what they might find when they arrived. At least, that was how it seemed to Buzz. Maybe Pa had some plan, something more specific than just finding the *Queen B*. But, if so, it had died with him. Buzz had no idea what it was or what he was supposed to do without Pa giving him orders. He picked his way across the heavy mud and marsh of the miserable, sodden Isles of Briton and felt for the first time a strange kind of lonely, frightening freedom.

CHAPTER FIVE

OLLU

OLLU MANNED THE tiller until the sky brightened, the wind dropped and the Great River grew calm. She knew which way to steer. That was the easy part.

Cassie's Farm had been on their trade route all her life. Cassie Daso was a powerful woman with wild black hair and skin as dark as midnight. Her voice boomed louder than the Ark's fog-horn, her laugh made the ground shake, but her smile made everything seem fine. Her bulk was a sign of her success as a farmer, and all her men were well fed and cheerful. Joe G, the twins' father, was one of Cassie's men – though Ma had never made any claim on him. If all else failed maybe Joe G could take the twins. Ollu did not want to think about what would have to happen for Joe G to take the twins.

Ma would pull through. She was as tough as Cassie herself, though not quite as large. Ma was a fighter: she'd fought to keep the Learnings of the Bargers alive, to keep the Ark pure and safe, to make sure she got a good price for their trade, for everything that mattered. She'd never let anyone on the barge who was not family. Even for the birthing she'd staggered landside. Men were never allowed, not even Davy now that he was grown. Joe G had never placed a foot on her planks.

And that was another problem. Ollu couldn't carry her

mother off the barge on her own. And then there were the twins to worry about.

Ollu secured the tiller to steer a straight course back through familiar water. Good water that was usually safe and clean, though who knew what the storm might have disturbed? It was quiet. The perfect moment to fix the tide turby, but Ollu hesitated. This part of the river should have been thronged with small craft of all kinds, not just the rigs of other Bargers. But there was no one there. She toyed with the idea of going landside and seeking help, but she did not know who homesteaded in this part of the river. The land here was often flooded and all but barren. Whoever scratched a living there, they were not trade partners of theirs and Ma was always very cautious about bringing the Ark into unknown berths. The Ark was all they had. It was too much to entrust to a stranger's honesty.

It was risky to fix the turby alone but she had no real choice.

She wrapped the scarf tightly round her hair and stripped down to her underthings. 'With your permission, river,' she mumbled and slid into the river's chilly embrace. The damage was not so bad, but it took several massive breaths to untangle the debris caught in the turby. And then she had Ma to see to and the babes to change and feed. She was exhausted. Ollu didn't need Ma to tell her that she couldn't manage like this for long. When the tide was against the Ark the tide-turby kept them moving well enough, but so slowly they could have been sailing through porridge, which reminded her that they had oats in their emergency stores. Ma might eat a thin porridge.

They had little food left. Ma had given away a lot of what they had in return for help with the birthing. The twins had come early so they'd not made it to the Island of Spring. They'd had to buy in help from a couple of travelling animal physickers and slaughterers and the long difficult birth had cost them most of their food supplies. Now they had nothing to trade and nothing for their keep even when they finally got to Cassie's. They could not just throw themselves on her mercy. She was not known for giving out charity.

By late afternoon, Ollu was struggling to stay awake. They were not as near to Cassie's as she'd thought and she did not know how long her mother could live without help. There was still no traffic on the river. It should have been teeming with trading craft, before the winter ice came. What was going on?

When Ollu was small they'd stayed in touch with other craft by radio, but parts got harder to get and somehow they'd fallen to using a system of flags and markers. Ollu found that she was scanning the land for any sign that Davey or one of the cousins had left a marker, some explanation for the ominous silence on the river. Her guts told her there was something wrong.

'Ma?'

Her mother stirred a little where she lay in her sweat-stained, bloody dress. She mopped Ma's glistening forehead and opened the porthole window to get rid of the rank smell that made the cabin, usually so clean, stink like a shore-side midden.

'Ma, I think there might be trouble. There's no one about. What should I do?'

'Joe?' her mother croaked and Ollu didn't know if her mother thought she was Joe or that she should find Joe to help them out. Her mother opened her eyes to look at Ollu, but they were shiny and blank as marbles, and she knew her mother could offer her no help

She loosed the catch on the spear gun, strapped on her belt knife, checked the spike release was working and locked the cabin from the outside, putting the key round her neck and inside her blouse. She was trembling as much from tiredness as from fear.

There was nothing else to do but stand at the tiller and wait.

*

SHE SPOTTED IT a short way from Cassie's Holding – a 'red' – a scrap of old plastic tied just at the base of a bush. It was their private signal for danger and it made Ollu's hard stomach knot even tighter. It could signify anything – sickness, savagery or death.

The Great River was fast flowing in these parts and she would not risk manoeuvring the barge towards the river bank. She dropped anchor and pulled the lever that released the kayak. That, at least, had stayed secure in its special place under the barge. It was old as the Ark and bleached white with age. It rested on a mechanical arm which tilted to empty it of water and then laid it to rest right side up on the river. Ollu lowered herself inside it, uncoupled the paddles and undid the catch which released the kayak from the Ark's securing arm. At least something still worked.

The tide and current were both running fast so she had to battle to reach 'the red.' The bushes by the water's edge scratched her arms while the tide tried to drag her into the heart of a water thorn. She held herself steady with her paddle and groped around for the message she hoped to find near the marker. She found it, wrapped in old plastic. The message was scrawled in blue crayon 'CASIYS HMESTD TAKN – REFUGYS @ RS' It was Davey's writing and he never could spell. 'Cassie's Holding taken refugees at Roberts" she translated, hoping that anyone else who might see the message might also have the wit to decipher her brother's terrible writing.

Ollu blinked back tears of frustration and resealed the message in its plastic bag. That's why the river was so quiet. The new invaders might have craft of their own and no one who had ever fought a river battle did it twice if they could avoid it. Ma had fought one way back. Ollu felt sick at the thought.

The trouble was she could not easily get to the Robert's place without going past Cassie's former homestead. There was a way, but it was only usually passable after the winter floods. Should she risk it? She feared holing the Ark like she feared death itself. If she waited till it was dark perhaps she could risk passing by Cassie's? There wouldn't be much moon and there was every chance the cloudy day would dwindle into a cloudy night. Ollu had to decide. She had to. There was no one else.

Not for the first time she missed her brother's strength and easy-going optimism. He and his wife managed his Mother in Law's barge now and, while he couldn't write very well, he could do most other things with ease. At thirteen Ollu knew that she hadn't yet grown into her full size and strength. It would come, Ma said, with all else that she was heir to. She prayed fervently for more strength now, as she battled the current back to the barge. 'Great River, give me ease of passage please,' she mumbled under her breath, just like one of the River Cultists Ma made fun of. Somehow she made it back to the anchoring arm of the Ark and locked the kayak back into place.

Ma was no better and the babes seemed worse. She needed help fast. Ollu would have to risk passing by Cassie's homestead.

Cassie had taken that land years back, when Ma was young. She'd been a refugee from Bad Water herself, with a husband then and a small company of land-hungry, blood-thirsty machete-men. Ma always said Cassie was the kind of woman you would want on your side in a crisis. If she were dead, who would help Ma? The Roberts were long standing trading partners but their land was not as rich as Cassie's and Ma had little time for timid Missis Roberts, who she privately called 'Rabbit Roberts.' Ollu on the other hand, had rather liked shy Missis R because she had snuck her a half round of short bread once – for nothing.

Right now, she'd take help from anyone. Ollu chewed at the inside of her mouth. Would the Roberts be able to help her if they were awash with refugees from Cassie's land? She pushed that worry from her mind. First she had to keep Ma and the babes alive long enough to get to the Roberts', and then she would have to do whatever she could to make them help. There was always a way, Ma said. Always

Ollu found something to eat from the diminishing stores. It wasn't enough but she filled up with Brit-tea. She washed the nappies, cleaned the cabin and tried to amuse the babes. Ma said you had to sing and talk to babes or their brains didn't grow right. It was nice in its way – their softness, the way they grabbed her fingers and hung on like birds with a worm. Their eyes watched hers as if they knew things that she didn't, which wouldn't be hard.

When she was done with all the caring and housekeeping Ollu put on her darkest clothes and tied her hair in the black silk scarf that had been Ma's. It was special and she hoped it would be lucky. Once more she readied the weapons, and with a sick feeling in her guts, she started the engine, heading across to the wrong side of the river, far from Cassie's land. The holding on the other side was poor, full of rubble and not much else. All the salvage there was long lost. No one lived that side and the night noises might disguise the sound of the Ark's engine? She clutched the tiller and hoped.

CHAPTER SIX

BUZZ

BUZZ HAD NO plan. He just wanted to stay away from the neobarbs. He had never met anyone who was not a Gaian Scientist, dedicated to keeping man from falling yet again into savagery. 'Man' meant 'woman' too Pa had explained, though women had a special purpose, given to them alone, to fulfil the promise of Gaia for whom the Lord died, and keep their wombs full so the earth might be repopulated with men worthy of the name. Pa never said much, but he was pretty disappointed that Buzz's mother had managed to produce only Buzz before succumbing to some 'weakness' and dying. Buzz had never known her. It was a new thing for him to be alone and worse to be without the constant contact with the comp. His head felt so empty, devoid of data. He had lost not just Pa, but the most reliable part of himself. Maybe that's why it was so hard to think for himself. He wasn't used to it.

Pa had been at the heart of everything: doctor, engineer, gen-engineer, leader and pastor. Why did he have to go and die when Buzz needed him more than ever? Why had he not, at the very least, told Buzz his plans?

The trouble was, Buzz wanted to stay away from people but he also needed to find a town or somewhere with organisation, somewhere that might have a comp. He had to have data. He couldn't decide what to do without it.

Buzz knew that before The Purge, these Isles had been full of people living so close to each other that, when the plagues followed the floods, hardly anyone survived. He'd seen sat-views showing the shape of the Isles before and after the sea rise. What had once been one land was a series of small islands and archipelagos, depending on the tide and rain. Buzz did not see why Pa was so desperate to fly all that way to such a small, chilly, waterlogged part of the earth. He'd been stubborn about it even for him. He'd been convinced the dangerous, extraordinary flight across the roiling ocean to this – nowhere – would be worth it. Buzz wished he'd asked why.

He found the bank of the broad river easily enough. It was just on the other side of the woods. The water looked brown and uninviting. He threw a twig into the centre and saw how fast and wildly it flowed. The water must be full of bones and the debris of long lost towns. He would not like to swim in it. It smelled strongly of waterweed and silt and other things he could not name. The day had warmed up and, with all the walking he had done through the thick wood, he was thirsty, but he was not fool enough to drink from such a river without using his filtration unit. He unpacked it carefully and filled it from the slower water at the bank side and wondered why there were no boats. Surely, if there was any kind of civilisation, there ought to be boats?

He waited a while for the water to be cleaned and then sipped it gratefully. He felt so weary suddenly that he could barely keep his eyes open. His arms still ached with the efforts of burying Pa. He'd slept badly on the plane too. When he wasn't at the controls he'd dozed to the engines roar and the strange almost-silence when the plane creaked and shifted as they rode the thermals.

He found as safe a place as he could – the hollowed base of some kind of tree. Pa would have known its name. Buzz squeezed his bulk into the shelter of its trunk. It was cool and shady. It reminded him of his den when he was a little kid with all the other compound brats. Back when he was safe.

It was dark when he woke, to the unmistakable sound of an

engine. He thought for one brief, perfect moment that he was back at home. Then he remembered all of a rush – Pa! His blind eyes staring. He did not want to think about that. Instead to distract himself he fumbled in his backpack for water, crawled from his hiding place and stretched. He felt safer at night, more in control. The night was cloudy and the moon was nothing more than a pale curve, like a clipping from a finger-nail. That was as he liked it. He got his automatic out, just in case and walked confidently back to the water's edge and the source of the sound. It was way over on the other side of the river. A long, narrow boat – a house-boat. He'd seen them in pictures. Buzz could see the round, blank windows that suggested a cabin down below, and a flat deck. He spotted a goat and a small figure, all in black, hugging the tiller. He had a weapon cocked over his shoulder and was scanning the river and the shoreline with anxious eyes.

There was something else. He felt a faint electric buzz at the base of his skull – a comp! Surely the boat had a comp! The sensation was faint, so it was either broken or dark-shielded. Oh, Christ in Gaia! How he'd missed the rush of data, the slick, metal taste of it in his mind. Hope flickered: dark-shielding suggested sophistication, which suggested civilisation. He opened his mouth to shout out, but then it occurred to him that the black clad figure might be trying not to draw attention to himself. There was something furtive as well as alert about the way he stood. Buzz pushed himself forward, out of the safety of the bushes and waved.

He thought his heart would stop when the black clad figure levelled his weapon at Buzz's exposed chest. Buzz had tucked his own weapon in the waist band of his under shorts and he raised his empty hands, palm forward, high in the air, the old timer's signal for surrender. The figure lowered the gun, and Buzz tried to signal that he was a friend and wanted to come aboard.

The figure watched him steadily for a while. Buzz repeated his dumb show in case he had not been understood. The long boat seemed an answer to his prayers. There was a comp there, however damaged and the craft had solar cells plus the stump end of a wind turbine. Civilisation. Pa was right. There was civilisation here. He signalled desperately. Could the boy on deck not tell that he too was a civilised man?

Obviously not. The figure remained impassive and then shook his head firmly, as clear a rejection as Buzz had ever received. The boy kept the weapon levelled at Buzz until the boat passed out of sight.

Buzz could not quite believe the boat man would not take him, though a moment's consideration made the decision seem more comprehensible. The neobarbs he'd seen were armed for combat, so perhaps he had landed in the middle of some war. Any stranger could be an enemy. His own home compound protected itself ruthlessly; perhaps the boat man did the same. Maybe he shouldn't have buried his tech trade goods alongside his father's grave? He might need them to show that he too was a civilised man with something to offer.

'What have you learned, Buzz?' Pa's voice in his head interrogated him. He had learned that he had arrived at a place of danger in which some tech survived. A rig like that had to have been maintained from the old timers' day, from the days of The Purge. Where there was one engine and a comp there would perhaps be others, and among people with comps, Buzz might find a welcome.

CHAPTER SEVEN

OLLU

OLLU TIGHTENED HER grip on the spear gun. The figure on the bank was tall and hefty. He wasn't dressed like a machete-man, he was barely dressed at all from what she could see, but his eyes glinted in the darkness like a cat's. He seemed to be waving his arms around. Perhaps he was signalling to someone else. She slumped further down into the shadows of the Ark. At least he didn't shoot at her. She put him from her mind.

The engine was too loud – the loudest thing around. No wolves bayed to mask the sound, which was as well, she supposed. She was terrified of the beasts of the land – both the human and non-human varieties.

She found herself holding her breath as she approached Cassie's land. As if the sound of her breath would make any difference. A huge fire was burning, and the stench of it caught in her throat. She knew the stink of a funeral pyre when she smelled it. She whispered a prayer for Cassie under her breath. If someone as powerful as Cassie was dead, then what chance would Ma have? The smoke made her eyes water and she blinked back tears. Ma would not die. Ollu wouldn't let her. The bonfire was quite a distance away and she had to hope its light would not make her more visible. Surely they would have set guards at the water's edge? It was their most vulnerable boundary.

The engine's sound suddenly seemed trivial compared to the sound of her blood pounding in her ears. She was so afraid she thought she might faint – though of course she was not that feeble. Just ahead she could see the dark silhouette of a ship, a big one that dwarfed the Ark. It was a Preeker ship from way back, even older than the Ark. It was lit at its prow by pitch burning torches; their smoke as acrid as that from the pyre. There would be a watchman. How could she not be seen? She could not turn back; that would draw even more attention to herself. She moved the barge so close to the furthest bank that the bottom all but scraped the river bed. Ma would have her guts if she damaged the kayak or the other kit stored there. There was a crack as a branch of a willow broke off. Surely someone would hear that?

'There's one of your ghost drudges, Fred. Do you hear it?' The voice was heavily accented. Loud male laughter came from the boat. There were watchmen. Oh God. What did she do? Should she cut the engine? Her fingers had already taken the decision. She switched the lever. The vibration under her feet ceased and her knees started trembling as if to compensate. The night was suddenly quieter. The tide had turned some hours back and was flowing again in her direction. She abandoned the tiller, and with shaking hand detached the long, hooked pole they used in shallow water and began to push it against the bank. The willow leaves battered the barge in a cascade of blows. Pus! She'd messed up. She'd gone in so close she was entangled and there was no getting free without making more noise. There was another guffaw from the ship, short and sharp as if someone had made a joke. She was almost alongside it now. The river was wide and with any luck the light from the torches might make it harder for the watchmen to see her, so far away in the dark night. It was the noise that was the problem. The river made its own noise, of course, but she could not keep the boat from scraping the bank or colliding with the trees – sounds that the river did not make all on its own. Perhaps they might mistake the sound for that of a nocturnal animal. Perhaps fish might fly and flowers bloom on Sheppey.

There was nothing else for it. She had to leave the shelter of the bank. She was making more noise than the engine. Much as she wanted to stay half hidden by the riverside shrubs, it wasn't safe.

The watchmen weren't doing a very good job, but there was always the chance that the watch might change or the gaffer might come and the men would suddenly shape up. She had to use all her strength to push away from the bank and its illusion of safety. She had to risk the deeper, faster water, further from the shore and closer to the enemy ship. At least the barge moved almost noiselessly through the water, though Ollu was all too aware that it was not quite silent. She heard the water lapping against the Ark's sides and the odd slap of a rogue wave seemed loud and sharp as the report of a gun. This was the quietest way, she reassured herself, relax and let the tide take her.

The idea of relaxing was a toxic joke.

She laid the pole carefully on the deck and grabbed the tiller. The voices of the men were carried on the gusty wind so that the volume was variable. Like their old radio when it still worked. There were two, no three, distinct voices. It sounded like their owners were drinking, but they were far from drunk. She wondered if perhaps they were celebrating the dead. Some people drank a toast to the spirits of the lost, to send them on their way and to keep the spirits from haunting the living. Ma said that was a superstition, but Ollu had seen her celebrating the dead all the same.

She was close enough now to get a good view of the ship, with it's long deck, it's tall mast and its crew. She could see one of them, a broad-shouldered man in a homespun jacket with an antique hunting rifle over his shoulder and a purple band around his head. He was leaning his back against the metal rail at the prow of his vessel, some fifteen meters above her.

By the Great River, God and Allah, do not look down. She prayed fervently and silently. She had to remember to breathe. She secured the tiller and lay down flat on the deck as she drew level with the great ship. It had been spray-painted long ago, in the style her mother called 'Twentieth Century Graffitti' The part lit by the torch was neon orange and luminous pink in great swirls of what might have been letters or random patterns.

'The bones are burning well...' one of the men said, and his voice sounded so close to Ollu she physically jumped.

'That fire's not hot enough to burn bones, you ignorant bastard. You need a furnace for that...'

'Hey! Who're you callin' ignorant?'

She was almost past. The voices of the men rose. Maybe they would fight, but there was a sudden burst of laughter.

'Hey what's that?' The man's voice was loud, and surely he was pointing her way. She thought her heart might stop.

'Where?' Ollu's head was flat against the deck. She could smell the wood and the varnish they used to preserve it. She shut her eyes as if she were a little girl who still believed that she couldn't be seen if she couldn't see.

'It's another of your drudge ghosts!' One of the babes chose that moment to wail, a strange thin cry.

'Pus and boils! What was that?'

'Fox. I reckon. You should have heard them last night.' There was more laughter and she heard the men moving around. There was a clink of tin mugs and a man's voice started to sing, a song her mother used to sing about the drowning of London town and the loss of a lover 'to the water all arown'.' The rhyme used to make Ma smile. Ollu's face was too stiff and frozen with fright to move at all, but at least it felt as if her heart was beating again. She got to her knees and looked up. She hadn't been seen. Then she spotted another watchman at the stern of the boat. She ducked down again quickly. Had he seen her?

He called out. 'Lads!' but no one answered. She expected to hear a gunshot at any second though common sense told her that no one would waste precious ammo on an unclear target. The Ark had to be an unclear target, moving in the night, didn't it? A stone from a slingshot plopped into the water beside her, but it was just a stone and not a charge. There was no explosion.

She waited; counted a hundred and then another. There were no more missiles; no more shouting. She could restart the engine if she'd a mind to. She hadn't a mind or a body to do anything but lay on the deck like the rag doll her mother had made for her when she was small.

Chapter Eight

Ollu

SHE MUST HAVE slept because the next thing she knew was that the babes were crying loudly and dawn had broken. It seemed they had survived the night. No thanks at all to her vigilance. She was ashamed. Ma would have killed her if she'd known. The tide was about to turn and would shortly take them back towards Cassie's homestead. Moving quickly, she restarted the engine and only then reluctantly opened the cabin door. It smelled foul enough, but not of death. Her mother was still breathing. There was still hope.

She did the bare minimum to settle the babes and the livestock and get some more water into her mother and then resumed her position at the tiller. A broad strip of marshland separated Cassie's homestead from her nearest neighbour. It flooded in high water times, when the rains or snow-thaw were heavy and at Spring Tide. She could smell the stagnant water, the stink of mudflats and reed beds. They were almost at the borderland. It was only a matter of luck that they had not overshot the Robert's place while she slept. She thanked the River for that, and carefully stowed away her weapons. She had to hope that they would not be needed now. She brought the barge in towards the bank as she saw the old walls of the Robert's holding, running parallel to the river. Things had changed since she was last there. A wall of shards – old barbed wire, broken glass and twisted pieces of metal too small to merit reworking, formed a barrier between the river's edge and the windowless wall of the fortress. It had been a factory or warehouse once, and a solid fortress in the violence of the Chaos. She could see a couple of machete-men parading in the space between the two walls. She did not recognise them, but then she wouldn't expect to. Even without the refugees, the Robert's clan was large and what with paid help and drudges it must have numbered upwards of a thousand people – a number Ollu always found overwhelming. Something high up glinted in the sun light. It was not the wind-turbys, which were white and barely noticeable, but someone keeping watch with an eye glass. Ollu squinted upwards. It wasn't an eyeglass but binos. Someone had come by some top salvage. It was a stupid thing to think given the circumstances, but she hoped they came from her brother and not an outsider. They could not afford to lose trade, not with the loss of Cassie's business.

She had not thought much about what she would do when she got to the Robert's, but as both the guards had turned to stare at her with their weapons raised, she had no time to think very hard.

'Identify yourself!'

'I am Ollu, daughter of the Ark, and a legitimate trading partner with this household.'

One of the men stepped forward. He was unkempt and gaunt with the hungry eyes of someone who had slept and eaten too little and seen too much.

'What proof have you got? I can't see no trade goods, little girl.' Ollu didn't have time to argue with jumped up flunkeys. As if on cue, one of the babes started to wail and the guard stepped back from the barge as if he had been assaulted.

'What you got there, more refugees?'

She shook her head and drew herself up to her full height. 'Look, I want to talk to the Missis here, to Missis Roberts. She can vouch for me and I need her help.'

'I'm not falling for that trick! D'you think we was borned

yesterday. I'll go and then you'll storm my mate and get through the barrier.'

Ollu wished she had her mother's ability to command respect. She wanted to beg that if they didn't help her Ma would die, but by the look in their eyes hers wouldn't be the only loss in this homestead. She would have to come up with something better than that. What would Ma do? Ollu put some steel in her voice.

'Look, fetch Missis Roberts or I'll take my business proposition elsewhere. Trust me. She will not be happy – particularly when the Mister finds out.' The two guards exchanged glances and the one who had remained silent nodded briefly. The one with the mouth and the attitude threw Ollu a baleful look, punched a security pad on the main door and was allowed to enter. That fitting was new too. What if the Roberts' were doing business with someone else? Maybe she'd no longer be welcome. She tried to keep the anxiety from her face, tried to look bored.

'This your rig?' The guard was young and looked sickly. She wondered what else had gone wrong on the Robert's farm recently. It was only a matter of weeks – six maybe – since they'd passed this way. They'd traded machine parts, placky yarn and bricks, in exchange for foodstuffs, seeds and some farm-stilled voddie to trade on. Ma would have logged it. Pox and piss, Ollu had not kept the log since she'd had to take control. Ma would be furious: trading, record keeping and educating were what Bargers did. 'Markets, Memory, Minds,' a braid of duties.

She couldn't let her distress show on her face. She couldn't think about her failures, or about Ma lying in her own filth in the cabin. She couldn't let the guard guess she was bluffing.

It took an unreasonably long time for the guard to return with a woman. Not the Missis, but her sister who had been badly scarred by smallpox. Ollu remembered her, Nada. Ma had supplied her with the thick makeup to cover over her pocked face. It seemed that she remembered Ollu too

She came up to the wire mesh of the door and peered short-sightedly: 'Ollu? Where's Lizzie? Why are you alone?'

'Ma's sick, Missis – not plague – baby fever. I...' the woman took a step back as though Ollu herself was diseased.

'You've come at the wrong time if it's charity you're after...'

'Not charity, business,' Ollu said firmly. 'Give me a list of what you need and I'll get it. In return for you taking Ma,' Ollu swallowed hard, 'and the twins.'

'Ah yes the babes. They live?' Ollu nodded. The woman must be deaf not to hear them screaming in the cabin. 'I'll come aboard!'

No. She could not. What would Ma say? The woman untied her headscarf as the guards both looked discreetly away. She then retied it over her mouth and nose as a barrier against contagion. She had a large and impressive bunch of keys tied in a chain round her narrow hips.

'I will send for a bearer but if I think it is plague or pox you'll have to go on your way.' Ollu nodded her agreement. The guards accompanied Nada with a self-important air. Ollu guessed her arrival was a welcome break in the boring business of protecting the long river-boundary.

The gate in the shard wall was 'A' grade salvage, a vault-door of bomb-proof construction. It looked more impressive than it was. Ollu knew well enough that the shard wall itself was not bomb proof and would have fallen to ordinary ballista, let alone explosives. Still, it suggested that the Roberts' had drudges aplenty and tekk and that, she supposed, was the point.

There was a certain amount of fumbling while Nada opened the door. In spite of the fancy Preeker key-pad, it was secured by nothing more than a padlock. The guards kept their weapons trained on Ollu. They both had rifles of the simplest kind, modified to take shrap ammo. Each of them also carried a sheathed machete and the quieter one had a quiver of arrows and a bow strapped across his back. They meant business.

Nada stretched out a tattooed hand for Ollu to help her on board. She was wearing heels as a sign of her rank, and was in real danger of breaking something important as she climbed down the steep bank towards the barge.

'I'm afraid you can't come aboard in those,' Ollu said. In truth, she shouldn't come aboard at all. She was not a Barger and a Barger's boat was sacrosanct: several generations worth of yarn spinning, tradition building and respect earning had made it so. Nada handed her antique, gold-coloured heels to one of the guards, who held them as if he had never seen the like before.

'It is not allowed...' Ollu began, trying to seem firmer and more impressive than she felt. The look the Missis' sister gave her was impatient

'I will not let you into the homestead if your mother has a contagious disease. Either I come on board or I do not help you. Are there words I need to say?'

Ollu had no choice but to tell her the traditional polite formula used even among Bargers' when boarding the barge of another. She found it hard to get the words out. She knew that telling a stranger these things was wrong, but she could not think of any other way to get help. 'You have to bow – to me, to the river and to the engine – over there.' She indicated its position with her head, 'And then you say, 'As you are gracious, and you have our oaths of discretion and honesty, it would be an honour to be permitted to board.' Nada performed this small ritual without hesitation or embarrassment.

'It is an honour gladly bestowed,' Ollu said quickly to hide her own shame, and extended her hand to help the woman aboard. The sleeve of her robe rode up and Ollu could see that the religious tattoos and healer's marks extended up her arm in a complex swirl of blues and greens. The woman was a priestess and healer in a unitist sect. Ollu was not certain which one. She had not known that Missis Robert's younger sister was an educated woman. It made her feel a bit better about breaking the rules. Such a woman would be used to secrets. 'I am afraid that what with the storm and everything I have been too busy to keep things in proper order...' She had let Ma down badly. Nada waved a dismissive hand. Without her wildly impractical shoes, the woman was not a great deal taller than Ollu and her brown eyes seemed both intelligent and inquisitive in her orange-tinted face.

'Is your sister...? It seemed rude to ask after Missis Roberts, and rude not to.

'My sister is well. She is confined and I am temporarily taking over her duties.' Ollu was surprised. She had always assumed Missis Roberts was too old to be with child.

She couldn't prevent her stomach tightening in dread when, once more, she opened the cabin door. The smell was overwhelming despite the open port hole. Missis' sister's face remained impassive. She ignored the mess and knelt on the floor next to Ma's prostrate body. Ollu picked up the crying boy baby and began to rock him in an effort to quiet him. She did not take her eyes off the healer as she placed her hand on Ma's burning head.

'How long has she had the fever?'

'A day? Two?' It was hard to remember: it felt like forever. 'When did she have the twins?'

'Three – maybe four days ago – they were early I think, and she just hasn't got her strength back at all.'

'Who supervised the birth?'

'It was so sudden there wasn't time to make the usual arrangements. There were some animal physickers on board the 'Safe Haven' – they helped.'

'And did these animal physickers also act as slaughterers?' Ollu nodded. The woman made a noise somewhere between disgust and disbelief. 'Were they so ignorant that they did not cleanse their hands?'

'They rinsed them in the Great River and said their words. They were cultists.'

'They should have scrubbed them hard with herbalist's soap. Your mother knew that. She must have been sick to let such fools anywhere near her. Well, what's done is done. We have to get her out of here.' Nada glanced at Ollu's face, and correctly interpreted what she saw there.

'Can you carry your mother? No? Well then, we need some help. Bring the children.' Ollu wiped her face, which was damp with sweat. A healer was one thing, but she could not allow Roberts' machete-men on board the Ark.

'If you would be prepared to help, we might drag her in a sheet to the deck and then perhaps your men may be able to take her without coming aboard.'

The healer pursed her lips and Ollu was afraid she had overstepped some unknown mark and committed an error that might cost them further trade. Or, worse, her mother's life.

'Take the babes out one by one. I have called for bearers – stead-drudges – and you may safely give the children to their care. I will think about how we might move your mother without causing her pain or putting her in further danger.'

Ollu was grateful the older woman appeared to understand her worries. The Roberts' clan knew well enough that the Ark was a matriarch boat. It was a relief to be told what to do, and she did what she had been asked gladly. When she emerged from the barge, a group of three women and four men, all dressed in faded work-darks, were waiting. All of them had their right shoulders exposed to reveal an ugly weal of burnt flesh in the form of a linked chain – a slave brand. The Robert's had always used indentured labour, but never branded them as slaves. Ollu swallowed down her shock. One of the women held out her arms for the baby, and then when the guard nodded she stepped through the gate to accept the child. The guard kept his rifle trained on the slave, as if she was likely to make a break for it. Ollu suppressed a shudder. Her Ma had brought her up to believe that no one could own another human being, but some desperate people would prefer to live as slaves than die of hunger. Ollu smiled at the woman, but her gesture went unseen as the woman kept her eyes lowered. The baby cried a little as Ollu handed him over and for one bleak moment she wondered if this was a terrible mistake.

She had no choice. She could not care for the babes without

help. She brought the girl child out in the same way, handing her into the arms of another woman with downcast eyes and a seeping slave brand. When she returned to the cabin, the healer was checking her mother's pulse. Ollu found the clean linen. Ma's clothes were soiled and she could feel the hot flush of shame creeping up her neck. She had not cared for her mother as she should have done. Ma would hate to be seen by a stranger in this squalid and desperate condition.

Between them they managed to roll her Ma onto the clean sheet and half lift, half drag her inert body out onto the deck. It was undignified and all, but no other outsiders had to cross onto the deck of the Ark.

The male bearers responded to an imperious click of the healer's fingers and were able to lift Ma off the deck onto a more suitable stretcher, and then onto a trolley. Ollu watched helplessly. What did she do now?

Chapter Nine

Ollu

The healer was about to follow Ma, but Ollu stopped her.

'I need to safety-up the barge.'

'The barge will be well guarded, I can assure you.'

Ollu did not to point out that the Ark would be a useful weapon against the river invaders, and was at much at risk from the Roberts' guards as from outsiders. Something of her thinking must have showed on her face, however, because the healer sighed and signalled for the remaining female bearer to wait to escort Ollu to the reception room at the heart of the homestead.

The girl waited with bowed head. Ollu felt uncomfortable.

'There are things I must be doing,' she said, awkwardly, but the girl gave such little sign of having heard that Ollu wondered if she were deaf, or if she perhaps spoke another language.

Once back on board she began to set the cabin to rights, running through all the drills her mother had taught her. First she cleaned the floor and stowed the hammocks. She washed herself quickly and changed into trading clothes – 'A' grade salvage flat, leather boots of ancient manufacture, light trousers, a fitted shirt and a jacket with many pockets in which she could hide sample salvage, as well as weapons for her own protection. It had been made for Ma by her own Ma and was cut to deceive, for it seemed to fit like a second skin. She quickly tidied her wild frizz into a high bun, which she covered in her best silk scarf – another ancient artefact that had somehow survived the chaos. She painted her eyes with kohl and put on her golden ear and nose rings, her ropes of pearls and chains of gold and silver. She found bracelets and bangles for her arms and several watches of antiques design – one of which contained a still working voice rec. Then, making sure no one could see her, she lifted the panel hidden behind the back of the stove and safety-upped the barge, instructing the ancient ay-eye so that only Ollu herself may set foot on board unhindered. It was a shock when the machine spoke to her. In the past it had always been her mother it had addressed, but today it spoke to her in its detached female voice

'Good morning Ollu, daughter of the Ark. The barge will be secured in sixty seconds. Commencing countdown. Please exit with care. Have a nice day!'

'Haveaniceday.' Ollu responded with a bow and then raced to leave. As her feet landed on the shore there was the familiar grinding sound as the whole side of the barge sprouted lethal spear-sharp spikes, like a startled hedgehog, and the tell-tale red light flashed on the underside of the tiller. The guards shouted some comment that she did not hear, but she ignored them. From now on she would have to use all her ingenuity and training to trade on the Ark's account. Until her mother was fit, she was captain of the Ark.

Even though she was brought to it by bad times and she wished she had not to stand in Ma's place, there was pride in her heart as she stood in her full Barger's regalia and followed the young female slave along the rough gravel path towards the homestead.

Ollu had no previous dealings with slaves, and couldn't ignore the girl by her side. She was very tall and kept her eyes downcast. Ollu guessed that was because she was in pain from her brand. There were raw red weals around the scar and Ollu was sure she had taken a beating. Her skin was the pale brown of Ollu's own.

'Is it very bad?' Ollu asked when they were out of earshot of the guards. 'Please – you can look at me. I am not your master.'

The girl seemed to struggle with herself before she replied.

'I can manage. I am strong,' she said flatly. She gave Ollu a swift glance. Her eyes were very sharp and calculating. 'My brother though... he's junked.'

'What do you mean?'

'Back home he's a prophet – famous for it. He doesn't know when to shut up about his visions. He's had the lights beaten out of him already and I can't protect him.' She sniffed, and Ollu thought she might be trying not to cry. 'There's nothing of him, he's skinny as... He can't survive long. He looks to be about your age.' Ma had raised Ollu to be without superstition and yet there was something about this girl's presence that spooked her. When she spoke about her brother Ollu knew that she would somehow meet this boy. She shivered.

'What does he see?' she asked.

'What will be,' the girl said simply. 'The last time I saw him, he whispered that his future lay on the water, that he wouldn't die a slave.'

Ollu was not falling for that one. 'Why would he think that?' She guessed the girl would tell her that her brother had seen someone just like Ollu coming to rescue him, but instead the slave shrugged.

'He is touched by something – madness, God, Allah or the evil one – I don't know. Skinny slaves don't last long and those with big mouths don't last at all.'

'Where do you anchor? I mean where do you come from?'

'C-Crew Code. Pirate slavers came and caught us. My brother was fitting, stuck in one of his visions. I couldn't run out on him, so they hobbled us both.'

'Who would do that?' Ollu said. Ma wasn't fixed on many things. She always said it was a hard world and everyone did what they could to get through it, but she didn't hold with slavery and neither did Ollu.

The girl looked her up and down with a kind of a sneer and said, 'Your kind. They called themselves Bargers.'

Ollu was so shocked she could not speak. Whoever else The Roberts' were trading with were no true Bargers. but some polluting pirates pretending to be Bargers. No one she knew would stoop so low. Ollu did not ask any of the many questions that were on the tip of her tongue. Even thinking about slave gangs posing as Bargers made her feel sick.

'I'd like to meet your brother,' she said.

'If his vision's true, you'll see him sure,' the girl answered and met Ollu's eyes properly for the first time. One eye was a startling green, the other swollen shut and purple with bruising.

'Oh, Pox and Piss!' Ollu exclaimed.

'This is nothing to what they'll do to my brother. Take him with you. You could buy him for a handful of shards.' She lowered her eyes again. 'They have him working the fields as a land-drudge...he's not strong. He'll be binned before the month is out.'

'I can't. It's taboo to take a man on a Matriarch boat.'

'He's nine years old!' The girl spat.

Ollu shook her head. 'I'm not a drudge, but I'm not free either. I can't defile the Ark.'

'Whatever you say, missis.' The girl's voice could have frozen sunlight.

They were almost at the main homestead. The Roberts had fabricked up yet another wall of shards around it, with four rough wooden gun towers guarding each corner. They had a lighting rig too, floodlights, though they were all rusted up. Ollu doubted they would work. They looked good though. She wished she knew where these 'Bargers' were getting their salvage. It had to be where they got the slaves, down river in the worst of Bad Water, in the Old City.

The girl did not speak to her again, but led Ollu to the armed guards of the Main Hall.

'The Missis' sister commanded the presence of the Captain of the Ark,' the girl said in a low voice. The senior guard, an older woman with the scarred face and hard expression of a fighter, looked Ollu up and down. She didn't laugh, which was something.

'Enter and be welcome,' she said grimly.

The slave girl led Ollu into a small room off the main one, guarded by a single machete-man. He had rotten teeth and his face was a mess of pimples. 'The Captain of the Ark' he announced grandly, though he didn't bother to keep the smile from his face as he said it.

As Ollu walked into the room, her heart was beating like a broken bilge pump. She did not feel like she this was the safe anchorage she needed. She turned on the recording device at her wrist and squared her shoulders. She was the Captain of the Ark and she would not be mocked.

Chapter Ten

Buzz

Buzz kept on walking all that night, following the direction of the barge. There was tech on that barge and somehow he had to find it. That was why Pa had risked everything. What else could he do?

He kept on, through the endless bog and marsh. There were no obvious predators around and, although he was cold, wet and shivering, he didn't feel threatened. By the time dawn arrived, he could see the outline of some big fortified building looming in the distance. A row of large wind turbines made of a mix of wood, plastic and metal turned in the breeze. They looked more like the old-timer windmills he had seen in pictures than the ones they had at home, but still they were wind turbines – a sure sign of civilisation. There were gun platforms too, he thought, high up at the level of the forest of vanes, and a high wall from which a variety of sharp objects protruded. It was obviously designed to put off would-be intruders. Was this civilisation? He could not see any people, but he could hear voices carried on the air – guards perhaps? He followed the direction of sound and found the river again. He kept the wall to his left and the river to his right until he began to feel that low buzz at the back of his head, the one that made the hairs on his neck prickle and rise: a dark-shielded comp.

He finally caught sight of the barge long after he'd sensed its tech. It was moored beside a great metal gate. A series of spikes protruded from its hull so that there was no possibility of boarding. He hunkered down low behind some foliage and watched until he got cramp. The flashing red light under the tiller was a status indicator, and the high-pitched beep it emitted confirmed the fact that it was armed. He could not access the comp, shielded as it was. It didn't matter. Pa was right: whatever the status of the place behind the wall, this barge represented civilisation, from before Gaia's Holy Purge.

No one could get near the vessel without triggering some alarm and, as long as he kept the barge between his body and the gate, he ought to be safe from danger coming from that direction. Wearily, he laid his pack on the ground beside him, by a scrubby tree. The temperature was gradually rising and his whole body ached with the physical effort involved in walking all night. He was desperately hungry, mud splattered, and more exhausted than he had ever been. Before he knew what was happening, he began to doze.

The smack of a gun barrel roughly pushed between his shoulder blades woke him.

'Put your hands in the air and scramble up.' It was a woman's voice, deep and harsh. Buzz did as he was told. He could not believe he had been stupid enough to fall asleep. What kind of brain whacked fool slept in daylight, right next to the perimeter wall of some fortress? What would Pa have said? The woman kept her rifle trained on him and moved round to look into his face. He did not know what she would see there, but he tried very hard to make sure it wasn't fear.

The woman was short and ill fed, but she was the one holding the gun, which may or may not have been loaded. It was a bodged together weapon, but he figured she wouldn't have held it with such confidence if it did not work and so he made no attempt to escape.

'Bob, I've got a poxing stray. Shall I bring him in?' She yelled at an unseen companion.

She pushed Buzz forward with the butt of her rifle so that he was walking ahead of her. He did not think she'd seen his pack, hidden in the tree roots.

She shoved him through the door of the perimeter wall which was opened briefly for that purpose.

'What are you doing on our land?' Perhaps it was 'Bob' who spoke, Buzz did not know. He shrugged a reply. 'Where did you come from? You a spy for the barbarian dogs on Cassie's farm?'

Buzz shook his head. He had a lot of trouble understanding the man's accent, let alone his words.

'Someone cut your tongue?'

'No sir.' That made the man laugh 'Nosir' he echoed, copying Buzz's own accent which it seemed was as strange to him as his was to Buzz.

'The Fam is busy with that Barger's kid. Take him to the slave barracks. If the Mister wants to see him, he'll let us know.' The woman looked him up and down. Buzz was embarrassed; he wasn't exactly dressed for that kind of scrutiny.

'He's big and well fed. He's come from somewhere. He might be a player.'

'He's not from over the marsh then. Cassie's mob were half starved.' The two guards looked at him curiously. 'You'd better tell us where you pitch. It'll better for you if you do. If the Mister wants you questioned, you won't look so pretty after.'

Buzz swallowed. 'I was travelling with my father. We were looking for old friends, but he got killed and I got lost. I was hoping someone might help me...' He tried not to sound pathetic. Although it was the truth, it sounded so crazy he didn't think anyone would believe it.

It was clear that the soldiers didn't. 'OK. Well, it'll be the Mister's puller tomorrow then. Take him to the barracks, Gina.'

The woman pushed him again, through another check point and then on to a squat, timber building, a long shed with shuttered windows. She opened the door and the stench of unwashed men made him reel. It was very dark, but his eyesight adjusted quickly. The room was empty but for about twenty mattresses on the floor. 'They're at work now.' Gina opened one of the shutters to illuminate the dirty room. She threw him some long trousers and a kind of shirt of thick sacking. 'It gets cold round here at night,' she said and he scrabbled to put on the clothes. When he had dressed, she took out a pair of rough handcuffs and cuffed him to a steel hawser attached to the ceiling beam. 'I'll get you some gruel and water for now. If what you told us is the truth, you'd better come up with a better lie.'

She disappeared for a while and returned with a bowl of grey stuff, some darkbread and a beaker of sweet water. 'You don't look like a runaway to me, nor a machete-man, a drudge or a scroungerman. If you want to live, keep your head down and tell the Roberts' what they want to hear. They're not villains, or at least there are worse out there. It's three meals a day winter and summer and a roof. Not much in the way of prospects, but keeping breathing is half the battle, yeah?'

Buzz nodded, barely understanding her. He thought she'd been kinder than she might have been. She was right about keeping breathing: he'd understood that bit. He waited till Gina had left before he ate the food. There was enough slack in the hawser to allow him to reach the bowl. It was messy without a spoon and he didn't want to be observed eating like an animal; he was civilised. The porridge tasted disgusting and the bread was hard but it didn't matter: it was food and he was very hungry.

So, Pa would have been proud of him. In less than forty-eight hours he'd lost his survival pack, got himself arrested and stood every chance of being made a slave. Good job he was made of the right stuff, or something really bad might have happened to him.

CHAPTER ELEVEN

OLLU

NADA, THE MISSIS' sister, was waiting in the room for Ollu, along with a figure she recognized but had never expected to see again. 'Cassie?'

The big woman smiled. She wore a patch over one eye and a bandage over one broad shoulder, but her white-toothed beam was as powerful as ever. It gave Ollu hope. 'Ollu,' she said, 'I am sorry your Ma is ill, but happy to see you so splendid in her place.' Her words were much the same as ever, but she sounded weary.

'I thought you dead.' Ollu could not quite keep the quiver from her voice.

'So, I think, did the polluted invader scum,' she said vehemently. 'They killed my boys, and Neil. They have my work gangs labouring for them now.'

'I'm sorry,' Ollu said. She had liked Neil, Cassie's last husband, a thin white man with a waxed moustache and a gift for making Cassie laugh with body-shaking abandon. Cassie no longer looked like a woman who laughed.

'The invaders will be the ones who are sorry.' Cassie's tone was hard and cold as salvaged steel. Ollu shivered, though her coat was warm. 'The Roberts' clan have agreed to help me take back what is mine, but I need certain things to seal the deal.'

Ollu felt a tightening in her stomach. She had not expected

to have to trade so soon, and not with Cassie. She was not ready. Her mouth was dry.

'Where is my mother?' she said, pleased that her voice sounded near normal.

'I have left her with one of my assistants,' Nada said, 'She is comfortable. We are bringing her temperature down, but she needs meds. We have some, but as you know they are costly.'

Ollu wanted to scream: *Give them to her and I'll pay whatever you want!* but she didn't. Her mother had trained her better than that. She closed her mouth tightly, counted to a hundred slowly and waited. Nada broke the silence first.

'If we are to treat your mother and find a wet nurse for the twins we will need substantial payment and sureties.'

Ollu shrugged. 'What had you in mind?'

'Tekk weapons, K4s preferably, top salvage – a couple of dozen at least.'

Ollu nodded, keeping panic at bay. 'If I could source them they would be worth more than a few pills and a wet nurse.' She was pleased that she sounded calm. If she could do this right, her Ma might one day hear this recording, and she did not want to be ashamed of it.

'I will throw in the standard food supplies under the usual terms, plus risk bonus less the cost of feeding the wet nurse and your mother.'

Ollu nodded. 'And repairs of course. I may need to use your workshops on my return – as usual.' She paused. 'Two dozen is too many. There's not that many in the whole of the Isles. I can get you six.' Six was still an impossible number, but it was better than two dozen. The silence lengthened between them and Ollu schooled herself to look relaxed, confident, the kind of person who could lay their hands on Preeker tekk in quantity. She counted to three hundred in her head and, at last, Nada nodded. 'Six K4s – if that is the best you can do.' She paused for a beat, then added, 'Of course, there is the issue of surety.'

'The Ark has traded here for fifty years.'

'Yes, and the Ark has served us well, but such arrangements need not be exclusive. As you must be aware, the world is changing.' She waved her arms vaguely in the direction of a late twentieth century ipad, resting in pride of place at the centre of the room. It had no power cable and it did not appear to be on, but Ollu doubted the Missis' sister had ever seen a working one, and she may not know the difference. 'You aren't our only trading partner any more... Times have changed and so have our terms. You need to know that if you fail to return,' she paused for effect, 'we will take the twins.'

Ice flowed in Ollu's veins. 'What do you mean – take the twins?

'We would usually take them as tied drudges, but as Lizzie has traded us with us for so long, I would keep them from that. The Missis birthed a daughter, but she died before her first breath. It would help her to take your mother's girl child as her adopted daughter in place of the girl she lost. As for the boy, he will be raised as her bodyguard. This is, of course, only if you break the trade, either by not returning or by not delivering.'

Ollu looked at Cassie. She could not believe what she was hearing. Cassie would not meet her eyes.

'No!' Ollu said. She wanted the twins to be safe, but not on those terms. 'No. The twins are not mine to trade. They belong to themselves. I don't trade in babies. If I fail to find the salvage you may take me as a tied-drudge, but not the twins.'

'If your mother dies, this would be a good deal for them. They would be given the best of everything.' Nada dropped her voice so only Ollu could hear it. 'How can you care for two babes?' she asked, gently.

'If my mother dies the deal is off.' Ollu said. 'You keep her alive until I return with the goods and then we'll talk. If I live, I will return with the goods or pay the price, but the twins must be free. I do not sell anyone, least of all my own.'

Nada looked at Ollu for a long moment, and then nodded.

'We will keep your mother and the twins alive until you come back and then we will talk again if you do not have the trade.'

'Do you have the right to speak for the Roberts' clan?' Ollu asked.

'Of course!'

'Then this is binding before witnesses and the word of the Ark's Captain.' Ollu said.

'It is binding before witnesses and the word of the Roberts' Clan,' Nada agreed.

They shook on it while Cassie looked on. She could have done more to help Ma's only daughter. Ollu had to fight to keep resentment and anger from her face: the older woman had let her down. Cassie was a refugee, it was true, but she was not without power, even here.

Ollu knew she should have asked for double the normal exchange of tekk for food, but the business with the twins had confused her, as Nada had known it would. It wasn't a good deal, but it was a deal and the first she had negotiated alone. It was up to her to make it work, and to live with it.

The slave girl arrived with the traditional brit tea that sealed the bargain.

'You will have dinner with us?'

Ollu nodded. 'I would be grateful for a small packet of supplies to be advanced against my return payment too. You will want me to start to salvage on your behalf straight away and I will not have time to trade for food elsewhere.'

There, she had said it. Ma had always said that you must trade from strength not weakness. Even Nada looked surprised. She hadn't realized quite how bad things were. She'd never seen the Ark in all its glory and so hadn't noticed its lack of trail barges. 'I will see to it at once,' she said, courteously enough, but Ollu guessed by her expression that she was cross with herself that she hadn't made a better deal.

'I would also like to see my family before I go,' Ollu added, while the conversation still seemed to be going her way.

'I'll take you to see your Ma,' Cassie said, 'We've time before we eat.' Nada did not argue, but her tight smile told Ollu she wasn't pleased to leave the two of them alone. She insisted the slave girl with the black eye went with them. Ollu tried to catch the girl's attention but she stared resolutely at Ollu's feet.

Ma was quartered in a sunny room that may once have been a meds-house. It smelled cleanly of soap and Ma had been washed and placed in a proper bed with fresh coverings. The Roberts' had a reputation for doing things neatly, if not always well. Ma's eyes were closed, but she was breathing evenly and Ollu thought she looked a little better.

'They'll have given her something to make her sleep.' Cassie said softly. She stared at her friend for a moment, stroking Ma's forehead, that was as smooth as the face of a Preeker placky doll. She looked beautiful but unreal, not like Ma at all. As if she were already dead.

'Oh, my dear, I am so sorry,' Cassie hugged Ollu tightly and subtly slipped a note up Ollu's long embroidered sleeve. 'We have all lost so much.'

'What happened to the boys?' Ollu asked, because she had to know.

Cassie's eyes filled with tears. 'They are dead. They defended me and the farm with everything they had. I can't talk about it. All I want now is revenge. I want those tekkless thugs to suffer and go on suffering. They'll cry tears of blood before I'm done.'

Cassie did not sound like Cassie anymore. Ollu pulled away from the big woman's embrace. Nada was right in one thing at least: everything had changed. Not even Cassie, her mother's most trusted friend, was the same.

Chapter Twelve

Buzz

No one came to bother Buzz for a long time. He slept; there was nothing else to do. He made a feeble attempt to free himself from the handcuffs but his heart was not truly in it. He'd found the tech he was looking for, only to get locked up. And the worst thing was that since Pa had died and left Buzz alone, the idea of company and three meals a day didn't seem so bad.

He changed his mind once the daylight faded and the slaves returned from the fields. They looked worn out and thin. Each man was branded on their shoulder and each man was almost too weary to talk. They followed their gaffer into the shed and accepted the bowl of slops he wheeled in on a rickety trolley with mismatched wheels. It was porridge with small pieces of chicken in it. The slaves ate it with their fingers without embarrassment, and fought each other to be first in the queue when more was offered. Buzz ate his slowly, to trick his stomach into thinking he was full, but the trick worked no better than it had with own rations. There was plenty of sweet water and he drunk his fill. Only when the gaffer had gone, taking his trolley squeaking and rattling across the boards and out of the hut, did anyone speak.

'You want to get out of them cuffs?' a man asked him casually. Buzz nodded, then realising the man could not see his gesture in the increasing darkness, said 'Yes. Can you do it?'

'Yes – in exchange for your breakfast tomorrow and the next day.'

Buzz weighed it up. In the back of his mind his father's memory roused him with accusations of having given up, of being pathetic, of only being fit for slavery if he could not show more gumption. He was going to have to try to escape, wasn't he? He owed that to his father's memory.

'OK.' Buzz said. He did not add the rider 'If I'm here' because he wasn't that stupid.

The man scrabbled under the floorboards and conjured a pin with which he sprung the catch of the handcuff. Even in the short time Buzz had been wearing the cuffs they had chafed, and his wrists were rubbed raw.

'They don't cuff you at night?'

'What for? There's no light except by the house and the fence and the dogs get anyone out and about at night. There's nothing but Roberts' land for about twenty miles except the marsh that would take you to Cassie's old place and the river. You don't want to go in the Great River or her tributaries – she's hungry as – is that river.' He paused. 'You thinking of going anywhere? Think again because I want your breakfast.' The man sounded threatening, but he didn't look like there was much fight in him. Buzz's body tensed anyway and he realised that the slumped and listless men all round him had suddenly began to take an interest in their conversation, as if they had sensed the chance of violence in the air.

Buzz paused. 'I don't know. How bad is it working here?' There was a silence and then a deep man's voice answered, 'It's better than starving, but not by much. You'll starve if you leave here, or get killed by the dogs or the machete-men, but don't let Glenn put you off. You give it a go if you want to.'

'Hey, shut it, Frogfart, don't interfere. We had a deal...'

'He must go,' a boy's high voice interrupted.

'Oh, don't tell me – another vision. Haven't you got enough stripes on your back yet, Ratter?'

'Leave it runty – we haven't got the energy...'

'Shut it!'

'We've got to find the boat and get my sister...' the boy they'd called Ratter said firmly, ignoring the interruptions. And then a row broke out over whether he should be allowed to believe in his visions or if that was just pandering to his superstition or his madness. Buzz did not think the boy was mad at all. In his self-pity, he had almost forgotten about the boat, and about his pack and his automatic lying in the long grass beside it. If he could get on that boat, he might find a way to live that was better than just not starving. He waited until the argument ran its course. The man who had removed Buzz' hand cuffs was spoiling for a fight, but no one else seemed to have the stomach for it.

Buzz waited until everyone had lapsed into silence and then said, 'So, if I was going to escape, how could I avoid the dogs?'

There was a long pause and then the one called Frogfart sighed. 'You're not from round here, are you? If we knew that, a few more of us might have tried it. A couple of men were killed last month – savaged. They showed us the bodies, just to be sure we'd got the message. We got the message.'

No one spoke for a moment and then the child, Ratter, spoke, 'We've got to do it. Me and you. We've got to find the boat and get my sister.'

Buzz looked at the speaker – a tiny, skinny boy of not more than eight with the narrow head and starved, feral look of the rodent which had given him his name. If Buzz had to choose a companion, it would not be this kid, who looked like a strong gust of wind would floor him.

'Can you run, Ratter?'

The boy flashed a surprisingly good set of long teeth. 'Running's what I do.'

'What? When you're not getting beaten?'

Buzz felt sick and it was hard to say whether it was because of the disgusting porridge, the thought of being savaged by dogs, or straightforward fear. He kept remembering his father's savage

Rottridges. Nevertheless, he took one of the blankets that lay on the stained and stinking mattresses and wrapped it round his shoulders as a cloak. He was tall enough that it did not tangle in his legs.

'All right. I'm going. Anyone else coming?'

The man who had released him yelled and tried to tackle him, but Buzz had the advantage in the dark and swiftly moved out of his way. Several hands reached to grab him and feet were suddenly extended to trip him. Maybe the men would be blamed for his escape. That made him feel bad, but he had to go. It was his duty. He dodged the hazards easily and pushed past the elderly man who had stationed himself by the door to prevent his escape. The man did not put up much of a fight, and whispered 'God speed' in his ear as Buzz threw himself through the door and into the cold night.

'Leg it!' Ratter was somehow by his side, leading the way in spite of the darkness.

'Smell that river stink!' he said, panting 'and that cow shit. That's good, that.' Without a second's hesitation, the small boy flung himself on the floor and began to writhe around enthusiastically in the sizeable cow pat that lay there. It had a hard-frosted crust but underneath it was soft and easily smeared. 'Get down and roll on it. It might confuse the dogs!'

It was a good idea. An idea Buzz should have had himself. Reluctantly he dropped to his knees and followed Ratter's example. The stench made him gag, but he covered himself in the ordure anyway.

'Doesn't smell much worse than the poxing slave shed,' the boy whispered. 'Now all we have to do is scale the wall.' Buzz was not sure when the initiative had passed to the younger boy, but his wits were as sharp as his teeth, which was as well because Buzz appeared to have lost his altogether. Ratter was about to run for the wall, but Buzz stopped him. In the far distance, illuminated by the faintest of artificial lights, he could just make out the silhouette of a man, and beside him on a short leash a huge and wolf-like dog.

'What?' Ratter hissed.

'A guard and his dog, over there.'

'I can't see anything. You bottling on me?'

Buzz didn't know what that meant, but he denied it anyway. 'We need to find some cover. Do the guards patrol the perimeter to some schedule?'

'I don't know nothing about a 'schedule,' the boy said, mimicking Buzz's accent. 'But we could hide in the cow sheds – over there.' He was off before Buzz could argue. The boy was right – running was something he did as naturally as breathing, Buzz, for all his greater height and stride, struggled to catch up with him. Taking the boy with him no longer seemed stupid. Besides it seemed more as if the boy was taking Buzz.

Chapter Thirteen

Ollu

THE SLAVE GIRL escorted Ollu to one of the guest rooms, in what Ma would have called a 'hotel'. Such buildings had not generally fared well and this one was no exception. It was much weathered and boxy in appearance and smelled of mould. The lower floors had been abandoned entirely and were used for storage. Ollu knew this was meant to tell her how unimportant she was as a guest. The Roberts' had better rooms and they would not have treated Ma in such a way. At least she had got help for Ma and the twins. She did not want to think about what she had promised to do in return. Not yet.

When the slave girl's back was turned, Ollu took Cassie's note and read it in the bathroom. 'I will help you when I am restored to my land. Don't worry about your Ma. I'll keep her safe. Be careful who you trust. Not all Bargers are honest.' The words were hastily scrawled in Cassie's loopy, childish, handwriting. Ollu had hoped for more. She already knew some Bargers were capturing and trading slaves, and that was neither honest nor honourable. What she needed to know was which ones. Why had Cassie found it necessary to write that down?

Ollu tore up the note into tiny pieces and put it in the double-yousee and then wondered if it would flush. Many did not. She tried it. The cistern seemed to dry retch and then released a cupful of brown, untreated river water. She turned on the shower and out came a trickle of more or less clean, hot water. Ollu scrubbed herself thoroughly and washed her hair. Who knew when she would get such a chance again?

When she emerged from the shower the slave girl was investigating her coat with interest.

'What are you doing?' Ollu was furious.

'Yours is a trickster's coat. My uncle had one once. I was looking to see if you had anything useful to steal.'

'And what would the Roberts' say to that?'

The girl shrugged. 'Do I care? Look, girly, I've been beaten before and I'll be beaten again, but I won't be a slave for ever, you can bet on it. My sort – we take what chances get tossed our way. Looks like you might be joining us too. You were a fool to offer yourself as a tied-drudge. You don't know what it means.'

Ollu watched the girl's hands while she was talking. The girl had found Ollu's propelling pencil and hidden it in her clothes. Ollu doubted she knew what to do with it. Not many people learned to read and write these days, apart from the Bargers and those who wanted to trade with them.

'What do you want the pencil for?' she asked evenly.

'What 'pencil'? I was trying to tell you that you've lost a screw. You wouldn't last a day as a slave.'

Ollu ignored the girl's attempt to change the subject. 'That thing you just put in your dress.'

The girl's expression remained innocent.

'Well, I don't mind you having it , if you know how to write or draw, but I don't see what use it will be to you if you can't do either.' The girl's expression was resolutely impassive. Ollu could see she wasn't going to get her property back, so it was her turn to change the subject.

'Those Bargers who brought you here. Do you know the name of their boat?'

'They never said.'

Ollu did not bother to mention that the name would probably

be written on the barge's side.

'There's no need to look at me like that. There weren't no writing on it. The Captain was called Flo, that's all I know, and she had a strong whip-hand and a voice that would make you lose your dinner – if she'd ever given us any.'

'Was she a tall, white woman with pale eyes?'

'Know her, do you?'

Ollu's heart sank. She knew all the River Bargers that served these waters and there weren't two called Flo. The last time Ollu had seen pale-eyed Flo it had been at the shindig to celebrate Davy's wedding. She had given away the bride – her youngest daughter and, as she too ran a matriarch's boat with no men allowed, she had put up a half share for a full stake in Davy and Stell's new barge *The Good Hope*.

Davy couldn't know about the slave trade; surely he'd have nothing to do with such an abomination?

'You *do* know her? I can see it.' Ollu's throat had gone dry too, and she felt as though all her life blood had drained away. She cleared her throat:

'I thought slaves were supposed to keep quiet and keep their eyes down. Not harass their master's guests.' She regretted her words as soon as they were said. The girl shot her a look of pure malice, lowered her eyes and refused to speak again. Ollu cursed herself. A light-fingered girl with a sharp eye and a quick wit could have been an ally in this unexpectedly hostile place. It was time she learned to keep her emotions in check. Bargers ought not to go around insulting people

Ollu was surprised to find that Nada had arranged a grand dinner for her after all. The Great Hall, with its window of coloured glass and the high vaulted ceiling, was lit by flickering leckie lights and candles. An array of eyetekk, pads, and fones were arranged in a huge display across one wall, to show off the Robert's wealth and sophistication, but Ollu's expert eye could see that very little of it was in good condition and none of it worked. In space of the speaker system which was 'temporarily faulty' they were entertained by three slaves with a limited repertoire of songs and a boy with a guitar. They would have been better to employ a song-peddlar. It was cold too. The Mister was dressed in a combination of antique synthetics and wolf skins: he would have been warm in a snow storm. The slave girl had brought Ollu a fur to borrow and though it smelled unpleasantly of bad meat, Ollu was grateful for it. She could not see why they did not modify the building to be more heat efficient, but her Ma had always told her not to discount the value of show.

The tables were covered in good white linen and the cutlery was all of silver, at least on the top tables. The harried looking Mister sketched her a bow and then ignored her. His wife excused herself from dinner because Lizzie's babes needed her too much. Ollu sat beside Nada, who sat in place of the Mister's wife.

'The arrival of your siblings has given her heart. She is feeding them and I begin to hope she may recover her strength after all, and that my hours in her place, may, thankfully, be numbered.' Nada whispered to Ollu, as if Ollu cared about the Missis' condition. It was good to know the twins were being fed and cared for, but she didn't look forward to hearing what Ma would have to say about Ollu's deal. The more she thought about it, the more impossible her task seemed to be.

There was not too much to eat – mainly a kind of gruel of grain with tiny bits of meat and fat. Ollu was offered a beaker of farm-stilled vodka but turned it down. So did Nada. Cassie and the Mister barely spoke, and apart from the music and the scraping of plates there was little noise at all. It was a cheerless meal, very different from the last time she was here. Then there had been dancing and anyone in the household who'd wanted a message passing on up river had talked to Ma, who'd written down their words or memorized them.

The Roberts' had to help Cassie and her refugees, just as they had to fight for them, but that did not mean any of them had to like it. The Roberts knew that they would be next. The marsh that divided their land from hers made a land-based attack tricky, so it was likely any attack would from the river. What the Roberts' needed most was a boat, which set Ollu worrying about the Ark.

While Ollu ate her food and complimented Nada on her hospitality, she surreptitiously estimated the likely size of the Robert's fighting force. At a push, she reckoned maybe three hundred fighting men and women, excluding the guard detail outside and the farm drudges. She wondered how many men had been needed to take Cassie's holding. The large ship she had passed could have carried at least a hundred.

'Where do you think the invaders came from?' she asked Nada.

'Some say from the far North, or the Uropp. Cassie claims they spoke English though, and she reckons they come from Bad Water. You Bargers heard nothing?'

Ollu remembered the men she'd overheard. They sounded like River-men to her ears, but she shook her head. Only a few weeks ago she was sure that Ma and the family knew everything that was to be known about their world – who had birthed a child, who had died, who had married and the whereabouts of all the best salvage. Since then she had learned that her brother's mother in law was a slave trader, that people had invaded Cassie's in a ship of such size that the whole known world ought to have known about it, and that her mother was not invincible. It was all too much. She no longer felt confident that she knew anything at all.

Chapter Fourteen

Buzz

Buzz did not want to hide in the cow shed for too long, though it was warm and the scent reminded him of home. Night was his time, and he did not want to waste his advantage.

There were no windows in the barn, so there was no way of knowing when the guard might have passed from view. Buzz tried to measure out ten minutes by counting to six hundred very slowly. He knew he counted too fast but it didn't matter, the guard had moved out of view. They sprinted for the wall. Ratter wanted to scale it where it was still faintly lit by the security arc lights. He was like some untrained puppy let out for the first time. Buzz had to grab him by his skinny shoulder and shove him towards the darkest section of the wall.

'Don't worry I can see well enough,' he said, when Ratter protested. 'I am going to lift you onto the top of the wall. If you can find something to help me climb over, all well and good, otherwise ...' He pulled a face. 'Otherwise, good luck.' He didn't think he could get over the wall without cutting himself to ribbons, though that was no reason for not helping the smaller boy. His father had always praised Buzz's size and strength and now for the first time in his life it wasn't an advantage.

'I'll find a way. Our fates are braided together like my sister's hair,' Ratter whispered by way of reply. He didn't seem surprised by

Buzz's revelation that he could see in the dark, or by his generous offer to help him over the wall. Buzz's night vision was supposed to be his big secret. Ratter's lack of interest in it was almost funny.

Ratter weighed almost nothing and was agile as a squirrel. He smelled foul, of course, but Buzz could ignore that. Ratter clambered on to his shoulders. Somehow he managed to maintain his balance while Buzz lifted his feet so that they were in line with the top of the wall.

'Open your hands – I can balance on your palms and jump,' Ratter said in a loud whisper.

Surely he'd fall? Ratter wriggled his foot out of Buzz's right hand and placed it on the top of Buzz's head while Buzz opened his left hand so that Ratter could stand on it, as if it were a platform. Ratter's foot was no longer than Buzz's hand. He repeated the manoeuvre with his other foot until he was standing on Buzz's raised hands, like a circus performer in an old deevee. Buzz could not hold him for long. Ratter's weight was a strain on his arms and the back of his shoulders and neck were on the brink of cramping. Just as he thought he might buckle, Ratter jumped and landed so perfectly that he miraculously missed every protruding shard of mangled metal and razor glass. There was a thud and a muffled expletive as Ratter jumped from the top of the wall to land on the other side. One of the guard dogs barked.

There was no way Buzz could get over the wall, and even if he could scramble his way to the top, the shards would rip his feet to pieces. There was no foot space for someone of his size. The wall looked like a picture of a stegosaurus that he'd seen as a child in one of his father's books. He toyed briefly with using the shards embedded in the wall as foot holds, but his feet would be shredded before he could climb halfway up.

'Think laterally, Buzz. Don't give in!' Again, his father's voice in his mind; loud and clear and faintly irritated.

If he could not get over the wall, perhaps he could get under it. There was only one way to find out. He began to dig. His hands were still sore from burying his father, so he found a couple of broad flat stones to use instead, and began to clear away the soil.

It would surely take all night, perhaps longer, but he could not think of any better way. He kept an ear out for the dogs, but nothing approached. He heard scuffling on the other side of the wall, but he presumed that it was some small animal about its business. He did not think about Ratter. He wished him well, of course, but his world narrowed to the small piece of ground before him and he worked with mechanical efficiency. Perhaps he was not as intelligent as his father had hoped however, he *was* strong and gritty. And he would not be a slave.

The soil was not easy to shift; it was full of small stones, pieces of glass and metal that had not made it into the wall. He cut his fingers more than once and developed blisters from gripping the rocks. After a long while, he heard someone or something else, digging from the other side of the wall. He stopped what he was doing to listen, his heart hammering.

'Ratter? Is that you? What are you doing?'

'I'm helping you get out. A braid, cuz, we are bound like a braid. There's no way over but I found some metal to dig with.'

Buzz did not know what to say. It was too early for friendship, for loyalty. Maybe the boy really did believe their fates were linked. Buzz made himself dig harder, though his hands stung and his shoulders ached. He was about to stop and rest when he suddenly saw Ratter's skinny arm appearing on his side of the wall.

'We're through. Come on, shift! It'll be morning soon. Everyone starts work at dawn.'

This was the bit Buzz was dreading. He did not like small, confined places. He had overcome his fear to fly with Pa, but the damp, cold earth under a wall was another matter. What if he got trapped?

He had to do this. If he did not, the dogs would get him, or someone worse. He might have got three meals a day as a slave but what did an escapee slave get? He guessed it was nothing he wanted. He took a deep breath and tried to squeeze his bulk under the wall. It was tight. He shut his eyes and wriggled. His shoulders grazed against stone but he pushed hard with his feet. There was dirt in his nose and his mouth. What if he got stuck? What if he had just dug his own grave? He couldn't breathe. He would be buried alive! Then he felt Ratter pulling at him with his bony hands. 'Come on! Push! You're through!' Suddenly, Ratter was scraping the mud from his eyes. Buzz opened them and then shut them again quickly, grit stung like fire in his eyeballs. There was earth in his mouth and in his nostrils. He tried to snort it away.

'Shush!' Ratter said, 'We've got to get the rest of you through.' The boy grabbed him under his arms, pinching his skin, and heaved. It was enough for Buzz to get his arms free and then it was easier to pull the rest of his body through the narrow channel. He was covered in cuts, but he was on the other side of the wall, and free.

'Thanks!'

'Quick, hide! There's someone coming!' Buzz blinked at the sudden brightness. Dawn was breaking and somewhere close by a dog was barking. He looked round desperately for cover. There was none, and the mound of earth told the story of their escape all too clearly.

'In the water!' he said grabbing the younger boy and pulling him into the River. There was no other place to hide. Ratter, terrified, started thrashing about, but Buzz put one large muddy hand across his mouth, taking care not to cover his nose too. 'It's OK. I've got you. I can swim. Hold onto my shoulders.'

Buzz released his hold on Ratter and slipped into the icy water. Ratter was shivering with fear, his eyes huge in his pinched and dirty face. He grabbed Buzz in panic round his throat and both of them went under. Buzz rose to the surface, gasping for air. 'Hold onto my shoulders and keep breathing. If you thrash around they'll hear us.'

Ratter nodded his understanding. The river was fast flowing here and Buzz grabbed a branch to anchor them to the shore. He had not survived death by burial only to drown.

Chapter Fifteen

Ollu

OLLU WAS DESPERATE to check the Ark, and to escape the noise and stress of so many people. It was not that she minded crowds, it was just that as Captain of the Ark she needed to take note of everything for the log. It was wearing, and she hadn't slept much for the last few nights. Back in the Ark she would be surrounded by familiar things. She could relax a little and sleep.

Nada had other plans. 'You must accept our hospitality tonight. You are still our trading partner and it is traditional that you stay at least one night on our land as a sign of the trust between us.'

There was no trust between them and they both knew it, yet Ollu had to smile and agree. She put more store by Cassie's promise to care for her mother than in anything the healer had said. She tried to copy her mother's dignified, formal tone.

'As you wish. It would please me greatly to see my mother again and, of course, the twins. I would not wish to upset your sister, but I'm sure that she would understand my need to say goodbye.'

The Missis' sister nodded. 'My sister will still be awake. She has not slept since she lost her own child. She may be prepared to see you.'

She sent a drudge ahead to check that all would be well,

and then guided Ollu into the more opulent sections of their holding. Hand-made, rag-rugs of bright placky-yarn covered the concrete floors of the most ancient of the family apartments and dim electric lights, mounted on metal wall fittings, lit their way. As they reached an impressive oak door, Ollu could hear the happy sound of a baby gurgling and a woman cooing. She felt a brief pang of jealousy. She had never heard such a sound from the twins when they were in her care.

Inside, Ollu could see that the Rabbit was much changed. She had become very thin and gaunt, as though her recent pregnancy had somehow eaten away at her. Only her smile was still the same, tremulous and uncertain.

'Why Ollu – you look so grown up in your finery! Here, come and see the babes.'

A fake fire burned in the grate, so that the plastic logs were never consumed but licked by an illusion of flame. It was a costly illusion, which wasted a good deal of fuel, and Ollu wondered at the extravagance it represented. Seeing her expression, the Missis smiled. 'The Mister has tried everything he could think of to cheer me up. Everyone has tried and only you have succeeded. Thank you for bringing me the twins.'

Ollu wanted to say that they were only on loan, that her mother would soon be well enough to reclaim them, but the lump in her throat, made such a speech impossible. The babes were clean and happily kicking, staring at an ingenious mobile of bright coloured shapes that the Missis had hung from the ceiling. They were dressed warmly and well and, for the first time since her mother had birthed them, they seemed content. She tried to smile.

She had never realised how much the Mister cared for his nervous little wife. If he had been prepared to waste power on her, surely he would be prepared to sacrifice Ma for her? Ma was so sick it would be easy to let her die. Something cold settled round Ollu's heart.

She stayed a little longer, admiring the many things the Missis had made or had designed to entertain the baby she had not had. She had birthed live children before, but all had died of the same disease that had scarred her sister. She wept a little for her lost baby, for her lost children, but was swiftly cheered when a slave put Ollu's baby sister in her arms.

'Ayesha' she cooed.

'But the baby has not yet been named!' Ollu said in horror. The Bargers counted it bad luck to name a child before it had survived a year. 'Girl' had been 'coochy' and 'bun' and 'dearling'. She was not 'Ayesha'.

The Missis' sister chose that moment to steer Ollu gently from the room. It was clear that the Missis was not to be upset by uppity Bargers who might disagree with her about anything. Ollu's face must have shown her distress. Nada called to a drudge to escort Ollu back to her room. It was the girl with the black eye.

'The Missis is not to be upset, Ollu. The children are lucky to have her care. Sleep well,' Nada said stiffly. Ollu waited for her to disappear down the candlelit corridor before she spoke to her escort.

'Look, I'm sorry about earlier. Please don't take offence. I need your help. I can pay.' The girl's green eyes flashed interest, held Ollu's gaze for an instant before she looked down in fake humility.

'What have you got?'

In truth Ollu did not have very much, but her Great Grandmother's coat always held some surprises. She put her hand in her pocket and came out with a knife of a strange design. The colour on it had faded, though it still retained some faint trace of red. The blades of several knives folded in on themselves. It was an artefact of which Ollu was fond, but she needed the girl's help more than she needed a piece of ancient design, however clever. She produced the knife with all the flourish of a village street conjurer. She demonstrated the arrangement of the knife's many blades, which included a device for removing stones from the hooves of cows and horses. The girl's eyes widened.

'What do you want me to do?'

'There is a man who used to work for Cassie. I didn't see him in the hall at dinner. His name is Joe G. Ever heard of him?'

'He's the guvnor short a right leg?'

Ollu hoped not. The slave girl expanded her comment, her eyes on the prize. 'He came with the Missis Daso. He may be dead now for all I know.'

'Where did they take the injured?'

'Same place they took your Ma. "The reaper's waiting room," they call it.'

'Take me there!' The girl looked away, with a fine display of reluctance that Ollu could not help but admire. She made a good negotiator. 'Please!'

'Please, Ally.' My name is Ally.' Those green eyes met Ollu's with pride. She was brave. Ollu could have done with some of her courage.

'Please, Ally. It is really important.'

The girl paused to weigh her up and when she finally nodded, Ollu felt as if she had been given a gift.

'You'll have to go quietly,' Ally said. 'The family retire early and we all rise with the sun. It's to save power, though they pretend it's good for our souls.' She pulled a face. 'My soul was better when it was free.' She took Ollu's hand. 'It is dark out of the house. They only light the bits the family see, or that guests might visit. You can trust me. I want that knife.'

Ally led the way outside. The chill hit her like the cold water of the Great River and she was grateful for her mangy fur. Ally had no such comfort, just a home spun shawl that exposed the raw blister of her branding. It made Ollu shiver just to look at her. She could not end up a tied-drudge or a slave. She hadn't the strength for it.

The medical facility was in darkness. Ally tapped a rhythm on the closed door of the facility and a huddled figure came to the door, clutching a stinking tallow candle.

'What you want, Ally? If you're on the scrounge you can forget it. I've run out myself.' Ally's face in the candlelight looked briefly embarrassed.

'I've come with the Missis' guest.' She inclined her head in Ollu's direction and the person holding the candle bowed.

'How can I be of service?'

'You can skip the spiel, Nerys. We want to see the Barger and the one legged guv – did he cark it?'

'No. Tough one that, though I can't see how he'll fight again with a peg leg.'

'I'll see the Barger first, and then Joe.' Ollu said firmly, taking the initiative. She handed the knife to Ally. 'I hope it brings you luck.'

'Don't worry. I'll make sure it does.' Ally's smile was brief and bitter, a baring of teeth. Ollu wasn't sure of much anymore, but she'd bet that Ally would not remain a slave for long.

Ollu got used to the darkness quickly. Ma was in a proper bed with sheets and warm coverings. There was a slave sitting by the bed sponging her brow. It was more than she had expected.

'How is she?' Ollu could not keep the fear from her voice.

'She's holding on. The healer has given her a bit of something and she's no worse.' Ally was still holding her hand. She would know how badly she was trembling.

'You can tell Lil your fears,' Ally whispered. 'She won't tell on you. There's no profit in it and she takes her job seriously.'

The woman Ally called 'Lil' lifted a candle up and squinted in Ollu's direction. The candlelight made their shadows in the bare walled room huge and menacing. Worse than that, it showed Lil's own face under her head scarf to be a mass of uneven weals. Her nose was barely there and great seams of thick scar tissue turned her face into a patchwork of skin. In the flickering light, she looked like the reanimated corpse of a river wraith, or worse. Ollu fought the urge to cry out, and succeeded. Bargers showed respect. She was not a child, to be frightened by deformity.

'Lil,' she began, 'This is my Ma and I think that someone from the Roberts' family might try to kill her, or allow her to die. I am going away but when I come back I will reward you if you keep her alive.'

'She might die naturally.' Lil sounded dubious.

'I know. I know, but please help her. I can see that you are a good carer. Please don't let anyone hurt her.' Ollu made herself look directly at Lil's ruined face and fought back tears. She felt as if the only thing that lay between her mother and death was this scarred slave with gentle hands. Lil reached out her right hand and touched Ollu's face, and Ollu saw the healer's tattoos there.

'You don't have much of a look of your Ma, do you?' she said.

'No.' Ollu swallowed hard. She had always wished to look more like her. 'But I am her heir, and she's a fighter.'

'I can see that.' The scarred face contorted into a grimace that may have been intended as a smile.

'You are a healer – how?' Ollu knew she sounded surprised. She thought healers safe from this kind of bondage.

'It's a long story and not one for here or now.' Lil made a dismissive gesture and returned to the point. 'I can't make any promises. Your Ma is very sick and she may be too sick to live. The crisis is coming and if she survives that she may be OK. The antibiotics we have, they are not so good and don't always work, but she'll get them. I'll see to it.'

'Thank you,' Ollu said, bowing to the scarred slave as she had to the Mister. Who could have more status than someone who had just agreed to try to keep her mother alive? She kissed her Ma's hot forehead, but her mother made no sign of being aware of her. 'Can we see Joe G now?' She could not bear to see her Ma in that state for another moment.

Ollu and Ally followed Nerys into an adjoining room with two rows of beds. The room smelled of old sweat and decay. Nerys' candle led her to the last bed in the row and the still form of a sleeping man. His hair had greyed and his skin had an unhealthy colour, but still she recognised Joe G.

She shook him gently and he jumped awake, his arm raised as if he would attack them.

'Hey, none of that,' Nerys said sharply.

'It's all right, Joe. It's Ollu of the Ark.' He squinted at her blindly for a moment in such confusion that she wondered if he'd lost his wits. Then he hauled himself up so that he was sitting. Wincing with the pain of movement, he scraped his wild hair from his eyes.

'Ollu? What are you doing here, child? Where is your mother?'

She told him the story, as briefly as she could.

'So the Missis has my twins and you are afraid that to keep them she'll let your Ma die.'

Ollu nodded. Thank God and the Great River he had not lost his wits after all, though he looked nearer fifty than thirty.

'I'd hoped you might be able to do something?'

He barked a laugh before Nerys shushed him.' Unless you can fashion me a new leg from salvage, I'm worse than useless.'

'You're alive.' Ollu said tartly, 'and you're here. I've got to try to buy our way out of this by finding a list of things I'm not sure I can get. It's risky, Joe, and I might not come back.' There. She'd said it. 'There is no one to look out for Ma or the babes. I was going to leave a note for Davey.'

Joe grunted, and she wondered if he'd heard the rumours about Davey's mother in law too. She did not ask – she did not want more bad news. 'The healer looking after Ma has promised to do her best and Cassie says she'll take care of her,' she dropped her voice, 'but Cassie doesn't seem like Cassie anymore and she seems to want revenge more than anything else...' She let the accusation hang there. Joe was Cassie's sworn man, one of her captains. He didn't leap to her defence.

'It was bad, Ollu. She's lost her boys – her future, and they didn't die easy. The invaders were as tough a load of bastards as I've ever fought.'

He wiped his face with his hands. 'You shame me. I need to get out of here. I don't know what I can do for your Ma or Cassie and as for the twins – your Ma would not acknowledge me as their father till the naming so I have no rights the Roberts' will respect...'

'Just promise you'll do your best for them, Joe. That you

won't let anyone kill Ma or hurt the boy. I think the girl is safe enough because the Missis lost a girl, but I don't want them to be slaves.' Her voice caught a little when she said that. She was shocked by the state of Joe. The last time she'd seen him he'd been a tall, muscular, laughing figure who had looked like he could conquer the world on his own. Here in this grim room he looked frail. All the people she'd depended on had changed in a few short weeks. There was no one she could trust but herself.

'Don't worry Lulu. I'll do all I can.' She smiled at his use of her baby name, but that Ollu could never exist again. She was Captain of the Ark now.

'Get well, Joe,' she said. Perhaps he only then realised how much she had changed, but he let out a huge sigh and as she turned to leave he caught her arm with his still strong hand. 'You have my word, Ollu, my word as Captain of the Daso Guard to the Captain of the Ark. I will get out of here and do all I can do keep your crew safe.' There was a glint of something in his eye, that caught in the candlelight like a scavenged diamond.

'I know, Joe,' she said. 'I will try to come back.' She clasped his hand, glad that his grip was still firm, and turned quickly away. She believed him. He would do all he could, but she wasn't sure how much that could be.

There was no one else to save Ma and the twins, no one but her. No one else who was up to the job.

Chapter Sixteen

Buzz

Buzz and Ratter kept their heads beneath the level of the bank. Someone was coming. There was the sound of the gate in the shard-wall clanking open. They were a good distance from that gate and Buzz knew that both his pack and the boat lay in the direction of that clank. He began to pull himself hand over hand in the direction of the sound.

'What are you doing?' Ratter hissed, clutching Buzz's neck with his small hands that were as strong as pliers.

'If you throttle me you'll drown. Keep your hands on my shoulders.'

Buzz wasn't sure Ratter understood. He was trembling with fear, so Buzz added more softly, 'You are safe. I'm not going to let you drown. You have to trust me.' Ratter's hands were clamped to Buzz's shoulders, but Buzz sensed him nod. Ratter was breathing hard, but as Buzz had already discovered, he was brave and not about to get them both caught because he could not keep his panic under control. Buzz's arms ached from all the digging and his fingertips were bleeding. He had to find his own strength and courage to pull their joint weight against the water, towards the only hope they had of getting away. He also had to do it slowly and pause after every movement to be sure they hadn't been heard. The water was cold, and his toes and the ends of his fingers were growing numb. When he finally spotted the moored barge, he almost sobbed with relief. He did not in fact make any noise at all because there were people nearby, close to the bank. Both voices appeared to be female – one old, one younger. The younger one spoke very quietly, and with her unfamiliar accent he found her words hard to follow.

'I will return as soon as I have the trade goods. I trust to your honour in abiding by the terms of our negotiation.'

'You may trust to my honour as I trust to yours.' The second voice was older and intoned the response as if it were part of some ritual. Buzz found himself holding his breath. It would be very bad to be discovered now.

He was watching the barge so he saw the precise moment it was unarmed. The red light under its tiller turned green and the massed spikes that had sprung up all along the side withdrew. He watched a small figure leap lightly from the shore onto the barge and bow to her unseen companion on the shore. Her head was covered in a scarf of a startling turquoise colour, and she wore a richly embroidered coat in a patchwork of colours and fabrics. She did not move for a while, but watched the shoreline anxiously. Perhaps she was waiting for her companion to leave. It was only when Buzz heard the door clang shut that the girl moved. She disappeared below and emerged a short time later in different, more practical clothes. She was thin and her hair without her scarf was a frizzy mass of pale, sun-bleached curls, vivid against her dark skin. He watched as she pulled slippers onto her bare feet and immediately got to work restarting the boat. Was she the figure he had seen that night, the one who would not stop for him? There did not seem to be anyone else.

It was no surprise to Buzz when the craft started moving of its own accord. This barge was indeed the work of civilisation: it had an engine. It was every bit as noisy as the engine on the plane, and for some reason it brought a broad grin to his face. His father would have loved it. He had to catch it. It was what Pa would have wanted. But how was he to do it?

Buzz knew there were guards on the watch towers above them, armed and likely to shoot if they spotted figures in the water. He could swim quite well under the water, but what of Ratter?

He whispered in the boy's ear.

'We need to catch that boat. We need to go under the water. You must take a big breath and hold my hand and I will pull you along.'

By way of an answer the younger boy gripped Buzz's neck so tightly in reflexive panic that Buzz had to forcibly peel his hands away.

'Think about it. The guards will shoot us if they see us. What other chance do we have?' Buzz pulled the boy round so he could see him.

Ratter was shaking uncontrollably, but he nodded. It might have been the bravest thing Buzz had ever seen. Buzz took a big breath and the boy did the same. Then Buzz put his arm across the boy's chest and pulled him down, under the water. For an instant Ratter fought him furiously, and Buzz feared that he would drown them both, or get them shot. Then Ratter seemed to gain control of himself by giving up control. He shut his eyes and went limp. Buzz hoped that he was all right, that he hadn't used up all his air in panic. There was nothing he could do for the boy but get to the barge as fast as he could, propelling himself through the water with strong frog kicks, trying to ignore the screaming of his lungs. He surfaced so that the barge was between him and the riverbank in the hope that the craft itself would keep them hidden from the sentries. Ratter surfaced a second later, making a horrible noise as he gulped in air. He was OK. He hadn't drowned, but his eyes were unfocused and strange looking. What was wrong with him?

Buzz shook him and yet Ratter stayed so limp that Buzz had to support his head in the water so the boy didn't drown.

The girl was looking away from them, downriver. Buzz could not see her face, but by the shaking of her shoulders and the general angle of her body he thought she was weeping. That seemed odd, but it gave them a chance to get on board undetected. A piece of rope trailed behind the barge, a surprisingly careless mistake, but a lucky one. He grabbed it with his right hand and wedged it under his arm so the barge pulled him and the slack form of Ratter behind it. He wanted a moment to rest and think about his next steps. Besides, every moment took him further away from the Roberts' homestead, and the threat of slavery.

Buzz watched the girl sobbing over the tiller of the barge for what seemed like a long time. He had to get Ratter safely out of the water, and he did not see any way of doing without being seen. Eventually, she wiped her eyes and tied back her extraordinary hair in the dark scarf that had been wound round her neck. She secured the tiller deftly and then went down to the cabin below. Now was his chance.

'Ratter,' he murmured quietly, 'can you hear me?' The boy's eyes still had that vacant, unfocused look that frightened him. 'I am going to push you towards the barge and give you a shove but you have to climb on. Can you do that?'

He nodded. 'Ratter can climb anything'. That was very likely true, from what Buzz had seen. Gripping the trailing rope more firmly with his right hand, he used his left to propel the boy by the scruff of his neck to the side of the barge and then shoved Rutter's skinny bottom upwards towards the deck. With mechanical efficiency, Ratter pulled himself onto the deck and then just lay there, unmoving. It was as if he had gone to sleep.

'Ratter?' he hissed, 'Are you OK? Ratter!'

Buzz got ready to pull his greater bulk on the deck when the door of the cabin door swung open and the girl returned. Dry eyed and hard faced, she gripped a spear gun in her hand.

'What is going on?' she said, in a voice that was colder than the river. 'By the thousand names of God, what do you think you are doing on my boat?'

She kept the gun levelled at Buzz as she approached the body of Ratter cautiously, turning him over with her toe. He looked very young and malnourished. The shadows under his closed eyes were dark, giving his whole face a hollowed out, skull-like appearance. He did not look much of a threat.

'He can't stay here.' To his surprise the girl pushed Ratter over board with her foot. She knelt, and with her belt knife sliced through the rope Buzz gripped so tightly.

Her face was set in a grim line as she upped the power and accelerated away from them.

'We'll drown!' Buzz wailed, with more desperation than he intended. Above the noise of the engine he could just hear her reply.

'Not my problem...'

CHAPTER SEVENTEEN

OLLU

OLLU WAS SHAKING with fear and fury. How could she have allowed the Ark to be boarded? When she was quite young Ma and Davey had fought off would-be invaders. Ma had shot one with the pistol and Davey finished off another with the spear gun. They hadn't hesitated, and she was angry with herself that she had. She should have shot the boy. Ma would never have cried so hard that she forgot to be alert for danger. How could she have been so unaware as to allow someone to actually land on the deck? It must never happen again.

She checked the engine. There was enough potential power in the battery cells to give her more speed if she needed it. She looked backwards. The bigger boy was screaming and waving his arms. He would be better off swimming for the shore. The tide was unpredictable in these waters and the Great River did like its sacrifices. She did not look back again. The Ark was not a charity. In the early days – after the chaos – only the strongest survived, and if being strong meant being ruthless then so be it. The Ark was not hers to lose.

Still, it bothered her that the little boy might drown. He couldn't have been more than eight or nine, so small and so thin. She had seen his slave brand too – like Ally's. Ally had a brother whose future lay on the water, but there was no reason to believe it was the same boy. There was no reason to believe it and yet Ally had said the boy could see the future. What if he had been right? What if his future did lie on the water, with her? Ma would have dismissed the very idea as unworthy superstition, but she was not Ma.

The Ark took a good deal of maintenance. She had to find more food: she would not grow plump or strong on the Roberts' rations. She still had to care for Lalo and the hens, keep the systems running, fill in the log. Doing all that alone seemed overwhelming. An eight year old boy was not a man. That would not break any laws, and as a former slave he might be used to hard work and following orders. She hesitated before she turned the barge around to rescue him. Even then she did not know if it was through self-interest, loneliness, guilt or compassion.

The big one could not come aboard, but she would take the child. She hefted the spear gun and rested it against her hip so she could keep one hand on the tiller. The engine laboured in the rough water but it did not take long to draw up alongside the big boy-man treading water.

'I'll take the little boy,' she shouted, 'but you'll have to fend for yourself.' She saw that it was only his strength keeping the smaller boy afloat. 'He looks ill – is he sick?'

'He was fine until he got into the water.' The bigger boy had a strange twang to his voice that made it hard to understand what he was saying, though the chattering of his teeth did not help. The Great River was not warm.

'I can't take him if he's sick.' The water was not so bad this far upstream, but the open wound on his shoulder where the brand had bitten into his flesh was raw and might be prone to infection. She leaned forward to peer at the boy's pale face and in a second the one with the strange accent had grabbed her by her ankle and pulled her with unexpected strength into the water. In her shock, she dropped the gun, which skittered across on the deck. She kicked with all her strength, and the man let her go. She hauled herself back on board, but the man moved faster. He was already ahead of her. He got there a moment before her and took possession of both the gun and the tiller.

A man had boarded the Ark! And that was not the worst of it. She was at his mercy. Piss and Pox! What was she thinking of, to have even considered taking a stranger on board? It was only because of that foolish impulse that she had made it possible for the Ark to be overwhelmed.

'Help Ratter on board!' The man had to say it twice before she understood what he meant. The boy was thrashing around, drowning, but he had at least lost the strange and vacant expression that had made her think he was ill.

Ollu knew better than to enter the water. Instead she threw him a line. 'Grab that!' she called and the boy must still have had his wits, because he caught it and she managed to haul him aboard. The two of them lay panting on the deck for a moment.

'Get us something to warm us up!' the boy with the gun demanded. He wasn't a man yet, for all his size, she could see that now. He was not a great deal older than she was – maybe fourteen or fifteen – and for all his bluster he looked almost as frightened as she felt. Not a machete-man or a hire-hand then, just a desperate chancer, fleeing the Roberts. In different circumstances she wouldn't have blamed him. In these circumstances she was furious. He had defiled the Ark.

Her anger made her bold. With a show of meekness she went to the cabin and brought out a couple of blankets and the revolver, hiding the one under the other. She threw one blanket over the shivering, choking boy, coughing out his guts on the clean deck, and went as if to throw the other over the shoulder of the bigger boy. Instead she pressed the barrel of the gun into his back.

'Drop my spear gun on the floor and kick it away. Not near the boy – over there. Put your hands in the air very slowly, and if you think I won't kill you where you stand, you don't know much about Bargers. You have defiled my boat and you will pay.' Her voice sounded coldly angry. She actually had to fight not to pull the trigger. She was so ashamed of what had just happened.

If pulling the trigger would have wiped away the shame, she would have done it, but it would only bring her trouble. They were not so far from the Roberts' that they would not hear the report of a gun, and the Roberts would follow, in canoe, kayak or dinghy. They had plenty of river-worthy craft to pursue them if they thought there was profit in it – the recapturing of a runaway slave might be enough. Besides, any gun would be useful in their fight against the invaders of Cassie's homestead.

The boy dropped the spear gun and raised his hands as she'd requested. Now what?

'Get back in the River or I'll blow your head off.'

'Please. I can help you.'

'Yeah, by shooting me with my own spear gun! Get in the water or I'll shoot.'

'Wait!' The boy called 'Ratter' levered himself up from the deck. 'You need him. I've seen it. We are all linked together like a braid. We all need each other. You will only get everything on your trade list to save your Ma if we stay with you.'

What did he know of her problems with her Ma? Had he been spying on her?

'What do you mean?'

'When I was in the water I had a vision – a true one, a sending. There's trouble ahead, Miss, and you can't take it all on by yourself. I know you're tough – I've seen that too, but you need backup. You need us.'

This was nonsense, a clever con. 'What do you know about Ma?'

'The man with one leg will help her – he's got guts. My sister, Ally, she's never backed down from anything in her life. She's mixed up with your Ma too. Your Ma needs you to come back and you most likely won't, not without us.'

How could he know these things? Had Ally told him? There was no doubt that this was Ally's brother, but she'd had no time to brief him about Joe G. Ollu shivered. The hairs on her neck were standing up as if a river ghoul danced with her soul.

She faltered. 'Why should I believe such nonsense?' Her

uncertainty had leaked into her voice and she hated herself for it. That was not something a good negotiator ever allowed to happen.

'You should believe it because it's true. I have seen a future where you lie dead on this deck and ditched in the water without prayer or ceremony, and another where you return triumphant, with a hold full of weapons.' The boy was weak after his experiences in the water, gulping for breath, 'The difference between the two visions is us...' he was not sure about that, she could tell. He had seen something more than he was telling and in that moment, she had made her decision.

'I cannot trust you.'

'You can trust me,' Ratter said confidently 'because I believe my own visions and if you need me, I need you too.' He glanced at Buzz. 'This mister has his own secrets. He's useful though. He can see in the dark – like properly see. But he'll need to convince you he's straight up himself.' Both Ratter and Ollu turned to stare at Buzz.

'You can trust me, because I am a civilised man and I keep my word.'

He thrust out his hand in Ollu's direction, as if he expected her to shake it. 'My name is Buzz and I'm pleased to meet you.' It seemed ludicrous to her to shake the hand of someone who had just thrown her in the water, boarded her boat and threatened her and yet for reasons she did not attempt to understand she stepped forward and shook his right hand, transferring the revolver to her left. She knew that he could have overpowered her easily if he wanted to do.

'I am Ollu, Captain of the Ark,' she said.

There was a horrible awkward silence and then Buzz said, 'I don't want to worry you and I'm not saying this just to distract you, but I think we might be about to hit something.'

Chapter Eighteen

Buzz

The girl, Ollu, was quick, he'd give her that. She had swung round to see what he was talking about, tucked the revolver into her belt, scooped up the spear gun and resumed control of the tiller in the time he took to finish his sentence.

'Thank God! That's one of our trail barges. Grab hold of it if you can. I need to recouple it. '

She sounded elated, though Buzz could not see what there was to be excited about. All he could see was a kind of floating lump of mildewed, semi-transparent plastic bobbing around on the river. He wanted to show willing, however, so he leaned out to grab it as Ratter leapt lightly on board the 'trail barge' and lay down flat on the top of it. The plastic was so thin it started to buckle under even his light weight. He started to manoeuvre it towards the rear of the boat by paddling towards the barge's side. Between the two of them they got it into position.

'Ratter! Can you see how it fixes onto the tow bar?'

Ollu appeared to have more faith in the boy than she did in Buzz. It was certainly true that Ratter's agility and speed of thought looked like being an advantage. Buzz was not accustomed to feeling useless. It was not a comfortable feeling.

Ratter's arms were not long enough to reach the mechanism, however, and not being able to swim he was reluctant to re-enter the water. Buzz found himself surprisingly eager to get wet all over again, just to prove to this skinny girl that he was worth having on board as more than extra baggage.

Coupling the two barges was a lot more difficult than he had imagined. The tide pulled them apart then forced them together unexpectedly, trapping his hands between them. He persisted only because he hated to give up, and because he didn't want to look ham fisted and incompetent in front of either Ratter or the girl. Ollu did not seem to regard his eventual coupling of the two barges as any kind of achievement. She just nodded at him as he hauled his tired body back onto the barge.

'I'm going down below. Don't touch anything,' she said, and disappeared into the cabin.

Buzz sank down on the deck, exhausted and let his head loll forward. For a whole five minutes he was no longer afraid. Somewhere in the back of his head he heard the familiar thrum of a comp. He couldn't reach it yet, but it was there. The pulse of it gave him hope. He had avoided being enslaved, killed by guards and dying through drowning. He had also missed a night's sleep and he found his head nodding down on his chest as the gentle motion of the waves rocked him to sleep.

Ollu's laugh woke him. It was not particularly kindly.

'Ratter says you can see in the dark?'

He nodded, trying not to look as fogged by sleep as he felt. 'You can do the night watch then. Here. There is not much to eat, but you can have a share – for now. If you don't make yourself useful though, you'll have to go. I don't haul dead weight.'

He nodded, not sure how the initiative had passed out of his hands once more. The bread and cheese she gave him was sour tasting but good, and although there was nowhere near enough of it, he was grateful.

'Are there fish in the River?'

Ollu gave him a look that suggested she had never heard such a stupid question.

'Of course. I'll put the lines out shortly. You're not from

round here?'

He shook his head. 'I blew in from a way off,' he said and then, so she didn't think he was uppity, he added, 'It seems like a nice place.'

The girl snorted. 'Go back to your beauty sleep, mister foreigner. I'll worry about the fish.' It felt as though she was putting him down, but he was too tired to argue. When he awoke again, Ratter was scrubbing the deck, and Ollu was nowhere to be seen.

'What you said earlier about us all being bound together, was that true?' Buzz asked.

'I don't lie about my visions.' Ratter sounded hurt, but his claim struck Buzz as quite unlikely. He was sure Ratter would have found it very useful to lie about such a subject. After all, how could his word ever be verified?

'Are your visions like a dream, or what?'

Ratter did not pause in his scrubbing. 'They're nothing like a dream. In a vision, you are like – there. It's hard to tell whether it's real or not sometimes. You can smell the people and I don't always know the people. Like, I saw you in a vision before I saw you for real.'

'Oh yeah?' Buzz could not keep the scepticism from his voice. It was his father's legacy, he regarded fortune telling as hokum. 'If there can be no scientific explanation, Buzz, the chances are that there is skulduggery involved. Beyond our own little bit of rational paradise, here in our compound, this world is full of tricksters and con men.'

His memory of his father's voice was almost as real as a vision to him, so he could see how a child such as Ratter might get confused.

Ratter was still talking: 'Yeah, you were in the sky – in one of those things that fly, like before the chaos. You were with an old mister, then I saw him with his eyes open, hanging from a tree. Not like with a rope or anything, just hanging out of the tree with his eyes staring. I knew you as soon as I saw you in the hut and I knew if I had seen you in a vision I had to stick with you.'

Buzz didn't know what to say to that. As far as he knew he had never mentioned the plane, or his father. Had he talked in his sleep? Had Ratter read his mind? He opened his mouth to ask him, and then shut it again. Ratter carried on scrubbing and chatting as if such insights were normal for him. Maybe they were.

'Yeah, Ally told me to keep my mouth shut about my visions. She was right. I told the Roberts' gaffer he'd end his days with an arrow in his eye before too long and he beat me till I bled.' Ratter showed Buzz the red weals on his back. 'Ally said if I got a chance to leave I was to take it, even without her. Still feels like I'm running out on her though.'

'Ally is your sister?'

Ratter nodded, 'One of them. I had three. One died in the raid. She was fighting to save us, but one of the men shot her.' He paused and pulled a face. 'She was called Grace. She was beautiful and brave and I'm going to kill the man who killed her. Then there is Bel. She got away, but I have to find her.'

'Why? Surely she's safe? She escaped the slavers.'

'She is beautiful too, which isn't good for a girl – at least not in the city. She's blind but she can tell when someone is lying just by touching their hand. Have you any idea what a gift that is? Before the slavers came she'd been picked as the Mainman's woman. Chances are his lackeys will have found her. I've got to get back to save her.'

Buzz was as puzzled by this as everything else Ratter had said. 'Won't she be safe as the wife of someone important?'

'You *are* from the sky, boy. That's worse than slavery. She'll be locked indoors in his roost and no one will ever see her again until he gets tired of her and one day they'll be news of another wedding and her body'll wash up somewhere and everyone will say it is a terrible shame and an accident.'

Buzz still did not understand, but he had the wit not to say so.

'Did you see that in your vision?'

Ratter nodded. 'I saw her married to the Boss, but it doesn't have to turn out like that. I can change it.'

'Has anything you dreamed ever not happened?'

'Not as far as I know, but that don't mean it can't be changed.' Ratter jutted his chin forward aggressively and suddenly looked horribly, vulnerably young. 'Will you help me?'

Buzz wanted to say that what happened to Ratter's sister was none of his business, but then, what was his business? There was his mission to find the Queen B, but he was not likely to find that ancient, powerful comp on a barge crewed by a skinny girl. Pa must have made a mistake with the comps coordinates or the storm had blown them of course, because he'd sensed no other tech anywhere close. Pa would have known where to look and what to do, but Pa was dead. The pause was a long one and when he ended it, he felt as though he had crossed from one world to another. As if he'd made some radical change of course.

'OK,' he said, sounding as casual as he could, even though his heart was thumping. 'I'll help you, but what about Ollu?'

'What about her?' Ollu's soft slippers had made no sound on the deck. She had a couple of fish in her hand and a grim expression on her face.

'We were just making plans for the future,' Buzz said, guiltily.

'Well, you won't have a future if you don't help me with these. You know how to gut and clean fish?' She threw him a knife at his nod. He wondered why she was trusting him with such a thing that could so easily be a weapon, but then he saw that she didn't trust him at all and this was a test. Somehow without doing anything she'd made him feel bad, yet again. On this boat his place seemed to be in the wrong.

CHAPTER NINETEEN

OLLU

OLLU HAD AT least managed to get the Ark back into some kind of shape while Buzz slept. The young one, Ratter, fell over himself to be helpful. Perhaps he was grateful to her for being rescued, but she didn't believe it. Life didn't work like that. She would not let them hijack the Ark to rescue Ally, or for any other cause. She had to be on guard. She could perhaps trust them with small tasks, but they must not know the Ark's secrets.

She did not open the aye-eye's secret compartment. She did not dare, not with strangers on board. Instead, she wrote up the paper log in her own made up code. Written down, her task seemed bigger than ever. She needed to meet up with Davey. Whatever his mother in law was up to, he was still Davey and he would help her. She knew he would. He would know how to get the salvage she needed. He couldn't have anything to do with the slave trade. If she saw him, he would explain. He'd help her save Ma and things could yet be all right.

The recovery of the crop barge was good news, but it barely lightened her mood. The inside of her mouth was sore, but she still chewed at it as she steered the boat. Things were out of control. Davey would be furious if he knew there was a man aboard the Ark. She had to find a way of getting rid of Buzz before she met with Davey. Indeed she needed to get rid of him before they met any other craft. Could she kill him?

'What do I do with the guts?' Buzz's strange twang cut through her thoughts, 'Do I throw them overboard?'

She shook her head. 'Put them in the bucket. We use them to make sauce and fertiliser and then we trade it.' He looked blank. 'We are traders. We grow luxury stuff on the barge – specially modified crops. We salvage and fabrick artefacts and materials. We catch fish and process the guts using secret techniques and we sell that too. We do everything we can to earn a living and we don't waste anything.'

Buzz looked shocked at the thought. 'But it is not waste to return stuff to Gaia, by water, by land or through the air.'

'It is waste not to use everything. Put the guts in the bucket and the bones in the bag. Fish bones make good needles and pins. We use everything.' She wished he would just disappear. His bulk on the barge's deck was an affront, and yet she could not imagine getting rid of him. She could imagine fetching the gun while he slept, but she could not picture herself pulling the trigger.

If he left before they arrived in market waters, she might get away with her mistake. 'There is a good place near here with plenty of work. They don't have any slaves so far as I know, and they are not so suspicious of visitors that they shoot on sight. You and the boy could find a place there and, if you prove yourself good workers through what's left of the summer, there's a good chance they'd keep you through the winter.' She tried to sound friendly. It was not easy. Something about Buzz made her uncomfortable.

It was his eyes, that was it. He had very strange eyes and she didn't like looking at them.

No one in any village would look kindly on a boy with eyes like his. They had a silvery sheen to them, as if coated in something metallic. The village of Newtown was liberal in its attitude to incomers, but taking Buzz in might be a step too far.

'Why can't we stay here?'

'Because this is a matriarch boat. It's not for men. You aren't safe here.'

He turned those eyes on her. 'Who would hurt us? You?'

She shook her head. She would if she could, but she did not seem up to the task. 'My clan. This boat has always been a matriarch boat. Your presence defiles it.'

'Always been, doesn't mean always should be,' he countered.

'Round here it does,' she said firmly. 'Our traditions have seen us through the tough times. We aren't going to give them up now. I'm just warning you. I think you should take what you're offered and let me put you shore-side. By the day after tomorrow we'll be far enough away for you to be safe from the Roberts'. The village is on my way.'

'What would you trade us for?' Buzz asked.

Ollu felt herself blushing, 'Grain, and maybe some meat,' she answered, honestly enough. 'I haven't enough to last me. They wouldn't own you or anything, but traders always take a finder's fee. If you didn't work out they'd want a refund next time I came by – something for nothing. So, it sort of means that I vouch for you. It is the best offer you'll get.'

Buzz threw the last of the fish guts into the bucket and the air was full of the scent of fish.

'I'll take a rain check,' he said.

Ollu had no idea what he meant. It did not matter. She had taken the island route which bisected a busy and much settled region. They were approaching market waters. The river was bright with painted craft, with flags and pennants and picture-signs advertising local produce.

She and Ma had been away from these parts of the river for too long. She loved the bustle and the smells of the summer market even though, being tekk specialists, they had never done much business there.

'You have to get down below!' she yelled at her unwanted guests, 'There will be trouble if you're seen, so stay away from the porthole window. Touch anything and you're dead.'

She had taken care to leave the cabin neat, and she had made doubly sure the Ark's secrets were as well hidden as she could make them. She did not much like the thought of the two boys being in her private quarters, but allowing them to be seen would be worse. She was not sure she could live with the shame.

She'd missed the chatter, the laughter and the music of the song-pedlars. With the brightness of the boats, the summer market always had a festival feel: traders rigged out in their best to make a good impression, rafts that bumped and rocked their way through the crowd full of village children in holiday mood. Hastily she tied a clean, multi-coloured headscarf round her hair and steered for the centre of the packed boats and the faded neon pink of the 'Punk Panther.' They were not Bargers, just market traders, but they were old friends, and likely to know if Davey were already at the Island of Spring for the birthing of his first child.

'Dizzy!' she called out, temporarily forgetting her dignity as Captain of the Ark in her delight at seeing the portly white man in an ancient sunhat haggling over a lamb carcass.

His smile of recognition gave her heart. She cut the engine and poled her way through the tightly packed barges. Most were not really boats at all, but rough rafts loaded with food and textiles, simple clinker built craft or much repaired ancient wherries that were just about fit for the shallow water of the Chert-sea Summer market.

Traders hurried to get out of her way. That was natural, as Bargers were important here on their native element, but this time she detected a certain fear in the eyes of the wool merchants and grain sellers, something more than respect. The sudden silence of the song pedlars seemed ominous too, though they always took a break from time to time to wet their whistles on local meadow ale.

'Ollu – you trading today?' Dizzy's broad arm indicated the bloody carcasses piled at his feet and she reluctantly shook her head. She had, as yet, nothing to trade except whatever was still left in her coat and she was not yet desperate enough to part with that.

'Just passing through,' she said. 'Have you seen Davey or the rest of the clan heading upstream?'

Was it her imagination or did Dizzy's eyes narrow at the mention of Davey's name? Did his warm smile cool by a fraction? He shrugged, like a man who knew more than he wanted to say. The noisy flow of barter seemed to ebb for a moment, as though those round them were straining to hear his reply.

'The market's been off what with the high water after the storm and all. We've had some drying out to do. Still, we have the weather for it.' He settled on the neutral subject of the weather with obvious relief. Anxious to avoid a lengthy discussion on how the latest rains had affected the condition of the village herds, Ollu clucked sympathetically.

'It was quite a blow,' she said. 'I'm guessing the Great River took what it could.' She kept her response conventional while she searched his face for some clue as to what was going on. She relaxed a little as the song-pedlars started up again, an unfamiliar haunting air. Dizzy turned back to his business. On the surface, all seemed much as usual, and yet for some reason it felt to Ollu as if the whole market, like the music, was subtly changed, as if everyone was performing in a different key. Perhaps it was only that she herself was changed.

If there had been time she would have liked to stay and gossip, renew old acquaintances even drop anchor and explore with the kayak. She felt suddenly nostalgic for the time before the twins, and then immediately felt guilty.

Ma had always let her do a little trading on her own behalf when their stocks were good, selling fermented fish sauce and medicinal herbs in exchange for trinkets. Ma did most of her salvage on contract, but they occasionally sold sheet plastic or reusable metal for a haunch of meat. No one in the villages bothered much with tekk. It was unreliable and expensive and they preferred to trust to brawn and human guts rather than to the vagaries of machines. There had never been primitivist tekk burnings round this part of the river, but there were more than a few primitivist sympathisers round and about. Ma worked hard on keeping them sweet. She was surprised Dizzy did not ask after Ma and seemed reluctant to talk to her at all. Maybe he already knew what had befallen them, though she would have been surprised as there was little contact between the Island villages and the Roberts' homestead. The river, and a generation of suspicion, lay between them.

She worked her way through the throng of craft and the shouting traders, adding her own voice to the cacophony. 'Ware the Ark! Coming through!' She waved at a few people she recognised, Missis Grebefarm with her barge of vegetables acknowledged her with a wave of one mucky hand, Councillor Edgar Village nodded at her while he grappled with his oar. His boat was full of caged birds.

It took a good half hour to negotiate her way through the melee and once through she could feel too many eyes staring at her. The traders of the summer market were glad to be rid of her, and she did not know why.

Chapter Twenty

Buzz

Buzz approved of the neat, wood-lined interior of the cabin. He admired the clever arrangement of sink, stove and cool cupboard, the pumped heated water, the small, well designed shower, the waste digester and the bunks that stowed away into the wall. It all smacked of organisation, intelligence, of civilisation. Ratter seemed less impressed. He took one look at the room, sniffed the air, and then lay down on the wooden floor and fell instantly asleep. He did not even attempt to lower one of the beds or untie a hammock from the ceiling where it had been neatly rolled and secured on a large metal hook.

It was true the cabin smelled less than sweet. That's what happens when you housed animals – chickens and goats – where only people should live. There was something else too. The comp was somewhere in this room. It was unlikely to be anything like General, but even the simplest old timer comp would be something. Gaia's blessings! He craved the feel of data slipping like silken threads through his thoughts again. He licked his lips. He was trembling, and he needed to get a grip on himself.

He followed the sonic hum. There was a comp there, he just couldn't reach it. He knelt down on the old, well-varnished boards and listened harder. Yes, the sound was unmistakable. Checking that Ratter was indeed asleep, he ran his fingers cautiously along the edge of the boards. There was no obvious hinge or break in their smoothness to suggest a secret door or some hidden compartment, and yet he knew it was there. In his enthusiasm, he tried to lift the boards with his fingers, which was a stupid idea and he got nothing but a splinter for his trouble. He didn't want to scrabble around like some desperate dog trying to unearth a bone. That was not the action of a civilised man. He looked around the room to see if there was a latch, something he should press or twist or pull to reveal what he knew to be hidden. Nothing suggested itself; the walls were the same aged, varnished wood as the floor. The few hooks on the walls held useful things: onions, rope, an oil lantern, a tinder box, a couple of rolled hammocks, several scarves and a couple of waterproof jackets. Nothing that suggested high technology, nothing to suggest his instincts were right. He knew though. He knew that there was a working comp on board. It's sound was only slightly out of the range of normal human hearing.

The sound of music, shouting and chatter from outside dragged him from his search. Out of respect for Ollu's worry that he might be seen, he found a bright scarf hanging from a peg by the door and wrapped it round his head before peering out of the porthole. Anyone glancing his way might mistake him for a woman. The scarf smelled of Ollu, and of herbs, lantern oil and fish.

The market was an amazing sight. All kinds of boats filled the river so that a nimble boy, someone like Ratter, could have leapt from one side to the other without touching the water. Everywhere there were crude home-made flags and pennants with pictures of bread, cakes or fish appliquéd and embroidered on them. They billowed in the breeze. And everywhere there were people: young and old, dark skinned and fair, pockmarked, scarred, wrinkled and smooth fleshed. All the women wore the bright scarves favoured by Ollu though hair of all shades and textures escaped such loose binding. The smell of the river was strong, but still he could detect the stench of butchered meat, the yeasty smell of beer and the tart freshness of apples. He was leaning forward too eagerly, and had to remind himself to hang back, to remain unseen. Something about the way the women turned from Ollu worried him. Was there danger here? It seemed to him that their presence caused a certain consternation. Was this a hostile place? He wished he had not left his pack by the outer gates of the Roberts' place. He would have been glad of a weapon of his own. For all the smiles and the waves in Ollu's direction, something was not right.

A sudden noise startled him. Ratter! He was rolling around and groaning as if he was in pain. He was still asleep and in the grip of a nightmare.

'Hush. It's all right,' Buzz said, as soothingly as he could. Ollu was jumpy and Buzz wasn't sure what she'd do if they drew attention to themselves in the crowded market. Ratter still thrashed around, moaning. In desperation Buzz shook the younger boy awake.

Ratter was wild eyed and flushed with sleep. He stared at Buzz without recognition.

'I have to go,' he muttered to himself, and was on his feet and heading for the cabin door before Buzz could stop him. Buzz had to lunge for the door to get there before him.

'No.' Buzz barred his way. 'What are you talking about? Why do you have to go? Where do you have to go?'

Ratter's eyes still wore a strange, unfocused look. 'They will come for us,' he said, and there was real terror in his voice.

'Who will come?' Buzz's own voice shook a little, as if Ratter's fear was somehow contagious.

'Slavers, invaders,' he whispered and then, shuddering, he shut his eyes. When he opened them, he was Ratter again.

'You're creeping me. Why are you staring at me like that?'

'I think you had another dream.'

Ratter shrugged. 'I have them all the time. I don't remember them all. What did I say?'

'That we should run.'

'Let's go then!'

'What, leave the boat and just go?'

'Why not? If I saw something bad, I'm not sticking around to see it again. My dreams are true.'

'I don't want to leave.'

'Well, I'm going.' Ratter's face was set, obstinate.

'I thought our fates were linked?'

That shrug again. 'If they're linked, you'll follow.'

Buzz wanted to find the comp beneath the floor of the cabin. He needed to find it. Without the stream of data that he'd known all his life, he felt only half alive, but at least he was half alive and without Ratter he'd be dead, or still rotting in the slave hut. Ratter was the nearest thing to a friend he'd got, and he didn't think he had the courage to let him run away alone. The girl on the boat would kill him the first chance she got. There was no friendship on offer there.

'We can't get off the boat here. There's some kind of water market and, I don't know, it doesn't feel right.'

Ratter grinned his sudden illuminating grin that made his gaunt rodent face look mischievous and human. 'What, are you the prophet now?'

Buzz shook his head. 'No, but it feels wrong.'

'OK. Tell me when it feels right.' Ratter settled back down on the floor, as if he intended going back to sleep.

'You're just going to take my word for it?' Buzz knew he sounded incredulous. He found Ratter's abrupt change of mood baffling.

'You believed me when I said we should go. I believe you when you say we should stay. Running isn't always the right thing to do. We might run into bigger trouble. I always want to run; not running got me slaved, and killed Grace, my sister...' His face darkened, as if the sun had gone with his grin. 'We go the moment you think we should, yeah?'

Buzz shivered, in spite of the warmth of the cabin. He didn't know what was safe or not. He knew less than Ratter. He wouldn't know what a slaver looked like if one sailed past the window. He took up his station by the port hole again, watching the receding market, the way the traders gratefully turned their backs on the barge. When he could see no sign of any people and the river seemed quiet again, he risked leaving the cabin, though he kept the head scarf wrapped round him.

'What was all that about?' he asked the girl, cautiously.

'Get down below. You might be seen!' She hissed at him angrily, 'And take that ridiculous head scarf off.'

'There is something wrong, isn't there?' he persisted.

'You mean apart from the fact that my mother is dying, I've abandoned my siblings, I've got an impossible trade list to meet and *you* are on a matriarch ship,' she said, spitting out the 'you' as if she hated him.

'Look, maybe it is best if we leave. Ratter seems to think you're right and we're in danger here. You could drop us outside the village like you said.'

Ollu seemed to have forgotten to yell at him. She looked grey with worry and fatigue.

'What did Ratter say?'

'Something about slavers. He had a dream but he can't remember it.'

'I suppose it could just be a dream, couldn't it? Not everything he dreams is a toxic prophecy?' She sounded as uncertain as he felt.

'I don't know,' he said, unable to keep his own terrible weariness from his tone. 'I think we might as well assume we're in danger all the time.'

She nodded at that, and smiled. 'So that's all right then.'

He wasn't sure what she meant, though he thought the smile had to be a good sign.

'Do you know how to steer? Just hold the tiller for me, will you? Keep us heading through the central part of the river.'

'I thought you wanted me to go below?' Buzz was not used to being with such volatile people. At home, people were steadier.

'No. I mean, I do, but I need a break. The head scarf is a good idea too. Keep it on. Ma will kill me when she finds out I've let a man wear one of her headscarves, but then she'd kill me if she knew you were on the barge, so there's no point in worrying.' She turned to look at him with her sharp, observant eyes. 'You're right about there being something wrong too, but by the Great River I don't know what. I've been going to the summer market all my life and I've never felt less welcome.' Then she disappeared into the cabin with a sigh.

Chapter Twenty-One

Ollu

IT WASN'T A good idea to fall asleep and leave the strange boy in charge of the boat. Ollu knew it wasn't a good idea, but somehow it happened anyway. She was exhausted.

Buzz was at the tiller, as unconvincing a woman as she was likely to find. His orange scarf blew wildly around him like a flag, but he was steering the barge carefully, his eyes never leaving the river even as he spoke to Ratter. In spite of her foolishness no harm had come to the barge or to her. The Island of Spring was looming. If she had been going to drop them off landside she ought to have done so long before this.

'Thank you,' she said and took over. Ahead, she could see the bright boats of the Bargers moored under the shade of the trees. There was music too. Uncle Hari was playing his fiddle and the wild strains of a fast Barger reel lifted her heart despite her worries.

'You'll have to stay down below while I do my business,' she said. 'I can't drop you here. This is sacred land. Our own place, the place for birthing and marriages and funerals too. My family would kill you if they found you here.'

Buzz's nose wrinkled with distaste, as though he could smell a bad odour. 'What's wrong?' Ollu asked.

'Can't you smell it?'

Ollu sniffed the air, but could detect nothing but the familiar smell of the river and the scent of barbecued meat. She shook her head.

'What's that in the river? It's coming from there.'

She followed his pointing finger. In the far distance was a lone trail barge, the kind sometimes used to transport horses. One of her cousins had made a good business transporting breeding livestock from farm to farm. It was quicker by river and the beasts tended to arrive in better condition.

'It's just the horse barge,' she said, 'My cousin, Melinda, trades horses from time to time. Why?'

Buzz had gone pale. 'It's not horses in there. Can't you smell it?'

Ratter looked frightened, but Ollu didn't think he could smell anything either.

'We have to go there.' Buzz said

'Hey! This is my barge and I say where we have to go.'

'Please steer towards the barge.'

'You go down below now and I will. Hurry, you will be seen! The family will have set a watch!' Reluctantly Buzz and Ratter did as she asked. 'Stay away from the port hole!' she called after them. She was taking such risks. She did not know what would happen to her if anyone discovered she had allowed men on Ma's barge. She did not think it had ever happened before.

The horse barge was not far beyond the island, and though the scent of the barbecue made her stomach growl, Ollu's curiosity was aroused. She steered towards it. Soon she could smell it too, the animal stench of ordure, sweat and death. Her appetite disappeared instantly, replaced by a sickening sense of dread. Whatever she was about to find was not going to be good.

She was stopped, as she had anticipated, by a couple of her cousins in kayaks. They were armed, and more hostile than was usual.

'What are you doing at the tiller? Where's your Ma?'

'She's sick. Is Davey here?

'What kind of sick? You can't bring disease to the island.'

It had been a stupid, thoughtless thing to say. For some reason, she had expected more of a welcome from her own kin.

'It's baby fever. I've left her shore-side along with the babes. The barge is clean and disease free, as am I.'

The two scrutinised her closely. 'You look just the same as always,' the elder one said grudgingly. 'Shouldn't you have grown by now?' She stuck her chest forward to show off her mature figure and Ollu tried not to mind. She was older than these twin cousins by a year or more, but showed no sign of maturity except in her thinking. She reminded herself, as her mother was apt to do, that brains outdid brawn in most things. She thought of Buzz down below. True as that might be, there were times when brawn helped.

There was no point in bickering with the watchers. It was more important that she found her way to the island and to the source of the stench that so offended Buzz.

'Davey's on the island, of course. It is his baby we're all waiting for and if it isn't here soon everyone is going to go flood-mad. Stell looks as big as an egg and keeps moaning and half the aunties claim she's in labour, the other half that her body is still practising.' She pulled a face. 'She's making a lot more fuss than you might expect. You'd better anchor up. If you hurry you'll get some food. Remind them to save us some.'

'How long are you watching for?' Ollu said, in an effort to be friendly.

'Until Ma decides she's proved a point. It wasn't our turn but...'

'Never mind,' her sister interrupted. 'We'll see you later. Be sure to remind Davey that you should go on the watch rota too. You're not really the captain, just a stand in. You have to take your turn.'

The two girls left in opposite directions with a splash of oars and a toss of thick auburn hair. Their scarves were worn so loosely that their beautiful hair escaped in all directions. Such immodesty was very likely what had got them put on watch duty.

If either of them cared to watch her they would see her draw close to the horse barge, but Ollu was confident that neither of them would bother.

She felt a chill at their talking of Davey's child. She had never thought of childbirth as particularly dangerous until she'd seen Ma go through it. Now she knew, and she couldn't help being frightened for Stell.

That wasn't the only thing she was frightened about. As they neared the horse barge, her stomach churned, as if her guts knew what her brain had yet to understand.

Slowly, she brought the Ark alongside the stinking horse-barge. Ratter and Buzz emerged from the cabin. They both looked as terrified as she felt. The horse barge had only one small barred window to allow the circulation of air, and three pairs of eyes peered out of it. Hands were thrust through the bars. Imploring, desperate voices begged for help.

'It's a slave barge.' Ratter wailed. 'It's like in my dream. The slavers are here!'

CHAPTER
TWENTY-TWO

OLLU

OLLU FELT SICK. The horse barge was not guarded. It was as if the whole clan knew about the cargo. Knew and didn't care. Whoever had brought this cargo to the island did not think to hide it and was not ashamed. But Ollu was.

'We've got to let them out!' Ratter's voice was shrill.

'Hush. Don't draw attention to us!' The two boys ought to stay below, out of sight. Ollu felt too numb to give the order.

There was nowhere for the slaves to go but on board the Ark. She could not let more toxic strangers defile her deck. It was all wrong.

'Help! Get us out of here! Please!' The desperate voices of the caged slaves could not be ignored. If being a Barger meant enslaving other people, she was not sure she wanted to claim that heritage. She had been brought up to be proud of being a Barger, of keeping tekk running since the days of Chaos. Everything Ma had taught her couldn't be a lie.

Ratter and Buzz were looking at her, waiting for her to speak.

'Yes,' she said, though her voice seemed to come from a long way away. 'We have to help them. You'd better bring them aboard.'

'Don't faint, Missis,' Ratter said. 'You're shaking. You'd better sit down.'

She was ashamed of this weakness too. She did not have time to sit down. She was already planning what she should do next. She could take the slaves to Newtown and Ma-Low – where she'd wanted to leave Buzz and Ratter. They would have to leave quickly. She did not want her own clan on her back. She didn't want to have to fight Flo, or Davey for that matter. Surely he couldn't be involved?

Buzz was speaking to her but she couldn't understand what he was saying. She slumped down, hit the deck heavily. She had to put her head between her knees till she could feel her own blood buzzing around inside her skull like a swarm of angry bees.

'What did you say?' She managed to speak at last.

'Have you got something to break open the lock?' Buzz was looking at her, his expression worried. She forced herself back up onto unsteady feet. The stench from the horse barge was overpowering. It smelled as though something had died.

'Wait here.'

She did not want anyone to see where she kept the tools. Chloe squawked and launched herself at Ollu as she went below. She tried to remember when she'd last given the hens any grain. Everything was falling apart.

She found the pair of bolt cutters and her gun. She took the gun and stuck it in the waist band of her cut-downs and covered it with her blouse. In a daze, she put on her trickster's coat, her leather boots, then re-tied her head scarf for good measure. It took her barely a moment. She was the Captain of the Ark. She needed to be in command.

Buzz and Ratter had been talking about her in her brief absence, that was clear, but they had also persuaded the captured slaves to be quiet. All those eyes – the eyes of her companions, the eyes of the slaves – were all fixed on her, watching to see what she would do next.

She handed the bolt cutters to Buzz.

'You get the door open. I'll keep watch and man the tiller.'

He nodded, but it was Ratter who leapt from the Ark to the narrow foothold offered by the horse-barge. Ollu's eyes scanned the water for signs that the twins might return, but all she could hear was the echo of their laughter and the distant sound of song peddlars, playing for Davey's wife and for the rest of the slavers. This couldn't be happening.

Ratter broke open the padlocked chain of the door in moments and then the prisoners were boarding the Ark, her boat, in silence. She flinched as they scrambled on board. There were five in all; three men and two women. All young, under twenty, she guessed, and all bloodstained and terrified. They had left a corpse behind in the horse barge. The survivors were trembling and none to steady on their legs. Ratter closed the door of the horse barge and tried to arrange things so it still looked secure.

Should Ollu make them say the traditional words for boarding a Bargers' rig? The words could not change the fact that they were not her people, and that three of them were men. It was way too late for all of that. None of Ma's training had prepared her for this. She made her own decision, and stepped forward to greet them.

'I am the Captain of the Ark. I'll take you upstream a way and drop you at a village I know. You should be able to find work or make your way home from there.'

'Have you any water?' It was the sturdier of the two girls who spoke. She looked dreadful, and Ollu could see her lips were cracked and dry. What could she do but help?

'We have to get you out of sight.'

Buzz helped her get them below. She could tell they didn't trust her. They were probably afraid she was another slaver. They shambled after her with Buzz herding them from behind. They'd been sharing the confines of the horse barge with a dead man. What if they were diseased? It was already too late to save The Ark if they were sick.

How could Bargers do this? Clan rules on the disposal of the dead were complicated, but with good reason. How could her own people beat a man to death and leave his body to rot, unpurified? She could not believe it, but she did not see how it could not be true.

She didn't like the way the slaves exchanged glances, or the way they filled the narrow cabin, watching her with hard eyes. The Ark felt suddenly small with so many people in it. She was overwhelmed: a child again, playing dress-up in her mother's coat. She had made a mistake in letting these strangers on the Ark. She knew it in her bones. She tried not to let her doubt show as she filled a couple of beakers with sweet water from the tank. Each person took only a couple of sips before passing the cup on.

'It's Ok. I have enough,' she said and refilled each cup twice so that everyone had a decent drink. They looked less sick immediately, which was good, but not reassuring. These strangers were likely dangerous.

She pumped hot water into a metal bowl and found a sliver of traded soap for them to wash their hands and clean their wounds. She had some farm brewed vodka too, and she felt their eyes on her when she pulled it from the cupboard. 'It's not for drinking,' she said hastily, 'It'll stop infection.' She poured a little of it into another bowl and tore up some rags they'd kept back to use as nappies for the babes.

'You can use these to clean up. When you are done, you can put the rags in this bucket.' She pulled out their battered pail. She would burn everything when she got the chance. She could risk no infection on the Ark, but she could not purify the Ark properly while the slaves remained upon it, and that worried her. She knew nothing about these people. Putrid Puss and all the thousand names of God, but everything was wrong.

'Thank you,' one of the women murmured. She did not see which. There was nothing more she could do. She did not want to hear their stories. She did not want to know who had captured them. She wanted nothing to do with any of it. She had to save her mother and the twins. She could not get involved in this horror. She nodded at them awkwardly and was careful to take the jar of voddie with her when she left the cabin. They had already fouled the air.

On deck, she took a deep breath of fresh, river air. Ratter's face looked more pinched and anxious than usual. 'We should skaddle,' he said quietly. 'The slavers could be here any second.'

'I have to see my brother.'

Ratter looked at her in horror, 'No! We must get gone fast before anyone notices. They'll kill us if they find out what we've done. That's cargo that we've just freed – salvage.'

She understood that all too well, but she was surprised Ratter did. The worst thing you could do to a Barger – besides killing him or one of the clan – was to steal cargo, rip off salvage. If you did that any Barger could take their revenge, take your life in payment, any time. The thought made her shake. Maybe it would have been better to leave the slaves where they were, to pass on by?

'I don't believe Davy's involved in all this. He wouldn't... I mean...' She didn't have the words to explain how much she needed to believe that this had nothing to do with Davey. 'Anyway, I need his help,' she finished lamely.

'If you go, we might steal the barge.' He knew he had her there. How could she leave the Ark in the hands of strangers? If she lost the Ark her Ma would kill her. If Ma herself was not already dead.

'If you steal my barge, I will go back to the Roberts' farm and kill your sister, Ally, myself.' She showed him the weapon in her waist band. 'You understand?' He nodded. 'Can you vouch for Buzz?'

Ratter shrugged. 'Buzz is not the thieving kind. Besides we're not stupid. I was blagging. We don't know enough about the river and the land round here. We need you as much as we need the barge.'

Was that even true? In the space of a few days every truth she'd clung to seemed to have turned out to be a lie. Everyone she'd trusted had abandoned her. She wasn't sure she knew anything anymore. Not that she was about to argue with Ratter.

'I'll take us further upstream and weigh anchor. I'll use the kayak and leave Buzz the spear gun.' She could not believe she was going to do this, to leave the defence of the Ark to a stranger and a man at that. Worse, she was going to arm him so he could fight members of her own clan. She must be mad. 'I have to talk to Davey. Get Buzz up here. I need you both to do something.'

Buzz emerged from the cabin, looking worried, his strange eyes shadowed.

'The slaves are in a bad way. One of the girls, Angela, her cuts are infected,' he said in his strange accent.

By the Great River, could things get any worse? Buzz clamped his mouth shut without saying more and looked at her expectantly.

'I have to go ashore to talk to my brother. I cannot take you there, but I can only leave you in charge of the barge if you pledge an oath – a blood one.'

'And if we don't?'

'I'll shoot you.' Those words were not the ones she'd planned to say. She was surprised to hear them come out of her mouth. Her hand had found her gun as she'd said them and she gripped it like a strong branch in a swollen river. It was not a sensible thing to say for, as Ma was fond of saying: 'a deal under duress wasn't worth a sneeze.' How much more true would that be of a promise?

But Buzz nodded, as though her response was perfectly reasonable. 'OK. What do you want me to promise?'

She released her hold on the gun, put on the safety and returned to her waist band.

'I would rather you gave it freely,' she said. 'I want to be able to pretend I can believe you.'

'What do you want me to promise?' he repeated.

Ollu sighed. She knew she was being ridiculous. 'I want you to promise to respect me as Captain of the Ark, follow orders and if I get killed...' she faltered. 'If I get killed I want you and Ratter to go back to the Roberts' holding and rescue my mother and the babes. Ratter seems to know all about them.' As she finished she found that tears were running down her face. What was happening to her? Had she lost all sense?

'I can promise that, 'Buzz said, his silvered eyes fixed on hers in a way she found uncomfortable. 'I'll take orders from you on the barge – it's your barge – but I can't promise anything off it. I don't know if I could help your mother, though. Last time I was at the Roberts' I was a slave. Can't see them letting me walk back in there to rescue anybody.'

'Would you try?' She was stupid even to ask, but the truth was she was desperate. Her brain kept running in circles, chewing over the same thought like a goat tethered to a post. What if she could no longer trust Davey?

'Yes,' Buzz said firmly. 'I can promise to try.'

'What about you, Ratter?'

The smaller boy shrugged. 'I've got a bundle of rescuing to do on my own account but, yeah, I'd give it a go.'

'What about the taking orders?'

'I'll try.'

Ollu trusted that more than a glib agreement. 'OK. Then let's seal the deal.' She pulled her good gutting-knife from the pocket of her cut offs. Both boys took a step back at the flash of silver. The knife was honed to a vicious edge. This was so risky, she couldn't believe she was going to go through with it. She chewed her lip, then, before she had time to change her mind, she sliced her palm with one swift, sharp cut. Blood welled and her eyes watered. Ratter looked wary, and Buzz shocked. There were so many blood-borne diseases, poxes and pestilences. No one who cared about avoiding sickness mixed their blood with another's, at least not from choice. Such a thing was foolhardy and they all knew it.

'If we do this, we are family, tied by blood, bound to keep our promises,' Ollu said and the boys nodded gravely. She passed Ratter her knife, in itself a sign of trust, and watched as he solemnly sliced his palm. He passed the knife on to Buzz, cupping his other hand underneath it to stop the blood staining the scrubbed boards of the Ark. That small, unconscious gesture comforted her. Already he cared about the Ark.

Buzz followed suit and when the three of them pressed their bloody cuts together so that their blood mingled, Ollu had a sense of having done something momentous. Foolish, but momentous. It had started as nothing more than a wild and desperate attempt to keep them from running off with her boat. Suddenly it was something else, something real. She barely knew these two, yet, for no reason that made any sense, it felt as if what she had just done was fated, inevitable.

'We are family,' Buzz said and Ratter grinned back at him.

'See! I told you so. Our fates are mixed together like the hair of my sister's braid.'

CHAPTER
TWENTY-THREE

BUZZ

BUZZ FOUND HIMSELF strangely moved by Ollu's impromptu ceremony. It was crazy. His Pa would have gone mad at the idea of his son's precious blood mixing with that of an undernourished, ill-favoured weirdo like Ratter and a half-grown girl of mixed race like Ollu. He was surprised to find that his own feelings were very different. He felt honoured to be adopted by them, grateful. He felt like there was somewhere in this strange and alien place that he belonged. He knew, of course, why Ollu had done it, but it didn't matter. It was done and couldn't be undone.

Ollu undid her scarf, and her wild, improbably blond curls blew freely around her head. She cut a portion of cloth from the bright fabric and bound his wound with it. He bound Ratter's, and Ratter bound Ollu's. Then they all looked at each, shaken and embarrassed. Ollu retied the scarf, covering her startling hair. It had been the work of a moment, like Pa's death. And like Pa's death, in a moment everything had changed.

'I should meet my brother,' Ollu said, as if to herself. She made no move. Buzz thought she too was overwhelmed by what they had just done. 'You might as well share out the fish that's left. There's enough water for them to have some more. Maybe I can get some provisions out of Davey.' She still seemed reluctant to go.

'You brother isn't involved with the slaves?' Buzz said.

'No. Of course not. Davey is a good man. We're in the salvage business. Slavery is not what Bargers do.' She spoke angrily, but Buzz did not think she was angry with him. She seemed to pull herself together then, moving with her characteristic suddenness to spring open a hidden panel on the barge's deck, bringing out her spear gun. It seemed so large and unwieldy in her hand, though he was sure she knew how to use it.

'You know how to fire one of these?' He didn't but he nodded anyway, fearful of seeming stupid in her eyes.

'Only fire it in an emergency, to keep the barge from capture. I do not know who in the clan are involved in slaving, but I won't have anything to do with it. My Ma would not want the Ark tied up in that.' She seemed unsure of herself. 'The Ark is in your hands until I get back. Please do not let me down.'

She barely met his eyes, just one quick glance; that was all. He took the proffered spear gun and slung it over his shoulder. He could examine it later. For now, he concentrated on looking as strong and reassuring as possible. He used the voice he used with Pa. 'You can trust me, Captain.' He could tell from the look she gave him that she thought he was making fun of her and so he added. 'It's OK. You had my promise.'

She nodded and then began the extraordinary business of getting out a bleached kayak of ancient fibre glass that was stored under the boat. He admired the mechanism which brought it out so neatly. The Ark was full of surprises, and so was Ollu. He had thought she was more likely to shoot him than make him her brother. Ratter seemed equally bemused.

'Did you forsee that then?' he asked the boy.

'Nah. I'd not have believed that one. You don't have any retrovees do you?'

'What?'

'Any bloodmungers, diseases?'

'No.' He didn't add that his father had devoted much of his

life to making sure Buzz had the kind of immune system that could withstand the plagues of the Holy Purge.

'What about you?'

'No. My sisters wrapped me up like an egg in 'strene. They wouldn't let me out of the flat if anyone round us had so much as a sniffle. That's why I climb so well – I had to get away from their fussing somehow.'

Buzz was reassured though. Thanks to his Pa's meddling, he was probably safe enough. 'What do you reckon to her?'

'Ollu?' Ratter gazed at her as she disappeared from view; each deft movement of her paddle taking her further from them 'I think she's healthy, if that's what you mean. As for the rest, I don't know. It was risky what she did. Risky, but right.'

Perhaps Ollu had been wise, because they both followed her orders to the letter. There was tech around. Buzz could sense it, hidden tech that sang to him just below the range of normal hearing, but he ignored it for Ollu. He carefully divided up the rest of the already cooked fish on deck, leaving Ollu's share to one side. He sluiced the deck carefully with river water once he was done. The barge was beautiful, and it was natural to want to keep it that way. As he went below to feed the slaves, Ratter acted as look out. The spear gun looked ludicrous in his skinny arms, but at least he held it like he knew what to do with it. Buzz toyed with the idea using the headscarf disguise again, but he quickly realised that no one of either sex ought to be on the Ark when Ollu was not. If they were seen at all they were in trouble. Particularly when someone realised that the slaves were gone.

The captives were on their feet as he opened the cabin door, and he sensed at once that they were positioned to jump him.

'It's me, Buzz, with food,' he said, his voice pitched just loud enough for them to hear him. The men looked edgy, and he was not sure that they wouldn't try to jump him anyway. They were clearly very suspicious people, but he couldn't blame them for that. 'Captain ordered me to feed you.'

The slaves eyed him sceptically.

'What's in the fish?'

'Bones, probably. Why?'

'That's how they captured us. Our Mainman, the Boss of the Minster crowd, held a feast in the Old Parley to discuss our problems with the poxing C-Crew. The polluted Bargers were there and they put something in the Brit-tea and when we woke up we were bound and locked away.'

Buzz looked pointedly at their bruises and contusions.

'We got these later, when we tried to fight our way out.'

That made sense, he supposed. 'Well, we are all sharing the same fish. Ollu, the captain, doesn't want you on board for a moment longer than necessary so she's got no interest in drugging you.'

They ate hungrily at that. Buzz waited until they had all finished before he asked them. 'So do you know which of the Bargers took you?'

'What do you think, we're stupid enough to share food with Bargers we didn't know? We've been trading with them for years.' The man pulled a face, 'We've had bad luck lately and not much to barter but even so...' He put a bruised arm round one of the young women's shoulders. 'I'll kill him when I get the chance. I don't care if I die in the attempt.'

'Kill who?'

'Davey of the 'Good Hope' of course. The pox-ridden polluter who captured us.'

And Buzz couldn't think of anything to say.

CHAPTER
TWENTY-FOUR

OLLU

THE SOUNDS OF celebration grew louder the closer Ollu came to the island. She found a mooring and scrambled out of the kayak. Only hours ago she had wanted nothing more than to find her big brother. Davey always made things better. Now it was hard to make her feet walk the few hundred metres to the centre of the island and the collection of bright marquees that marked the encampment. Davey's wife would be in the red tent, tended by relatives and the midwife, while the rest of the clan kept Davey occupied with songs and tales and dances. The birthing was not usually such a big event, the naming of a child after it had survived its first year was usually far bigger, but for some reason Flo, Davey's Ma in law, had decided to make a big fuss of this confinement. Knowing Flo, Ollu was certain she had some scheme and was using the birth for her own ends.

Ollu spotted Davey at once. He looked the same, tall and fair skinned, following Ma and his own father. His pleasant face was lightly freckled from the sun. Ollu was startled. People who had changed so much shouldn't look so much the same.

She was grabbed in a warm embrace by one of her mother's many cousins, Della of the 'Solace' a barge almost as old as the Ark.

'Ollu! What is this! You're in Lizzie's kit. Where is your Ma?'

'She's sick, Aunty. I need to see Davey.'

Della dragged her immediately towards her brother and then disappeared off to find them some food, which was lucky, because Ollu lacked the courage to approach Davey on her own.

'Ollu! You came for the birthing! Where's Ma?' He kissed her and fussed over her as if she was still the child she'd been at his wedding.

'She's at the Robert's 'stead. She's sick, Davey. We lost everything in the storm. 'A' grade stuff mainly – good fettling material for resiking and fabricking. We lost Dilly and Ludo too, and all the hens but for Chloe and Claudia. I have to scavenge K4s to pay for Ma's care and free the twins. I don't know where to start. Have you anything that can help?'

He stiffened noticeably. 'That's bad. But I'm sure Ma will get better, she's strong. She's battled more than a bit of sickness and survived. Don't worry.' He patted her reassuringly. 'We're going through a tough time right now, Lu. We have to cover the birthing costs and Flo is a hard gaffer. She wants the main share of everything I find. I can give you food for the journey and some shrap, but that's about all I can spare.'

Ollu could not keep her disappointment from showing. 'This is for Ma, Davey, for our Ma! It wasn't just Flo who put up for your barge, it was Ma as well. Doesn't she get a take too?'

'You know that's not how it works on a matriarch boat.'

'From what I've heard, Flo is doing well enough in her own dirty trade not to need your scavengings. I'm sure she can spare something to help us out.' Ollu pulled away from her brother, putting a good space between them.

'What does that mean?' Davey's face flushed.

'It means I heard a rumour she was slaving.' There, she'd said it. She held her breath.

This was the moment when he denied it all, when he made everything all right. When he told her it was someone else's trade but never his. She waited, willing him to say something. She was still waiting when Della came back with a generous plate of roast-pigeon pie and potatoes. Ollu was hungry and her stomach growled. She took a bite. It was hot and tasted of ash.

'I'll see you in a minute when you've done with your brother, Ollu. It is good to see you at least, and looking so well.'

Ollu looked at her brother expectantly. He would not meet her eyes.

'Is it true? You're a slaver now?'

There was a long, awkward silence.

'You have to understand. Flo has a big family – a complicated business. You know how hard it is to get decent salvage these days. Even when we do decent dreg most of it is so corroded and decayed, it's got to be fabricked into something else. Trade is our life. We've just moved on to a new kind, that's all.'

This could not be Davey, her brother, talking to her. He gestured for her to follow him further away from the noise of the clan. He held his voice low, barely above a whisper.

'Stell and me, we want to get away from Flo. She takes everything.' He paused, high colour in his face, as if struggling to control his anger. 'Last year Flo found an old Preeker bunker. There's stuff there! Big Sea-going ships, proper high-tekk guns. We haven't seen the half of it but it's in Bad Water – very Bad Water. There's a crew there, the Grennish-geezers. They own the turf. They don't know half of what they've got. There's real tekk there if we could only get to it – and weapons – a lot of weapons.' He sounded frustrated. 'Anyway, they've lost a lot of people lately. The land is real toxic and bad for growing things so we've been trading slaves – would be fighters and female drudges, livestock and grain for arms.'

He waited for her to speak. She didn't say anything. She couldn't.

'To cut a long fireside tale to the bone, I've been doing a bit of trading on my own account, for the ship. We don't want to trade slaves, Lu. We're just doing it so we can get away from here, get out. Go somewhere where we can earn a clean living – me and Stell and the babe.' He was looking at her, appeal in his eyes. She still couldn't say anything. Shock seemed to have frozen her throat.

'I've nothing left to trade right now and I can't leave Stell. She's too close to her time and Flo wouldn't let me. You want to get more weapons? You'll have to offer slaves. It's all they want. Three men for a gun, eight for two guns with ammo.'

'And how many lives will your ship cost you?' Ollu asked bitterly, recovering the power of speech at last.

'Other Bargers have done worse in their time, Lu. How do you think we survived the Chaos? When life is hard we can't afford to be soft. Don't judge me!' He looked uncomfortable, but stubborn. That was the thing about Davey, he was obstinate, and he would never admit to being wrong. Once, when he'd nearly holed the Ark with bad steering, he'd blamed the tide.

She shook her head. She didn't want to understand.

'Where can I buy the dreg, the K4s?' she said at last.

'You can't go there, Lu. It's not safe.'

'If you won't go, who else is there to save Ma?'

'Not won't go, Lu. I *can't* go. Flo would kill me if I left her daughter now. You've no idea what she's like. She's nothing like Ma, and if Ma had known her better, I'm sure she wouldn't have organised the alliance, but she did and now I'm stuck with it. The ship is our only chance.'

'You mean a ship like the one that was used to take Cassie's place? You are trading with our trading partner's enemies?'

He shrugged. 'Cassie's not my trading partner anymore.'

Ollu could not believe what she was hearing. Cassie had been good to Davey, had a soft spot for him. As a boy, he'd played with her sons. Her sons who were all dead now. Dead thanks to Davey.

Ollu did not want to believe it.

'Tell me it isn't true, Davey. Tell me this is a wind up.'

'I can't, Ollu. I've left the Ark behind. Now I'm looking out for me and mine. Isn't that all we've ever done?'

She turned away from him. 'I've got to go. Tell me where I

can find the arms. If you have any food, I'll take that too, and the shrap. I'm not in a position to be proud.'

He nodded curtly. 'Eat your food and talk to the aunties. I'll meet you by the cottage in half an hour.' Neither of them wore any kind of working time piece, but Ollu knew Davey still marked his days by the old chrono on the Ark.

She watched him go in a kind of shock. She ate her food mechanically, making herself swallow because she needed to eat to get through the next few days. She spoke with her numerous aunties for the same reason. She did not want them to know what she was about to do. What she had already done. She tried to be the little Lulu they expected her to be. She told them about Ma, but not in detail. They were family, but maybe family did not count for so much if there was profit to be made.

She had thought better of Davey. He had changed a lot these last years, and so had she.

She forced herself to smile and fabrick plausible answers under the questioning of her aunties. When she managed to escape, she found that she was desperate to get off the island, and away from the whole clan. Rather than cross it on foot, she headed back to the kayak.

Davey was waiting where he had promised to be, at the ruined cottage. It had become so overgrown she almost missed it.

'Here, Lu. It's everything I can spare.' Davey leant over the water to hand her a backpack, steadying the kayak with strong hands while she put it on. 'You must believe me. I would come with you if I could. Send me word as soon as you fix that transmitter. We've fettled up a new radio now. There's a note for Ma in the pack too. Please give it to her.'

He reached forward as if to embrace Ollu, but she pushed the kayak away. He almost fell, but with the natural balance of a waterman, he righted himself and waved.

He must know how she felt? If he did, he didn't let it show. His voice was upbeat – as if he had decided not to believe the seriousness of her predicament, or Ma's.

'Give Ma my love!'

She nodded tersely. She should have wished him well with his baby, but she could not get the words out. Her brother was a slaving stranger. She had to fight not to cry.

CHAPTER
TWENTY-FIVE

OLLU

IT WAS GETTING dark and Ollu could see no sign of life as she approached the familiar outline of the Ark. Tears blurred her vision. It was as if she was under water, as if she were drowning.

'Ollu?' Buzz's voice, pronouncing her name in that peculiar way he had. She wiped her face on her sleeve. At least she wasn't alone. What did it matter what Barger rules she had broken? At least she wouldn't have to face death by herself.

She stowed the kayak swiftly and with Buzz's help she scrambled back on board the Ark. He did not ask her any questions. Ratter appeared from the cabin with a beaker of hot Brit-tea for her. Lalo was chewing her way through a sizeable pile of fodder and the hens were pecking away at grain that had been thrown on deck.

'I was careful. I swam out to the other bank and brought some fodder. The goat was trying to eat my clothes.' Buzz answered the question she didn't ask. 'Ratter found the grain when he was searching for Brit-tea.' Both boys were looking at her anxiously.

'You did right. I should have mentioned the animals,' she said, forcing a smile. 'What about the slaves?'

Buzz and Ratter exchanged glances. 'We fed them like you

said. They're not big fans of Bargers.'

She nodded. There was tension in the air and she guessed its source. 'It's OK. I know it was Davey that took them.' She didn't want their sympathy. No one spoke for a moment. 'I need to get K4s to save Ma. I can get weapons by trading the slaves.'

Ratter looked like he might fly at her throat any second.

'Don't look at me like that. I'm no slave trader, but I don't know how else to get the dreg I need. If you have any ideas, I'd like to hear them.' Even to herself, she sounded more lost and uncertain than any Captain of the Ark should. She scrubbed her face with her hands as if she could rub away her doubts. It didn't work. 'I need to think.' Saying the words seemed to help. Their first task had to be to get away, to head back downstream. Their fate lay in Bad Water.

'Buzz, pull up that anchor there when I tell you. Then both of you get down below. We have to go back the way we came, past the twins and there must be no sound or sign that I'm not on my own. It is important the slaves lie low. We cannot fight our way out of here.' She noticed the spear gun was draped crossways over Ratter's narrow shoulders. 'You better hang onto that though, even so. Just don't let any of the slaves get hold of it.' She checked her waist band reflexively. Her revolver was still there, but she did not think she could fire it at one of her own, even to save her life.

It had been a brighter day and the solar had been working well, so there was more than enough power stored in the cells to keep them moving, back the way they'd come. Back towards Bad Water.

The twins barely acknowledged her. 'Not staying for the birthing then?'

'Got to do an errand for Ma,' she called back. Neither girl was taking much notice of the river. A small gaggle of the older cousins, boys almost of marrying age, were gathered round the prettier girl. Her sister was complaining plaintively that she was lonely, but no one had made an effort to rescue her. Flo did not suspect anything, or she would not have left two such ninnies in charge of security. Once out of sight of the 'watch,' she called to Buzz to take the tiller. She needed to consult Davey's map and see what he had given her. He had made his own choices, and now they were none of her business.

It was hard to unpack the ancient rucksack he'd given her. She recognised it as the one Ma had given him to take from the Ark when he came of age and was forever exiled from his home. It reminded her of all they'd shared growing up. She remembered his pleasure when they'd first found it, still wrapped in transparent plastic like liquid glass, its colours bright, its zips opening with the rasp of old tekk. She remembered his face when he'd shouldered its familiar faded bulk, years later. She had not thought about how he'd felt to be sent away from them to marry a girl of his mother's choosing, just because he was a boy who had turned into a man, and whose presence would sully the purity of the matriarch boat. If he'd stayed, she probably wouldn't be in this mess. He'd never have become a slaver and she would never have become Captain of the Ark. And what was the point of his leaving? The Ark was sullied anyway by her own actions, by everything she'd had to do because he was not with them. His going had achieved nothing.

Thinking such thoughts made her feel sick in the pit of her stomach: What would Ma say? Perhaps she would be angry enough to cast Ollu out too. Ollu had betrayed the traditions of the Ark. In Ma's eyes, she did not think there was a greater sin.

Davey had packed the rucksack with his usual practical efficiency. He'd given her a good quantity of cooked meat – pigeon mainly, but pork too, bread and a quantity of apples. Had she been alone it would have tided her over for a few days, but with Buzz and Ratter, not to mention the slaves, she would be lucky to get two meals out of it. Still, Davey had not understood her need and she couldn't blame him for that. She did not read the note for her mother, but tucked it away in one of her coat's many secret pockets. The map she took out and examined carefully. Davey was scarcely better at drawing than at writing, but she recognised the rough form of the river and her heart sank. The weapons were the other side of Bad Water, further downstream than she had ever been. On Ma's maps, down in the cabin, those waters were marked in deepest red. Red for danger; red for plague. She did not think the plague still raged there. Davey had, after all, survived his trading journeys. There was no point in worrying about it in any case. She had to go there and do whatever she had to do to get the weapons that would keep her free.

She checked the very bottom of the bag and was surprised to find that Davey had included in his gifts one small modified revolver, a shoulder holster and a bag of shrap ammo. She did not allow herself to wonder how many slaves that gift had cost.

'Are you all right?' Buzz was looking at her oddly.

She shrugged. 'Yes. Tell me do you think it can be right to do wrong things if you have to? If it's a matter of life and death?'

'You mean like, do the ends justify the means?'

She thought for a moment. She wasn't sure what he meant. 'I don't know. Maybe.'

Buzz looked thoughtful, his face clouded. 'Sometimes you don't do everything right because you can't, maybe because you haven't enough strength, but I think you still have to try. The right thing doesn't stop being the right thing just because it's hard and the wrong thing is still the wrong thing.' He smiled, embarrassed, as if he thought he had spoken out of turn, or somehow said too much.

If it was the wrong thing to sell slaves to try to buy a boat, surely it was wrong to sell slaves to pay for her mother's care, to save herself from slavery. She chewed the inside of her mouth savagely, until she could taste her own blood. She did not think she could do it. She was not sure that Ratter would let her do it, anyway. She had seen the look on his face when she'd suggested it and he had her spear gun. She was all too aware of how fragile her control of the Ark really was. She was Captain only if the slaves and her newly formed family of Buzz and Ratter allowed her to be captain.

She took off her coat and, after loading the revolver with the shrap ammo, put on the holster and replaced her coat. She did not like the feeling it gave her, having this second weapon so close, but she was small and afraid and she had promised to do an impossible task to save her siblings, her mother and herself. Buzz was watching; she could feel his strange eyes boring into her back.

'What are you going to do?'

At his question, she turned to face him. 'I need to buy the weapons on the list, to pay for my family's care. I have nothing to trade except...'

'Us?'

'Not you and Ratter – we are oath bound. I'm not a polluting oath breaker.'

'I don't think I can let you sell the others either. You said you would get a fee if you found them work in a village. Wouldn't that help?'

She shook her head. Either she traded for the K4s or she found some hidden cache of weapons for herself; she knew how likely that was. She was out of her depth and drowning and she knew it.

Chapter
Twenty-Six

Buzz

Buzz watched Ollu enter the cabin. She was exhausted. He didn't need good night vision to see that. He wondered what it would feel like to know that your brother had done something really wrong. He didn't have a brother, but he guessed it wouldn't feel good. Ollu seemed devastated, but she was carrying on the best she could. He supposed that meant she was made of the right stuff, even if his father wouldn't think so, even though he didn't think she was of Gaia, even though she did crazy things like make blood oaths with strangers. Pa would have wanted him to wrest control from her slim fingers, he knew that. Pa would have expected him to take control of this bastion of civilisation. Yet Pa had taught him to obey orders so well that without that stern voice in his ear he was lost. Ollu had that quality that other people followed, just like Ratter. It had nothing to do with size or skill, it had to do with something else. Somehow he wanted them to think well of him. Somehow he wanted their respect. So he didn't follow her into the cabin. He didn't demand to hear her plans or to help her make them. He stood quietly at the tiller, watching the dark water and the broken reflection of the moon's face on its corrugated surface.

He peered at the far bank for signs of life and strained his eyes, scanning the river for shadows of shadows, for any indication that they were being followed. He listened to the gentle hum of the engine, the slap of the water against the bow, the rustle of the wind in the foliage at the river's edge, and felt almost at peace. The pull of data was still there, a seductive hum that reverberated through the bones of his skull, but he was learning to live without it. And maybe it wasn't too bad. He felt more connected to people when he was less connected to machines. It was different, but not all bad.

Perhaps if he had not been concentrating so hard, he might have missed the early signs, but every heightened sense was trained on the river and he missed nothing. His suspicion had been right; they were being followed. He had observed how Ollu tied the tiller to keep their course straight when she had to be busy elsewhere. He did as she had done, as rapidly as possible, his fingers made clumsy by haste. He was across the deck in three paces. He pulled open the door with more force than he intended and almost tumbled into the cabin.

'Ollu!' All eyes were on him. The scene before him was like a tableau in a play, lit from above by the cabin's electric lantern. He had obviously arrived at a bad moment. The slaves must have overpowered both Ollu and Ratter. The woman, Angela, seemed to have recovered her strength most remarkably in spite of her infected wounds, and she was wielding the spear gun as if she knew how to use it. She seemed suddenly very large, very adult.

Ollu was struggling ineffectually against the strong grip of the largest of the men, the one they'd called Pyke. Pyke had the general air of being in charge. The eyes of the other slaves flicked between Buzz and him as if they awaited his orders. For a moment Pyke was too surprised to speak, which was good, because otherwise Buzz might have had a spear in his chest at any moment. Ollu must have been taken by surprise as she had not been able to get to her guns and, perhaps fortunately, her captor seemed unaware of them.

'We're being followed, Pyke. Unless you want the slavers to catch us, you'd better let her go. She's the only one who can save us. Give me the spear gun.'

'You're having a laugh. I don't believe you!' Angela said but she didn't sound entirely sure of herself.

'You don't have to believe me, but it's true! It's why I left the tiller. It's up to you. I'm not a slave who's about to be recaptured.'

Pyke seemed convinced by Buzz's earnestness. At least, he only hesitated for a moment before reluctantly releasing Ollu. Her hand darted inside her coat and she whipped out her weapon. It looked ludicrous in her small hand, but Ollu did not waver and the gun did not so much as tremble.

Her expression was fierce and her voice low. 'Throw Buzz the spear-gun and let Ratter go.' No one seemed in any doubt that Ollu meant business. Angela threw Pyke a murderous glance, as if somehow it was all his fault and tossed the spear gun in Buzz's general direction with ill grace. He caught it easily.

Ollu sighed. She did not holster the gun. 'How can I trust you now? How is trying to take me prisoner on my own boat going to help? I am tempted to give you back to Davey.' She sounded exasperated, but unafraid. Buzz couldn't help but admire that. She did not look at the slaves as she pulled open the cabin door and Buzz found himself acting as her bodyguard. He turned to face the slaves, keeping the spear gun aimed in their direction.

'That was stupid,' he said. 'She was on your side.'

'*He* said she was going to sell us to buy weapons to save her dying mother.' Pyke inclined his head in Ratter's direction and Ratter looked shamefaced.

'I was a slave yesterday. I don't forget as quick as you. I couldn't let her sell them. It's not right.' Ratter looked more upset than Buzz had yet seen him.

'She gave you a chance. She saved your life. You were oath bound to give her loyalty!'

Ratter looked deeply uncomfortable, his face flushed. He hung his head.

'What? Are you not going to claim some vision in your defence?'

'I have seen nothing of this in my dreams,' Ratter said in a low voice, 'That's part of the trouble. I'm not used to not knowing what comes next.' Suddenly he looked very young and vulnerable. The slaves merely looked confused.

'What are you talking about?'

'It doesn't matter. We have to help Ollu defend the Ark.'

'Against slavers?'

'Against all comers.' Buzz kept his weapon trained on the slaves as he backed out of the cabin. Ratter followed.

'Sorry,' he said softly. 'I am with you, and Ollu, it was just...'

'She wouldn't have sold them.' Buzz said firmly, with more confidence than he felt. 'Anyway, I thought we were a braid.'

'Yeah. All right. I said I was sorry. Leave it out.'

On deck Ollu was peering into the night, her gun drawn. 'I can't see anything,' she whispered.

'Buzz can see in the dark,' Ratter said flatly. Ollu gave Buzz a quick, unreadable look.

'Back there, a shadow moving, staying close to the bank. It looks like three or four kayaks. Listen! Can you hear them?' Buzz did not add that his father's genetic meddling had given him keener than average hearing too. Ollu raised a finger to silence him and shut her eyes, as if to help her concentrate.

'Yes, I can hear something. I am going to move onto full power, but if we can't outrun them we've got problems. I'm guessing it will be Davey's crew after the slaves. He can have them as far as I'm concerned.'

'Ollu, you have to give them a chance to fight for their freedom,' Ratter said.

'I don't have to do anything,' she said coldly. 'I'm tempted to let them take you too.' She snapped her mouth closed and adjusted the controls of the boat, which were hidden under a panel of wood. The Ark hid her secrets well. Buzz was irritated with himself that he had failed to notice the panel – especially as he had been standing next to it for such a long time. Ratter shot Buzz an uncharacteristically pleading look.

'Ollu, if it gets to a fight, we might need the slaves,' Buzz said, because it was the truth, and because he couldn't bear Ratter's anguish.

'If it gets to a fight, I'm handing them over. You think I'd fight my brother?' She sounded angry. Ratter was about to argue further, but Buzz silenced him with a quick kick to the shins. The kid didn't know when to quit. Ratter scowled a response but managed to keep his opinions to himself and for a moment no one said anything. The engine of the Ark burst into noisier life, the whole deck vibrating, and they powered ahead, leaving a wake of white foam on the dark water. Buzz wondered if it was wise to drain whatever stored power they had, but he had the wit not to mention it. The kayaks were hard to hear above the increased engine noise of the Ark, but Buzz knew that they were still there. He readjusted the weight of the spear gun and aimed it in the general direction of their pursuers.

'I don't want anyone firing until I say so,' Ollu said, though Buzz did not think she would have been able to see him very clearly. 'I don't want a fight – not with family. I'll explain that it was all a mistake.'

'How will you get the weapons you need for your Ma with nothing to trade?' Ratter said sharply.

'I don't know yet, but I'll find a way. Don't worry, your neck is safe enough. I don't want you to help me anymore.'

Ratter's shoulders slumped a little at that. Ollu's tone was hard. Maybe she'd offload them all on Davey, Ratter and himself too. A part of Buzz thought she had the right. 'We're with you Ollu,' he said softly, but Ollu only grunted in response and then the door to the cabin opened and the former slaves were with them on deck.

'What do you want us to do, Captain?' Pyke asked Ollu.

'Stay below and out of sight,' she answered grimly. 'I'll not give you up if I can avoid it, but I don't want you fighting my family.'

Buzz didn't know what would have happened had he not had the wit to get Pyke in his spear gun's sights once again, but Pyke was no fool. There was a long moment's pause when Buzz wondered if the slaves would try to rush him en masse. But maybe he looked more intimidating than he'd thought because nobody moved.

'Aye, aye, Captain.' Pyke said, in a voice which dripped with sarcasm and contempt. That was OK. They could live with sarcasm and even contempt if they had to. Buzz kept the spear gun steady as the adults retreated to the cabin. They would kill Ollu's family given half a chance, Buzz knew, and do it gladly if the family included Davey. Ollu knew it too, which was why she was burning the Ark's remaining power. Buzz suddenly understood. Ollu wasn't worried about saving them. She knew the slaves would fight back. She was running away on full power trying to be true to her family. Trying desperately to save Davey.

CHAPTER
TWENTY-SEVEN

OLLU

OLLU KNEW ALL too well who would be in the kayaks – Davey and the other men of Flo's clan. Flo's daughters had all married and Flo had picked all the men. They were all like Davey: strong, practical types without too much interest in right and wrong. Perhaps he would think she'd stolen the slaves to sell for weapons. Maybe that's what he would have done in her shoes. Was she so different?

Please Davey, she urged him silently, *give up. Lie about the Ark's full speed, make out that she would be impossible to catch, come up with something to keep them from confrontation.*

She stood awkwardly, hunched over the tiller, willing Davey to turn back. She did not notice Ratter standing miserably beside her until he spoke. 'I'm sorry, Ollu. I didn't know the slaves would go for you like that ...'

'You shouldn't have told them what I was thinking. I thought we were on the same side now, after the oath. At least, I hoped we were.' She didn't sound as angry as she felt. Ratter aroused her pity, even though she knew he was tough as the river rat he resembled and probably as poisonous.

'I'll make it up to you, Ollu. We are still supposed to work together. I know we are.'

She no longer believed in his visions. They seemed likely to be a scam to get him aboard. Right at that moment she was hard pressed to believe in anything beyond the reality of the great dark river and the black night. 'And do you know whether Davey will catch us up? Have you seen that?'

'I haven't seen Davey at all in any of the futures I've dreamed, but I never saw the slaves either.' He faltered. 'Maybe my gift is failing.'

He sounded so desperate that Ollu found herself reassuring him. 'Maybe the slaves aren't part of our future. Maybe I set them free and we go about our business without them. So far they've been nothing but trouble. It might be safer to let them go. I have to be practical.'

'You can trust me, Ollu. You have it on my sister's life that I will not betray you.'

'And that's worth more than your blood-oath, is it?' She was joking, but then the clouds cleared momentarily and she saw his face in the moonlight and she knew that it was no joke. 'I believe you, Ratter,' she said.

There was an awkward pause before Ratter spoke again, in a more normal tone: 'I should have said before. The thing is – I know Pyke and Angela and the others, or at least I've seen them before...'

'Where? I mean, how? In visions?'

'In real life. In the Minster. Pyke – well I've seen him plenty of times, though I've been lucky and he hasn't seen me. He was big – back in the Minster – he's a cousin-brother of the Mainman. Ran a fair bit of his stock business. I saw him in a couple of raids. Back home I'd become a peeper, eavesdropper and other things for the C-Crew Code Boss because I'm small and quick. There's a turf war going on with the Minster men. They took over some of our vertical farms. I saw Pyke's cousin-brother doing a deal with Bargers. I didn't think it was the same ones who caught us, but it might have been.'

'Why didn't you tell me this before?'

'We've not had much time to talk. I thought you'd think I was scamming you, trying to persuade you to go to my bend in the river so I could get my sister.'

Ollu scowled. 'I don't understand.' She was still gazing upstream, hoping that the familiar night music of the river did not include the sound of paddles in the water, hoping that needle shaped kayaks would not emerge from the shadowed bank. She could only give Ratter a part of her attention.

'Well. Davey drugged Pyke and the rest of them at a feast, or so they say. And if that's true you can bet that was only done on the Mainman's say so. Pyke'll want his revenge, maybe more than that, I'm guessing. If we're going downstream we could drop him off at the Minster, which just happens to be where I want to be too. It's where I last saw my sister.'

'Ally?'

'No, Ally can look after herself. My other sister, Bel, the one I need to find. If Pyke and his lot were around to help, I'd stand a better chance of saving her...' He said this last so softly she had to strain to hear him.

'And what would I get?' Ratter did not seem to understand that she was not some one-woman search and rescue operation. She was a business, and one that was about to go under, if she did not get the items on her list. Ratter's sister was not on the list. There was a long pause during which Ollu could almost hear Ratter's brain whirring and spinning like some mechanical gadget trying to fabrick a way that there could be something in this for her.

'Well, if the Mainman traded them for K4s, maybe they would repay us for our help in K4s.'

She could not help but laugh: 'Yeah. And that's what a clan about to wage a civil war always does isn't it? Give away their fire power to any toxic half-wit who gets involved. Great idea, Ratter.'

It was of course very far from being a good idea, but then her idea of trying to find an undiscovered, unexploited, not to say unguarded, cache of useable weapons in the next few days wasn't exactly a good idea either. She had to forcibly push the last image that she had of her mother from her mind.

'I think we may have lost them.' Buzz said suddenly. He did not whisper, and his voice sounded so loud in the quiet night it made her jump.

'Are you sure?' She tried to answer in her own normal voice, but it came out as a kind of a croak.

'I'm not cross my heart and hope to die sure,' he answered carefully and she had no idea what he meant. Sometimes he talked in riddles. 'But I can't see them or hear them either and all my senses are sharp. I think they turned back, unless there's any way that they could head us off?'

The whole region was a latticework of waterways, spreading like the veins on a leaf. Most of the smaller ones were risky, dreg-filled waters as likely to hole a boat as give safe passage. Most of them dried up in the summer, but this year they had been doused with such heavy rains it was hard to say whether some channels might still be navigable. She consulted her mental map, wishing she had her mother's skill of always knowing exactly where she was. There were a couple of tributaries around the island, but they were pretty clogged. Last time they'd been that way, Ma had struggled to steer round the rotting spire of an old church. There'd been a matched pair of slime-covered skeleton towers rising from the water like some corpse that wouldn't drown. Their old bones kept crumbling and a huge piece of masonry had fallen and only just missed them, scaring even Ma. She did not think Davey would risk that – not at night.

'There are ways' she answered Buzz, 'but I don't think Davey would be so desperate as to take them.'

Buzz nodded. 'What are you going to do about _them?_' Buzz indicated the cabin with a wave of his hand.

'I don't know yet. I should probably talk to them. You heard what Ratter was saying?' Buzz did not deny it.

'You've got good ears. Are you a peeper and an eavesdropper too?' Ollu asked.

'What?'

'Are you some kind of spy, Buzz?'

'Who would I be spying for?'

She shrugged 'Take your pick. Since the Chaos any man can be King, Judge and High Executioner.' It was one of Ma's expressions that seemed to fit. 'Ratter, you take the next watch. I'm going below.' Then she remembered what she had forgotten in the stress and confusion of the last few hours. 'I forgot to say, thanks for rescuing us – from the slaves, Buzz. I don't know what would've happened if you hadn't arrived at that moment.'

'I'm sure you'd have thought of some way out.'

It wasn't true, but it was a nice thing to say. She smiled and cut the power to the Ark's engine. The tide had turned and was bearing them downstream again. She checked the gauge which told her how much power remained in the cells. They were not entirely out of power yet. She had made the right call. Perhaps she _was_ fit to be Captain of the Ark after all.

CHAPTER
TWENTY-EIGHT

OLLU

OLLU WAS NOT so keen to save power that she would risk walking into the cabin in the dark. The only home she had ever known had suddenly become hostile territory. She flicked the lecky switch and opened the cabin door. The slaves were huddled together on the floor; they had not made use of the hammocks or the bunks. One of them– not Pyke, but a taller man whose name she did not know – leapt to his feet as soon as the light flickered into life. Like Buzz he was too big to stand erect in the cabin and Ollu took a step backwards, afraid. Her fear was the instinctive kind. She suddenly understood why there were no men allowed on matriarch boats. She had the gun in her trembling hand before she was even aware of reaching for it. The cool metal reassured her, and the man put his hands up in the ancient symbol of surrender.

'Don't shoot me, little girl,' he said with a lack of respect that made her finger unreasonably itchy.

'I am Ollu, Captain of the Ark,' she said testily, 'I came to let you know that we seem to be out of immediate danger. Do you want anything to eat?'

'My apologies, Missis,' the man said, sitting back down awkwardly between his companions who stirred and started awake.

The Ark had not been designed to sleep five adults on the floor.

Pyke opened his eyes and scowled at her weapon. 'What's this? Have you come to hand us over after all?'

All the adults were staring at her like a pack of wolves eying a stray sheep. She reckoned it would only be moments before they had grabbed the weapon from her hand. Then she heard Buzz coming down the stairs behind her and she felt a little more confident. He still had the spear gun, and she didn't think he would give it up easily.

'No. I came to say that we seem to have lost the kayaks for now. I was going to give you something to eat.'

'Why?' Pyke asked, and he seemed genuinely puzzled.

'I am hungry and …well…how could I eat alone?' The sharing of food was such a basic obligation among the Bargers that she had not thought to question it before.

'Then what?'

The other slaves moved to let her through, and she unhooked a couple of the hammocks with one hand as she considered what to say. She returned her gun to its holster, confident that Buzz would protect her. That was odd too, how quickly she had allowed herself to trust the large stranger with the silver eyes.

She pulled down the bunks which had housed her mother, herself and Davey in happier times. 'A couple of you can take the bunks. Then there will be more room on the floor.'

Pyke was not to be distracted, 'Then what?'

'I am headed for Bad Water. I can drop you off where you came from if that's what you want.'

She ought to have bargained their freedom for sureties, for future trade goods, maybe even for the weapons that she needed so badly, but her guts told her that no surety or promise could be relied upon. She had no trading partnership with these people and no way of exacting anything from them that would be worth as much as Brit-tea dregs.

'And what do you want from us? I know you Bargers of old. You give nothing without taking something back. What kind of Captain are you?'

Buzz bridled at that and shifted the spear gun into a more prominent position. He really was on her side.

'Fair. I'm a Barger sure enough, but you can't give me what I need. Besides, it was my brother who took you. If I take you back that ends the grievance —yeah? And there is no need for revenge?'

Ollu did not know much about the tribes that scraped a life for themselves in Bad Water, but, from Ma's stories, it seemed that honour killings were common and revenge a way of life. She did not want these men and women to hunt her brother down. Family was family: blood of blood and bone of bone. Davey had done wrong, yet he was still her brother.

Pyke exchanged glances with the others. Angela shrugged.

'I can agree to that,' he said, 'We will not set out to kill him if we meet him again.'

'Nor cause him harm?'

'No – not deliberately, not for revenge. But if he tries to take more of our clan as slaves...' he shrugged.

She could not ask for more. 'OK,' Ollu said.

'Will you allow him to stand down?' Pyke looked at Buzz with something approaching concern. Buzz did look intimidating – Ollu could see that. He was taller and better fed even than Pyke's men: he was probably the reason they were bothering to negotiate with her at all.

'No. This is my barge and I intend to keep it. I always keep my word but I don't know about you. You've not shown much toxic gratitude since I saved you.'

There was some muttering at that – quelled by a glare from Pyke. They sealed the deal with a captain's handshake and Ollu finally got to eat. There was little enough to share but when she offered a portion to Pyke and the slaves they looked at her wonderingly.

'This is the second time you've fed us. We count this sharing of food as a debt of honour,' Pyke said under his breath. They thought her foolish to share what little she had, she could tell. It was clear to all of them that the rucksack of food was all she had besides the livestock, now safely stowed on the recovered crop barge.

She slept a little then, while Buzz kept watch. She curled up on her own bunk, lying positioned to protect her weapon from even the most adept of thieves, and trusting to Buzz's solid presence to keep her safe.

At dawn she took the tiller and navigated a risky route round Cassie's land. The purple banded machete men patrolled the riverside but she sent everyone else below. She hoped they would see a young girl on a barge as unthreatening and let her go past unchallenged. She probably ought to have had a better plan, but she couldn't think of one. She'd instructed Buzz to keep the spear gun trained on the guards, while Ratter was to watch his back. She didn't trust her guests. She steered close to the bank furthest from Cassie's holding, keeping the decaying debris which clogged the channel between herself and the guards at all times. One of the guards saw her and raised his rifle, but nobody wasted ammo. She might have been in more trouble if he'd had a bow and arrow, because arrows were easier to replace than shrap, but luckily for her he had only his machete and his gun. She was barely afraid at all. She refused to consider the possibility that her Ma might already be dead and burning on some funeral pyre on Roberts' land. She could not bear to think of that.

Once they had passed beyond the furthest reaches of Cassie's former holding, Buzz and Ratter came back on deck and dozed while she steered. They wrapped themselves in her mother's old blanket against the chill of early morning. She found the sight of them cheered her up. They made her feel less alone.

It was late morning when Pyke came to sit with her on deck. Buzz woke at once, as if he had an inbuilt sense of danger. She knew he had no such thing or he would never have been captured and almost enslaved, but he seemed to move from a deep sleep to instant alertness. He came and stood beside her at the tiller, unspeaking and unsmiling. He stood so close that he made her almost as nervous as the presence of Pyke. Pyke himself was on his best behavior.

'I've been talking to Ratter,' he began which confused her a little until she realised that at some point while she had slept, the boys had swapped duties. She was ashamed to have taken a double rest while they had stayed awake all night.

'Oh,' she said as neutrally as possible. She wondered if Ratter had spoken of his visions or of his time as a peeper. Both subjects were dangerous.

'He told me more about the mess you're in.'

Great. Ratter had a big mouth and did not seem to know when to close it.

'I'm alive,' she said shortly, 'And that's good enough to be getting on with.' She did not want to be patronised by Pyke. He might not yet have called her 'little girl', but clearly, by his manner, he thought of her as a child.

'Easy,' he said raising his hands in defence. 'I'm not having a go at you. You've taken on a silting lot. Respect for that.' Ollu said nothing. She was not discussing her business with Pyke. He carried on. 'We munged our first meeting, that's for sure. Now's the time for some rewinding. By your Holies, I'm grateful that you rescued us. We all are. Chances are, we could help each other. You know how we were slaved?' She nodded, suddenly more interested. She was not in a position to turn down help from any quarter. 'I owe my cousin-brother a taste of his own physick. How would it be if I gave you him and some of his inner guard? You take him of my hands and you can trade him for whatever you most need.'

It was a solution if she could trust him, but she did not think she dare trust him. And doing as he suggested would still make her a slaver. She shook her head. 'This is a matriarch boat. I won't take men on board again. Besides, I'm no slaver. I don't believe in it.'

'You don't believe in it?' He looked at her as if she were a baby who had suddenly started reciting poetry, or a goat that had learned to sing. She knew she looked young, but she was not too young to know the difference between right and wrong.

'No, I don't believe in slaving. That's why I rescued you, why

I haven't dumped you landside the first chance I got and why I will not sell you, even to buy care for Ma.'

Pyke grinned. 'So you're an arms dealer, but not a slaver.'

She tried to adopt her mother's confident tone, 'I trade in tekk of all kinds... people kill each other with spears and machetes when there are no guns or bombs.' He was laughing at her and she did not know why.

'Ratter said you'd say that. We don't have a deal?'

'I'll not take your cousin-brother nor any other polluting men on my boat again. You can be sure of that.' He gave her a thoughtful look, but she couldn't tell what he was thinking.

'Do you want me to take a turn at the tiller? You must be tired.'

Buzz gave him one of his most unfriendly glares. Buzz certainly didn't trust Pyke, and he was probably right. 'No,' she said firmly. 'This is the Captain's place. You might as well go down below. There is heavy water ahead. We've a way to go before we're close to the Minster – if my map if right.'

'Can I see?'

'No. We Bargers keep our secrets. We'll take a break landside soon. I need to get supplies, reprovision the boat. We haven't enough food for us, or for the animals. You might be able to find some herbs and make a salve for Angela's wounds. I know which ones you need to find.'

'You want rid of us?'

'Of course. But I keep my word. I'll take you to the Minster, like I said.' She shivered at the thought. If Grennish was more savage than the Minster and its people even more hostile than Pyke, she was not sure she would make it back to Ma.

'It would be good to get off the boat for a bit.' Pyke agreed so easily that she was instantly suspicious. 'I'll tell the others.'

Even with the protection of Buzz's powerful presence, she was still relieved when the older man went back into the cabin.

'I don't trust him,' Buzz said through gritted teeth.

'Me neither,' Ollu agreed. 'I think he wants the Ark.' Word or no word, perhaps she should leave him landside?

Chapter
Twenty-Nine

Buzz

Buzz was relieved when Ollu finally anchored the Ark within striding distance of a small island. The cramped conditions on board were too much like his father's plane. Too much had happened too quickly, and the turbulent river was carrying him towards a future that he did not understand. He was aware that he was following Ollu as thoughtlessly as he'd followed Ratter's lead when he had escaped the slave shed. He did not seem able to develop a plan of his own. He hadn't even found the tech on board the Ark. Pa would be angry, but Pa was dead. Every time Buzz remembered that fact, it shocked him all over again.

He dropped behind the others. Pyke was issuing orders and Ollu had given Ratter the gear he needed to set some rabbit traps, along with instructions to find dinner and bring some kindling back to cook it; the Ark's efficient stove ran on multi-power sources. Ratter had skipped from the Ark without a backward glance to do as he was told. Buzz didn't think of him as a child, so it was confusing to see him acting like a little boy, eager and excited to trap rabbits.

Ollu had given Buzz a couple of baskets to gather any wild fruit or herbs that might grow there too, but he was not sure he wanted to do as he was told. Ollu was no older than he was, so why did he feel he had to obey her? There was the oath of course, but was there some lack in himself, some long ingrained habit of obedience that made him someone who followed orders and never gave them?

The island wasn't much of a place. Buzz had flown over many a site like it at home. It had been part of a town once, and probably not the best part. Much of the land was broken concrete and rubble, overgrown with weeds. Nothing much could grow there, though he had to fight his way through brambles laden with blackberries. He had been hungry since the moment of his arrival, hungry as he'd never been back home with its well-run farm and 'scientific' approach to nutrition. He missed the security of that ordered existence. More than that, he just missed home.

The blackberries were ripe and burst with sweetness as he bit them. He could not help it; he felt his eyes fill with tears. The taste reminded him of the compound, of the jam and pies their Missis Nile made for Pa. He did not know why he was crying. Missis Nile was an interfering busy body who had set her heart on marrying Pa. Now there was no Pa to be married and Buzz would never taste blackberry pie again. He was going to die, trying to help some girl he barely knew trade arms to save the life of a woman he'd never met. He sat down in a small area of cracked concrete, leaned his back against a decaying graffitoed wall and let the tears fall.

He did not stay there long. Although Pa was dead, his voice lived on, berating Buzz for weakness, for sentimentality. Civilised men did not cry. Automatically his hands began to fill the basket he'd been given with blackberries, picking fruit as if he, like Ratter, were a little boy again, safe at home. The activity helped him think. Would he ever fulfil his mission if he stayed with Ollu? Did he want to commit himself to her doomed quest? He'd lost Pa, but was he really ready to die? The tart taste of blackberries filled his mouth, the sun warmed his back even in this decaying wasteland of an island, and he could smell the rich woody scent of the vegetation, the sharp tang of the river.

No, he did not want to die.

Perhaps he could make his own way to one of the villages Ollu had talked of, places that had local government and maybe even the kind of civilization it was his mission to unearth. They might have comps, though he had sensed no live tech anywhere except the Ark and near the other Bargers. There had to be more elsewhere. Pa couldn't be wrong. The Queen B must be somewhere in these damp, unlovely islands.

He had almost decided he was not going to return the Ark when Ratter emerged from the bushes, red faced and panting.

'This place is full of rabbits! How many do you think we'll need?' His face was alight with enthusiasm. Buzz shrugged.

'You mustn't do it, you know,' Ratter continued, as if they were in the middle of some lengthy conversation. 'You mustn't abandon her. Without you Pyke will take the Ark and she'll be a skinny corpse in the river.'

He looked at Ratter for a long moment. He wasn't sure what Ratter knew or how he knew it, but he was impressed. Pa would have been horrified at how easily Buzz had begun to believe in the unseen and the unscientific.

'How did you know I was thinking of going?'

'I was too.' Ratter picked a handful of berries and ate them greedily, the juice staining his mouth purple. He was a little kid, nothing more.

'No dreams then?'

'No. But I have dreamed of the three of us, of the braid and I think we *are* meant to stick together. I think things are better for each of us if we do that. I don't know for sure, but I believe it.'

Buzz carried on methodically filling the basket, avoiding the younger boy's eye.

'Do you know that we won't die, trying to get these K4s for Ollu?'

He forced himself to keep picking fruit so that Ratter did not guess how urgently he needed a reassuring answer.

'Nothing's sure Buzz. I've dreamed your death and mine, before

I came on the Ark, but in those dreams, we were not together and we were not with Ollu. Maybe that will make a difference.'

'Do you really believe that?'

Ratter grinned. 'I don't give much for our chances without you. Ollu's tough, but she looks easy to kill and both of us together don't make a whole one of you. I can't keep Pyke from killing us and taking the boat, but I think you could.'

Buzz would have preferred it if Ratter had pretended he wanted Buzz to stay because he liked him, or even because he admired his grit. It was slightly galling to be valued only for his brawn, but perhaps that was better than not being valued at all. He had a sudden mental image of his father as he was in life: strong, determined, scornful. Pa would not be amused that his golden boy, his triumph of gen-engineering and careful breeding, was seen only as a muscle-bound thug.

He started to laugh. He laughed so hard that he dropped his basket of blackberries and they rolled onto the broken cement path. He laughed until his ribs ached, until he ran out of air, until he had to wipe his eyes.

'Are you OK?' Ratter looked at him dubiously. 'If there's something in the blackberries, tell me now and I'll spit them out.'

He pulled himself together with difficulty, 'No. It's not the blackberries. I just thought of something funny, that's all.' He bent to pick up the spilled fruit. He had made his decision and it wasn't a rational one. He'd stay with Ollu and Ratter, because of the blood oath, because they needed him, because Ratter was honest and Ollu was honourable and because he did not want to be alone.

Ratter didn't hang around, but left, hastily cramming blackberries into his mouth so that he could check the traps. He must think Buzz was half way crazy, best left alone until he'd got a grip on his madness.

'You may not like it, Pa,' he said aloud to the empty air, 'but it's my life now.' Of course, he wasn't at all sure how long he'd have any kind of life.

He wiped his face on the rough hessian of his slave shirt and ran his fingers through his hair in a half-hearted attempt to clean himself up. Right. If he was to be Ollu's body guard, the Ark's own thug, he had better get back to work. He collected the baskets of fruit and strode purposefully back towards the barge.

Chapter Thirty

Ollu

Ollu had not expected it to be so easy to persuade everyone to leave the Ark. She could not for a moment believe they'd all gone. She slumped on the deck, trying to understand how she had come to break all her clan's most sacred taboos, before she gathered her strength and went down to the cabin. It smelled of strangers, it smelled of men. She flung open the porthole window and began cleaning up. Ma would know she'd let outsiders on, of course she would. Ollu would tell her, eventually, but she would not know by the state of the Ark.

She scrubbed at the wood of the cabin as if she could scrub away her guilt. She saw to the animals and did all the housekeeping tasks she had let slide over the last day. When she was certain she was unobserved, she checked the recording device in her pocket, to be certain she had the details of the deal with the Missis' sister. When she pressed the replay button, she was shocked at how small and high her own voice sounded, the voice of a child. Had the Missis' sister actually taken her seriously? For the first time, she began to understand how desperate the Robert's must be if they were prepared to trade with her. Not that the deal cost them much. Ma was as likely to die as not, whatever anyone did. Ollu knew that in her guts. She doubted even the care and home-made physics of Lumpy Lil could save her Ma.

It felt strange to be alone on the Ark. She did a quick tour of the barge, to be certain that she could not be watched and then found the hidden place in the panelling which housed the aye-eye. She knew at once that it had not been tampered with.

'Hello, Ollu,' the aye-eye said, in that strange stilted accent which had so intrigued her as a child. It was a voice from the Preeker past, and in the empty space of the cabin she shivered.

'Has there been any contact?' she asked, just as her mother always had.

'There has been no English language messaging, mail or broadcast for the last three thousand six hundred and ninety-two days, four hours and six minutes. Some activity has been detected in the Chinese speaking world.' The machine spoke pleasantly, as if it did not matter. Ollu declined the opportunity to review the Chinese correspondence. The aye-eye's translations never made any sense and even Ma had given up worrying at them. If civilisation survived in China, the other side of a vast world, it was not a lot of use to them. Ollu wasn't entirely sure what she ought to do if ever the aye-eye recorded contact. She was glad it hadn't.

She dictated her log and ran a quick virus scan of the Ark's systems. To her relief and surprise the Ark had the 'all clear.' According to Ma, the Ark's abilities had declined over the years. Once the Ark had owned a system that allowed biological sampling and human virus scanning, but that was long gone. It would have been good to know that Buzz and Ratter were really disease free, especially as she had shared their blood. She had taken some crazy gambles since Ma had fallen sick. She was lucky to still be alive.

She washed her face, smoothed her hair and combed out the worst of the tangles with her fingers before bundling it back under head scarf. It delayed the moment, but not by much. She still wasn't sure if Ma would approve of what she was about to do, but it seemed to her the only thing to do. She could not trust anyone with the Ark. Ma always insisted that the barge's secrets had to be kept.

Ollu cleared her throat. It was a lonely, hollow sound. She spoke as clearly as she could, using the form Ma had taught her long ago.

'This is an emergency. Begin programme: 'Self destruct'. She repeated the string of numbers and words her mother had made her memorise since the moment she'd learned to talk.

'Are you sure? Please confirm.' The aye-eye's voice was as unemotional as ever, but Ollu's voice shook a little when she repeated the confirmation code.

'Choose a trigger word.'

It had to be something that she would not say accidentally, she knew that. Something that she could scream loudly, with a dying breath. What word did she want to die for?

She couldn't use her mother's name or anything weak like that, but there was a word her mother used when she talked about the past that made her eyes bright. Ma used it a lot when she talked about the way things had been. It seemed to sum up everything her mother wanted to preserve, with her endless worrying about how to keep things going.

'Civilisation; civilisation; civilisation,' Ollu said three times as clearly as she could.

'Programme commencing, please wait.' There was a pause, a kind of thrumming. She felt it through the soles of her feet, as if it were the pulse of the Ark itself. She had never felt it before, and it worried her. Had she awoken a sleeping monster, or had the aye-eye, the other mother of her childhood years, chosen this most desperate of moments to let her down? Ollu realised that she was holding her breath. She released it once the machine spoke again.

'The emergency programme, "self destruct" is now activated.'

Ollu's legs were trembling, as if she were still battling the storm that had started this whole disastrous chain of events. Forcing herself to breathe calmly, she completed the last of the system checks and then logged off. 'Haveaniceday' she intoned carefully, before bowing reverently in the direction of the machine and 'powering down.'

Is this what Ma would want? Ma had always said that the Ark should not fall into enemy hands. But who was the enemy? Was Pyke the enemy? Or would she meet the real enemy in Bad Water? What of Buzz, or Ratter? She had trusted them, but they were still male strangers who did not have the right even to board a matriarch boat. She loved the Ark and she was not having anyone take it from her. Its secrets were Bargers secrets and not for gadgers.

She had to unclench her bunched fists and make sure that all was as it should be, that nothing was out of place. She touched the all but invisible joint in the varnished floorboards which might betray the hidden cavity beneath. Could it be seen? She scrubbed the floor again. She dare not leave the slightest sign to alert the attention of a sharp eyed boy like Buzz, or Ratter.

That wasn't all. There were other things still to do; other decisions to make. She was going to Grennish, but who should she take with her? She drank a glass of sweet water, grateful that the purification unit was still working.

It was very simple. If she allowed Pyke and the others back on board, she needed Ratter and Buzz as back up. If the boys did not return to the barge for reasons of their own, she could not risk having the adult slaves on board. If Buzz came back, she would take the slaves downstream. There. That was her decision. Right or wrong, she had made her choice.

She washed up the glass. She had done all she reasonably could for the Ark and for herself. The rest was down to God, Allah, the Great River, and perhaps all three if they were not somehow one and the same. With a last check that the cabin was restored and as neat and clean as she could make it, she returned to the deck to wait for the others. The Ark's unwelcome but necessary crew.

Chapter
Thirty-One

Buzz

There was something wrong with the Ark, Buzz knew that at once. Something about it gave him a sick feeling in his guts. Ollu seemed fine. He thought that she seemed a little surprised to see him. The smile she gave him was warm, warmer than he had expected, and she brightened further when he handed her the blackberries. She seemed perfectly in control.

He wished he knew what was wrong with the Ark.

Ratter arrived a few minutes later, his face smeared with dirt and blood, clutching a brace of rabbits. If he was surprised to see Buzz, he did not let it show. He volunteered to prepare the carcasses, on the banks so as not to sully the Ark's pristine deck.

'You worked hard,' Buzz said to Ollu as he took in the neatly scrubbed deck. He liked things neat himself. Pa would not have stood for mess and disorder of any kind.

'So did you, with the blackberries,' Ollu said. He was about to deny that blackberrying was work when she surprised him with an abrupt question: 'Why did you come back, Buzz?'

It was hard to answer and the sense of wrongness on the Ark made him twitchy. 'You needed me,' he said simply.

'Thank you,' she said, startling him further.

'I thought you didn't want men on the Ark?'

'What I want doesn't seem that important any more. I have to save Ma and the babes, and Davey too if I can. I can't do that on my own.'

A cry from the bank prevented them from talking further. Ratter had abandoned his knife and was writhing around on the floor. Pyke and the rest of the slaves had arrived unheard and were watching him, their curious expressions tinged with revulsion. Everyone feared madness and disease, wherever they came from. The years of the Chaos had brought too much of both.

'What's wrong with him?' Angela asked. She looked ready to bolt at any moment. Someone had made a salve for her wounds and she looked better.

Pyke answered her. 'I should have guessed. This is Riki's peeper, the prophet. I thought the Mainman binned him last month?'

Buzz did not like to see Ratter so vulnerable. In three strides, he was by the boy's side and scooping him up. He weighed very little. Ollu rushed to help them both aboard. Ratter's face was as pale as the bleached wood of the deck. Beneath his closed lids his eyes moved rapidly as though he were dreaming and his long dark eyelashes fluttered.

'I think he's having one of his dreams again,' Buzz said as he clambered back on board. Ollu moved to bar further entry to the Ark.

'You have to lay down any weapons before I can allow you on board,' she said firmly to Pyke, reaching for her own weapon. Pyke looked abashed at being challenged by a child. Buzz kind of sympathised. Ollu looked so small and inconsequential but her voice rung with authority.

'Take off your coats and show me what is in your pockets.' There was a murmur of discontent. Pyke took a step forward.

Buzz turned Ratter on his side as his Pa had taught him, into the position that meant that if you were sick, you probably wouldn't choke. He did not think Ratter would be sick, but it was hard to say for sure. It was the work of a moment and then he was beside Ollu. Pyke took a step backwards.

'Give me your gun and you can search them,' Buzz said softly, stooping a little to speak into Ollu's ear. He wondered if she would trust him so far. He noticed the way she chewed the inside of her cheek, but she complied.

The slaves had not been able to come up with much: several objects Ollu dismissed as 'shankers', shards of glass they'd fashioned into knives, and a serviceable wooden club embedded with nails that Pyke had hidden in his sleeve.

'If I can't trust you why should I let you on board?' Ollu asked them. It was obvious that she couldn't trust them, and Buzz didn't think she should let them back on board, but it was her command and he didn't challenge it.

'We weren't going to use them against you,' Pyke said, his voice ringing with outrage. 'You can't expect us to turn up back at the Minster unarmed! I thought we had a deal – or do Bargers have no honour left?'

'We had an agreement, but it looks to me like you were thinking of breaking it,' Ollu responded hotly, and Buzz thought that it was perhaps a good thing that he was holding the gun. The two leaders, man and girl, stared at each other for a long moment. Buzz wondered if he could hold the slaves off if they decided to rush the barge. The silence lengthened, and then Ollu nodded at him and he herded the former slaves in the direction of the cabin. They had to step over Ratter's prone body on their way.

It was the wrong decision. There would be more trouble from Pyke, he was sure of it.

Ollu gathered up the makeshift weapons and stowed them in one of the many hidden cupboards of the Ark. He raised an eyebrow.

'I don't believe them, but they have a point. I gave my word.'

'You've taken a big risk letting them back. Are you going to trade them?'

Ollu pulled a face. 'I don't know. I can't help thinking that they might still be useful. Anyway I had a deal and Bargers are people of honour.' She stated this last defiantly, as if he were about to challenge it. He had more sense.

'Danger coming!' Ratter's thin voice sounded terrified. Ollu reached his side first. She shook him gently by the shoulder, cooing like a mother to her child. 'It's Ok – it's just a toxic dream. You're OK.'

Ratter opened his eyes. They held that blank, unseeing look that had so disturbed Buzz before. 'Get him some water from the cabin will you?' Ollu said.

It was not a request, but a command.

Buzz still had the gun in his hand as he moved to open the cabin door. The five slaves could still overpower him if they had a mind to. He hesitated.

'I don't think they'll jump you. They're better off letting me take them where they want to go, and I think they know it. If they try to take you, odds are at least one of them will die. They know that too.' He nodded. He did not disagree with her assessment.

She turned back to give Ratter her full attention.

Buzz opened the cabin door with a certain amount of trepidation. The sense that there was something wrong with the Ark was strongest here. He could taste the strange but familiar flavour of tech in his mouth. It was so powerful he found it difficult to speak for a moment.

'I need to get water.' The two women moved out of his way silently.

'Is the peeper OK?' Pyke asked casually.

'Can he really see the future?' the other woman, not Angela, said with a fake shudder.

'Maybe.' That was all Buzz was prepared to concede in answer to either question.

When he got back on deck Ratter was sitting up, and looking more normal.

'Ambush,' he said, taking the cup of water gratefully. 'Down river, we'll be ambushed.'

'Are you sure?' Ollu sounded shaken.

'Am I sure it will happen? No, but we were all in the vision.'

'Should we turn back? Avoid down river?' Buzz said, not at all sure they could defend the Ark from ambush, and suddenly afraid that he would see Ollu staring at him with eyes as dead and coldly judgemental as his father's.

'We have to go downstream.' Ollu said shortly. 'I've got to get the trade list.'

'Let's collect the rabbits and the kindling and get on with it then. What time of day was the ambush?'

'It was dark – night.'

'In your vision did Pyke help or hinder?'

'He fought beside us and took a bullet to the heart.' Ratter looked like he might finally be sick. Then Ollu asked the question that was on Buzz's own lips.

'Do we die?'

Ratter shrugged, 'Maybe. I don't know. I didn't see you dead. I just saw Buzz's eyes shining with silver light and fire. There were flames dancing all around.'

Ollu did not pause to listen to the details. She was already grabbing the rabbits and the discarded knife from the bank and raising the anchor.

'We'd better get going. We've wasted enough time here. Ambush or not, I'm going to Grennish.'

There wasn't much to say in response to that, so Buzz didn't say anything.

'Take the tiller, Buzz, I'm going below with Ratter to show him how to cook the rabbits. I need to talk to Pyke.'

Buzz nodded. So they were going to be ambushed? Was it still an ambush if you knew about it in advance? Pa would have known. It was as well that Ollu hadn't thrown Pyke's shankers overboard. It looked like they might come in useful after all.

CHAPTER THIRTY-TWO

OLLU

OLLU DID NOT bother reclaiming the revolver from Buzz. She believed in the ambush. Ma might have dismissed Ratter's visions as cultish superstition but Ollu could not. She was not Ma.

She opened the cabin door cautiously, unsure what to expect. 'Captain,' Pyke said with a little bow of his head. If he was making fun of her he made no move towards her or to Ratter. He gave some kind of hand signal and she tensed at once, but it was not that kind of sign. Instead of launching an attack, a man and the woman whose name she didn't know took the rabbits from her and, when she showed them how the stove worked, were happy to prepare a meal for all of them. Ollu wondered if they would have time to eat it.

'You all need to know something...' she began, awkwardly. 'The thing is ...' All eyes were on her – unforgiving, adult eyes. She wished she had Ma's presence, her natural authority. She wished she had not heard her own voice on the recording machine. It was not a voice to inspire trust. She was, however, Captain of the Ark.

'OK.' She just had to get this over with. 'Ratter has had a vision.' She spoke too quickly. No one laughed. 'Ratter thinks, I mean Ratter saw...'

171

Ratter himself interrupted. 'It's all right Ollu. I can explain.' To Ollu's surprise he entered the cabin and stood in the middle of Pyke's people.

'You may know me already as the prophet of Riki, the Boss man of the C-Crew Code.' There was a general nodding of heads. 'Well, for this time only, I guess we are on the same side. Ollu's side.'

There was a slight hesitation, and then Pyke nodded his head once in agreement. Everyone was paying very close attention to Ratter now. He seemed quite at ease. 'You know my rep. I foretold the fall of Wharf to the Steveners of Westamm, and the death of the six brothers of Chaz.' Ratter made eye contact with each member of his audience in turn. No one breathed. 'I've seen what I've seen and I'm telling you true and fair, by all your Holies, sure as the Great River bears our dead, there will be a fight. Tonight the Ark will be ambushed and, if we do not fight as one crew, not all of us will see the dawn.'

Still no one spoke for what seemed like a long time. Pyke broke the silence first.

'Did you see who?'

Ratter nodded. 'It was your Mainman.'

'You know if he sold us? As a prophet, do you know?' Pyke could not keep the anger from his voice.

'He did. He was worried you might build a peace with us, with the C-Crew Code, and that it might hold. He thought you'd be the hero and his hold on the clan would be broken.'

Pyke turned to Ollu. 'Is this true? Do you know if your Davey,' he spat the name and Ollu winced as spittle fell on the scrubbed boards of the Ark, 'Sorry. Do you know if your brother did a deal with the Minster's Mainman?'

She wanted to confess that she knew nothing, but that would make her seem too much a child. Captains knew about these things.

'Davey is no longer part of our firm. This is a matriarch boat. He works for his mother in law now, and I don't know her business. The Ark does not trade in Bad Water.' She folded her arms.

'And the Minster is in Bad Water?' She nodded, 'Well, you

got that right.' He grinned. 'It's chock full of corpses from one gang or other.'

Ollu could not keep the shock from her face. She could not believe that after all the plagues of Chaos anyone could be stupid enough to deliberately foul their main source of water. The Minsters must be mad as well as lawless.

Pyke spoke to Ratter again. 'Does your vision tell you why my Mainman would want to ambush the Ark?'

Ollu had no gift of prophecy, but she thought she'd understood nonetheless. If it had not been for the imminent birth of the baby it would have been Davey trading in Bad Water. As she understood it, his business these days was shipping slaves to Grennish in return for arms. If he was going to pay for his ship, chances were that he would be working double, trading for Flo as well as on his own account. Why wouldn't Pyke's 'Mainman' try to take Davey's cargo? Ma had always said they were a lawless bunch, and if Pyke was anything to go by Ollu believed it. The more she considered it the likelier her explanation seemed. The only flaw in Ollu's theory was that Davey would have been heading upriver with guns and downriver with slaves. She would have thought the Minster Mainman would prefer arms to slaves, and would have attempted to ambush a barge travelling upriver, not down.

'Reckon they could be waiting for Davey,' Ratter said, echoing her thoughts.

'Wouldn't they be expecting Davey to be travelling up river?' Ollu asked.

'Maybe he cheated them and they care less about his cargo than making him pay.' Pyke said. He did not seem particularly troubled by the thought of an ambush.

'Davey's no cheat!'

'Yeah, and he's no slaver either, I suppose.'

There was not much she could say to that.

'Look, it doesn't matter why we are about to be ambushed, we're going to be ambushed. Will you fight for your Mainman?' Ollu asked.

'He sold us.' Pyke answered, grimly.

'You don't know for sure. You've only got Ratter's guess.'

'And if I say 'yes' what are you going to do? Shoot me?' Pyke spoke with an edge of mockery.

'I'll drop you landside and save you from a fight.'

'And if I lie when I say 'no' what will you do then?'

'Save my first bullet for you.' As Ollu said it she believed it to be true. She was more savage than she'd thought. Pyke nodded, as though he found all her responses reasonable.

'We need to discuss this.' He indicated the assembled group with a wave of his hand. Ollu must have looked surprised because he added, 'We've all got a say in this. The Mainman is family. We're a clan too, like you Bargers, and we don't often turn on our own.'

Ollu left them to it. She was beginning to think she would have been wiser to leave them landside. Whatever they told her, she couldn't trust them. Ratter followed her out of the cabin.

'I didn't know you were famous back where you came from,' she said

He sniffed, 'I don't know if you'd call it famous. Pyke's lot have been trying to bin me for months.'

She went to stand beside Buzz. The sun had come out and the Ark was bathed in golden afternoon light. It made the planks gleam and for a moment her heart lifted. The Great River shone, its gilded ripples undulating like the back of some great and powerful snake. She loved the river; she loved the Ark and it hurt to think she might never see either of them again, that this bright day could be her last. She forced herself to be businesslike.

'You'd better take the spear gun and give me my revolver,' she said to Buzz. 'Ratter, you'd better have the other gun. I don't know if we're going to have trouble with Pyke's lot or not, but if we are, we'll drop them at the next bend. We'll haul them off the boat any way we can and then they can take their chances with the Mayor of Tonlock.' She looked at her companions, forcing both of them to meet her eyes. 'We might have to shoot them.' By their expressions, they'd already come to that conclusion.

She didn't feel that confident about arming Ratter. If he had another vision fit anyone could take the precious weapon from him. 'It takes shrap, so it'll knock you backwards if you're not ready for it,' she warned him.

Ratter nodded gravely. Ollu felt death was very close as she handed over the gun. How had she lost so much so quickly? Her Ma, Davey, the twins, and now the Ark and her two companions.

'Be careful, don't be too brave,' she said, almost without meaning to. 'The Ark isn't something you should die for.' She wondered what Ma would think if she heard her say that. Ollu would probably die defending the Ark because that was the Captain's duty, but she couldn't expect that kind of crazy loyalty from Buzz and Ratter.

The boys looked serious. Buzz handed her the revolver without a word and Ollu exchanged it for the spear gun. 'The slaves' weapons are in here if you need them and I can't get them out,' she said, indicating the cabinet where she had concealed them and feeling suddenly shaky.

There was a comb in one of the many pockets of her coat and she fished it out, undid her scarf and started combing out her hair. It was a strange thing to do, even she could see that, but it was something Ma had always done for her when she was scared. It was also a sign that she counted the boys as her brothers. Only loose women left their hair unbound in front of men who weren't family.

'Your hair!' Ratter gasped and then his knees buckled and he tumbled to the ground in what she hoped was a faint.

Ollu's first thought was that her reservations about giving him her weapon were entirely justified. How could she trust him with the gun if he was going to fall over like that?

He lay on the floor twitching. This seemed to happen a lot. Too often for her comfort.

'Do you think he's OK?' she asked Buzz, who turned him on his side once more and checked his breathing.

Buzz nodded.

'What was that about?'

'Your hair is very beautiful?' Buzz said, uncertainly, 'When it caught the sun just then it was dazzling – like you had a halo.'

Ollu shrugged. It did not seem like much of a reason to faint. She hurriedly covered her hair so as not to spook Ratter again, and knelt down beside him.

'Ratter are you OK?' He shuddered, but then opened his eyes. 'Ollu?'

'Yes, it's me. Here, have a drink of sweet water.'

He gulped from the cup, thirstily. She gave him a few moments to pull himself together. She was glad she was not a prophet. It seemed a very inconvenient gift.

'Why did you faint?' Buzz asked. Ollu thought he was scowling, but he may just have been squinting against the sun.

'Back home, I had a dream that the Mainman of the Minster would die. It was one of my earliest dreams – I had it before the current Mainman was even Mainman. It's been one of those dreams that kept coming back. I thought it was an angel would kill the Mainman. We used to live in a high place with pictures of angels made of glass. I never saw her face and then when I saw the light on your hair I knew it was you.' He took another sip of water. 'It's funny. That's why Pyke's lot tried to bin me, because of my vision of you.'

Ollu must have looked blank because Ratter immediately explained.

'The Mainman of the Minster is mean. I think even Riki, the Boss, is afraid of him. When word spread he'd be killed by an angel, my crew got bolder. Riki, got his henches to believe that they could not lose with an angel on their side. We've ripped off some of the Mainman's farms. That's how Riki first saw my sister –when he came looking for me to make me peeper and prophet. You see! Our fates were braided together before we even met.'

'But I'm not an angel,' Ollu said, bemused. 'And I don't want to kill anybody.'

'Maybe not,' Buzz said, 'but, according to Ratter, it is the Mainman who will ambush us tonight and you *are* carrying a revolver.'

CHAPTER THIRTY-THREE

BUZZ

BUZZ WAS NOT sure what to make of all Ratter's talk of prophecy. Ratter obviously had vivid and powerful dreams, and he identified the characters in them with real people that he met, but were they prophecies? Probably not and yet…

Buzz knew that he could do things that others could not. Perhaps Ratter was another kind of freak. An accidental one, a naturally occurring mutation. Pa believed in those even if he did not believe in the supernatural, in superstition. In fact, Pa had always defended his 'meddling' in genengineering as speeding up the work of Gaia. Buzz had always believed what Pa believed. Without Pa… well, it was hard to know.

What would Pa have made of this place? It was so much harsher than the compound. Pa had expected to find the *Queen B* in some place like the compound, a high tech, civilised, community. Buzz could not see how civilisation could exist in this mucky, waterlogged wasteland. Ollu's Ark had tech but it was all wrong, all broken. The thrum of bad tech made his head ache. Pa had made a terrible mistake. There was nothing for them here. No one knew or cared about the skill and ingenuity that had brought them across the Ocean. Pa was a genius, but he was just as dead as any fool. His remains lay in a shallow grave and soon Buzz would be dead too, his body left to pollute the Great River.

His introspection was halted by the strong, savoury scent of baked rabbit. Ollu and Ratter stopped their chattering to sniff the air like two small dogs.

'You take the tiller,' Ollu said to Ratter. 'Keep your wits, these are dreg waters. Buzz, come with me.'

Ratter pulled a face, but scrambled to his feet to take over the steering without argument.

Buzz didn't question Ollu either. Somehow you didn't when she gave commands.

In the cabin, Pyke was already distributing the food among his companions. He looked up briefly as they came through the door.

'I was going to bring some food out to you,' he said easily, as if they were workmates, or family, not potential enemies. Buzz tried to appear equally relaxed and unworried, but he wasn't sure he pulled it off. 'We've been talking,' Pyke continued as he passed them a generous share of the meat. 'We will help you defend the Ark.' Ollu nodded, as if this was nothing more than she had expected. Buzz admired the way she seemed so calm, so in control.

'And what of your Mainman? Will you fight him too?' she asked.

Pyke looked around the room as if daring anyone to argue. 'I will and so will the rest of us, apart from Angela.'

Buzz turned to her in surprise. She seemed the least likely of all of them to be squeamish about a fight. She looked upset. She may even have been crying, for her face was blotched, her cuts vivid where the salve had been wiped away.

'The Mainman's my father,' she explained. 'I can't believe he sold me. I think there was a mistake. I can't fight him. It's not right.' She looked at her companions defiantly. 'Pyke says you have to drop me off on one of the islands before nightfall. Is that true?'

'What if she warns him?' Buzz spoke before he could stop himself.

Ollu barely glanced at him. She was already tucking into her food. She spoke between mouthfuls, in a tone that suggested she was speaking to an idiot. 'She won't get to him before we do. The Great River is the fastest route round here and no sail boat, kayak or skiff will go faster than us – with or against the tide.'

She turned to Angela. 'Pyke is right. You can't stay on board if you're not with us. Say your goodbyes. I'll drop you off as soon as you have eaten. I know the Mayor of Tonlock a little; I can write you a letter of introduction. It might be better than being seen as a stranger. They're not fond of strangers in Tonlock.'

'You know how to write?' Angela's blue eyes grew even larger with astonishment.

'Yes and read too. All Bargers can. Did you not know that?'

Angela shook her head in wonderment. Pyke also looked interested. 'I thought the knack of that had died out,' he said thoughtfully, but Ollu was already extracting paper and pencil from her coat in between mouthfuls. Buzz did not know what to think. In the compound everyone was literate. It was a sign of civilisation. Pa should never have brought them here.

Ollu's writing reflected her personality, her letters small, but clear and bold. She wrote only that Angela was a friend of 'The Ark', and was not known to have any diseases or criminal tendencies, and that she was of a good and powerful family whose lands were located some distance from Tonlock.

'You can read?' Ollu caught Buzz following her script, watching over her shoulder. He nodded. He knew she wanted to ask him more about that, but there was no time. The light was already beginning to fade. 'Take this to Ratter,' she said, and he had to leave her alone in the cabin with their dubious allies.

'They're going to fight with us – all except Angela.' Buzz said to the younger boy who nodded and took the meat from him greedily.

'No worries. Angela is going to be important some day.'

'What, have you had a vision?'

'Nah, but she's good looking and she knows how to make things run her way. She was one of the ones I followed when I was peeping for Riki.'

'Is it true that her father sold her to Davey?' Buzz didn't want it to be true. How could a man do that to his own kin?

'Probably.' Ratter shrugged. 'She was slipping away from his block, sneaking out to meet someone. She was all set to cause the Mainman a lot of trouble. If I knew that, the chances were he did too. At least he didn't try to have her binned.'

'He sold his daughter into slavery?'

Ratter chewed and swallowed. 'He's got plenty more. Six living daughters, no living sons. There's no need to look like that. Crewmen do what they must to get through. Riki is thirty six and just about the oldest crewman I know. Angela is well out of it.'

Buzz concentrated on eating every morsel of his food. Perhaps it was as well that Pa had not lived to discover how wrong he was about this place. There was nothing he'd recognise as civilisation here.

Chapter
Thirty-Four

Ollu

Ollu felt slightly better when she'd eaten. Pyke was with her for as long as they wanted the same thing. He would try to take the Ark when the time was right, she was sure, but she'd already done what was needed to keep its secrets out of his hands.

'I am going on deck,' she said. 'I want Angela to join me there in a moment.' She handed Angela the torn scrap of precious creamy paper. 'Here, keep the letter safe,' she said in a low voice, while Pyke watched her curiously.

'What does it say?' Angela asked.

'That you are a friend to the Ark.'

Angela took the letter. 'Why are you doing this?' She sounded at once bemused, grateful and suspicious.

'Bargers are traders,' Ollu explained. 'We are always looking for new partners. It doesn't cost me anything to write the letter and one day you may be in a position to help me.' It sounded good, but it was not true. It was more than that. Davey had enslaved Angela, and all of them. Ollu needed to put that right.

'Thank you,' Angela said. 'If I can lend you a hand, I will, trust me.' Her intense blue eyes were earnest. 'Seems not all Bargers are polluters.'

Once Ollu would have defended her clan, but now there was nothing to say.

On deck she breathed in the sweet scent of wild honeysuckle, carried on the wind. The sun was setting and the whole vast expanse of the Great River was flushed with pink. The only sound was the waves, lapping softly against the boat. It was all so beautiful she could not speak for a minute. God, Allah, Great River keep them all safe! She wanted to see a dawn to match this sunset.

No. She just wanted to see another dawn.

Angela emerged from the cabin a moment later, followed by Pyke and the rest of his crew. Ollu steered the boat towards the shore. She did not like taking the barge into shallow water, but it was too cold to make Angela swim. She felt awkward. They were going to fight Angela's father, after all. 'Keep walking with your back to the river. This part floods at high water and the village is on high ground a short walk from here. Remember to ask to see the Mayor.' She looked at Angela properly for the first time. Her face was still cut and her clothes torn. Worse, her hair, a startling red and cropped short, was immodestly uncovered. In spite of everything, she was beautiful.

'Have you no scarf to cover your hair?' Angela shook her head. Perhaps it was not the custom in Bad Water. Ollu knew enough about the world to know that not everyone believed the same thing.

Ratter raced back down into the cabin and returned, brandishing one of Ma's least precious scarves. 'Can she use this?'

Ollu nodded. 'Up River women wear something over their hair unless they are at home with family. We don't show our hair to strangers.'

Angela took the scarf and tied it around her head. 'Will this do?'

Ollu nodded gravely.

'Gaia's blessing,' Buzz whispered ,just loudly enough for Angela and Ollu to hear.

Ratter leapt nimbly onto the bank to help Angela across. She walked off into the sunset, like a character in one of the films Ollu had watched when the old aye-eye could still show moving pictures, back when she was a little child.

'I hope she will be OK,' she said. Pyke looked at her curiously.

Angela's departure depressed all their spirits, especially Pyke's. He seemed so dejected that Ollu wondered about the nature of their relationship. Not that she could spare him any sympathy.

As the sun faded, Ollu handed out the weapons. This was a dangerous time. If Pyke wanted to take the Ark from her, he might do it now. She was all too aware that she could be arming an enemy. She chewed her cheek until it was sore. She had to battle to stop her hands from shaking as she gave Pyke and his three companions the shankers. The remaining woman, Jana, looked capable, holding the shanker as though she was used to the weapon. When she saw Ollu watching she gave her a fierce grin. 'Don't worry, Captain, we know what to do.'

It was the first time she'd spoken to Ollu and yet Jana might end up dying for her, and for the Ark.

There was no plan as such. Ollu would use the Ark's protections to keep off any invaders, while the others fought anyone who got close, in any way that they could. Ollu would stay by the tiller and try to keep the barge moving onwards, downstream, as it was much harder to fight a moving target. If their enemies had set a trap or a wire across the water, it would be Ratter's job to take it down. He was the most agile, apart from Ollu herself, and she was not leaving the deck.

While Ollu waited, the wind whipped up and the air grew chilly. Buzz found his way to her side. His strange eyes glittered in the fading light. It was clear he had something on his mind.

'Ratter and me – we were talking earlier and we think you should go below and leave us to do the fighting,' he said. He kept his tone low, so he would not be overheard by Pyke's lot.

'And why would you think that?' She could not keep outrage from her voice.

'Look, I know you're tough and all that, but do you really want to be in this fight? We will fight for the Ark and so will Pyke's crew. You don't need to.'

'If you think I'd leave this up to anyone else you don't know me at all,' she hissed.

'I know you're brave and all, Ollu, but...'

'Pox and Piss, Buzz. Even grown men die when you shoot them. I've strength enough to pull a trigger.'

'But do you want to?' She didn't answer him straight away. He understood her better than she'd expected, because no, of course she didn't.

'I am Captain of the Ark and it is mine to defend any way I have to.'

'OK,' he said, 'but at least hang back. And take out any light they might have. I can keep you safe in the dark.'

She shook her head. 'No one can keep me safe, Buzz. I have to take my chances, same as everyone else.'

They stood without talking for a moment. Ratter was on the trail barge feeding Lalo. They watched his complete involvement in his task, as if nothing else mattered. Ollu thought of his sister, Ally, back in the Roberts' land. He would have been safer staying a slave.

Buzz was fiddling with the strap of the spear gun. He was usually very still and controlled in his movements, and she guessed that he was afraid too. He cleared his throat so suddenly he made her jump.

'I just want to say, well, thank you, Ollu, for letting me aboard. It has been an honour.' Buzz shook her hand very seriously, in a way she might have found funny in other circumstances. There was a lump in her throat and she had to look away.

'Don't say anything else, Buzz. We'll make it through. I feel it in my guts. Ratter isn't the only prophet.' She didn't feel that she was anything of the kind, but Buzz grinned as if he believed her and that, strangely, made her smile at him in return.

CHAPTER
THIRTY-FIVE

OLLU

OLLU STEERED A straight course down the centre of the river, a good distance from each bank. She was straining so hard to see that her neck ached and her eyes were watering. She called Ratter over when he'd finished sorting out the animals.

'Where exactly did you see the ambush taking place?' she asked him.

'On the river, where it bends. Close to the Minster maybe?'

'Was there no dreg in the water? No ruins to mark the spot?

'I couldn't see the tower of the Old Parley, if that's what you're asking. I just saw moments. Visions don't come with a polluting map.' He sounded angry, but he was shaking and Ollu guessed he was scared.

It was not a stretch of river Ollu knew, but Ma had talked a little about what lay in Bad Water, and, of course she had Davey's map. She made herself speak softly. 'I know it's hard, but tell me again, Ratter. Can you think of anything that would help?'

'I saw flames, gunfire, Pyke, the Mainman and you.' He screwed his face up with the effort of memory. 'It was over too quick.'

'Right.' She had forgotten that he'd mentioned flames. Did

that mean she would have to self-destruct the Ark? She ran her fingers on the smooth, worn surface of the tiller and hoped Ratter was wrong, or that the flames did not come from the Ark itself. Every small sound made her jump and her heart was beating so hard and so fast it was a wonder her chest could hold it in.

The Ark floated down the deserted river, unhindered, for what felt like a long time. Bats flew overhead, and the stench of Bad Water grew ever stronger.

Ratter sniffed the foul-smelling air and grinned. 'Home,' he said and Ollu exchanged a glance with Buzz. Ratter couldn't like that stink?

Buzz wanted to turn out the lights and, though Pyke argued, Ollu overruled him. Pyke might have ignored her order, but she had her revolver in her hand, and Buzz stood beside her.

All of them clustered on the narrow deck, waiting. Her palms were damp and she was afraid the gun might slide from her grasp. Buzz kept licking his lips, as if his mouth were dry. Pyke started humming under his breath, until Jana pointed out that he might give away their position. Ollu strained her eyes to see signs of the enemy hidden on the bankside. She wanted the fight to start so it would be over sooner, and she would know the worst.

'To our left in the bushes,' Buzz said at last, his voice reassuringly steady. She peered in that direction but could see nothing. 'Look out! There's a fallen tree trunk in the water, steer right!' He grabbed the tiller and she did not stop him. She could see nothing except dark water, darker land and the blue black of the night sky. The enemy was near though. She trusted Buzz on that.

'Look out!' he yelled. Suddenly there was a terrible rattling sound and her eyes were dazzled by leaping flames. Twenty or more barrels of something stinking and flammable rolled in front to the Ark, their thunder making her heart throb in her chest. The fired barrels bobbed on the river, throwing up a wall of bright, leaping flame that prevented her from moving on. Their enemies must have used some kind of explosive. She hoped they had no grenades to fire the Ark directly, or they would be done for. She would not have the Ark burned unless it was at her own hand.

She cut the engine with trembling fingers. Whatever was in the barrels produced noxious, choking smoke that made her eyes stream. All around her she could hear her companions coughing. Pyke yelled out 'Don't breathe it in!' She covered her mouth and nose with her scarf. Beside her Buzz raised the spear gun to his shoulder.

Ratter shrieked 'Behind you, Pyke!' While the Ark was trapped by the burning barrels, the enemy was surrounding the barge.

Someone in dark clothes was clambering up behind the former slave. The brilliance of the flame made Ollu blind in the darkness. She blinked away the tears caused by the acrid smoke. Yes. Someone was trying to board her barge. She holstered the revolver. She would not waste ammo when a flat oar could do the job. With the ease of long practice, she grabbed the paddle of the kayak and swung it hard, hitting the enemy in the face. He spluttered and cursed but did not fall back. Buzz, watching over her like some private bodyguard, snatched the paddle from her hands and did what she could not. He swung the oar hard and fast, with enough force that the man screamed and landed in the water with a splash.

Ollu looked wildly round to spot the source of the next threat. Jana and two of Pyke's men were covering the portside. She saw the flames reflected off the glass and sharp edged metal of their blades, dancing as the shankers flashed in their quick and ruthless hands. They did not hesitate, even for an instant. She had to look away as Jana's knife found flesh. Everyone around Ollu was now fully engaged. Buzz had strung the spear gun across his back and was having more success with the paddle, repelling a second attempt to board the barge, while Ratter danced around him, firing whenever he could get a shot. She yelled at him to save his ammo, but she didn't think he heard her. By the thousand names of God, why hadn't she armed the barge? She should have done it at once, but the burning barrels had confused her. Her fingers were still punching in the code on the keypad when the man came racing towards her across the trail barge. In all the confusion, she had not registered the frantic squawking of the hens as a warning.

Her attacker was not a big man, but he was powerful, grinning a gap-toothed grin as he came for her. She must have looked like nothing, a child. He wore his weapon slung over his back, an original K4. He did not bother to retrieve it. He was going to kill her with his bare hands. She saw his intent in his eyes as he vaulted athletically from the trail barge to the home barge. Luckily her hands did her thinking for her. She was transfixed, unable to move her body, to back away or to run, but somehow her hand came up of its own accord. She held the gun level and her hand did not wobble or shake. It belonged to another, more composed, Ollu. It was that Ollu who fired, and the sound was the loudest thing she'd ever heard.

The man's face crumpled and he fell back into the trail barge, smashing through the plastic protector, landing hard on the bed of medicinal herbs.

She must have cried out because Buzz turned, leaving the defence of the starboard side to Ratter and his wild shooting. He was shouting, angry, but she couldn't catch his words because of his accent She couldn't move and he had to pull the gun from her unresisting hand. He must have known that she could not fire it again.

Everything looked strange in the flames from the burning barrels. It was as if the barge itself was flickering like a mirage, an illusion. The smoke caught at the back of her throat and she gagged, and then it seemed as if all at once everything had stopped and it was over and she was still alive, but she didn't think her attacker was. He hadn't moved the whole time she'd been looking at him, the whole time she'd been staring at the place where he lay, her own legs rooted to the spot.

'Are you all right?'

Buzz had to ask her twice before she could answer and when

she spoke she sounded frightened and stupid as the little girl he must have thought she was.

'Is he dead?' she asked.

'I think so. I think we killed four of them and the rest have gone back to shore. They have weapons, though and they could shoot from the bank if we don't put out those fires. Can you sink the barrels?'

She shook her head. 'Extinguisher.' she said. He frowned. She could not explain. Instead she leaned over to unhook the fire extinguisher from the boats' side. It was a relic, really, and neither she nor Ma knew if it would work, but it was manufactured just before the Chaos and in those desperate days, according to Ma, things had finally been made to last. She pulled out the kayak's lever and took the oar that Buzz still gripped in his hand.

'Don't let them shoot,' she whispered, barely able to talk through her cracked lips. The smoke had dried up all the moisture in the air. Buzz helped her get into the kayak, arranging herself so the fat barrel of the extinguisher was lodged between her churning stomach and the kayak itself. She manoeuvred the boat with clean, steady strokes, her body working automatically, her mind still frozen by the vision of the dead man falling from her, her bullet lodged in his chest.

They fired at her from the shore, and Buzz keep shouting at her to get down, but she was already as low in the water as she could reasonably be and she could not paddle, duck and navigate all at the same time. She got as close to the flames as she could. The heat burned her face and the smoke filled her eyes and mouth. She could only stay so close for a moment. She balanced the kayak paddle carefully, struggling to get the cumbersome cylinder into the right position. It took her three goes to move the ancient lever, which was stiff and made for bigger hands than hers, but she finally shifted it and – nothing happened.

She shook it, despairing. There was a strange gurgling from deep within the solid casing of the device and then at all once an explosion of white foam, so powerful it was all she could do to direct it at the surging flames. She battled to keep tight hold of it, to keep the force of the gushing liquid from making the cylinder buck out of her hands. There, she had it. A fountain of froth, pink and gold in the light of the flames. It expanded in the air to form a blanket of foam. It fell like an airborne snow drift, smothering the fire in its all-enveloping softness. It was a kind of magic. She watched in fascination as the flames died away under the silent onslaught of froth. She could not quite believe that the fierceness of flame could be undone so gently.

A bullet grazed her ear. That brought her back to her senses sharpish. She laid as low as she could, paddling with her spare hand and the oars resting across the front of the kayak, furiously trying to get round all the barrels before the miraculous substance ran out. She focused only on the job in hand, ignoring the danger. She needed to put the fires out to save the Ark from further damage.

When all the fires were extinguished, the darkness was shocking. The afterburn of the flames still danced in her eyes long after the last flame had been doused. There was a cheer from the Ark and then Buzz shouted down at her.

'Head back to the Ark, Ollu! I'll do the rest!' He sounded buoyant, cheerful, though she did not know what 'rest' he intended to do. She couldn't go back for a good while though. Her eyes were too full of tears. She gave the Great River the empty extinguisher case as an offering, a gift of thanks. She did not have the strength to carry it back and it slipped into the depths almost of its own accord. When it had gone she rested her face on the kayak and let the sobbing take her. She had saved the Ark. She had killed a man. She was still alive.

Chapter Thirty-Six

Buzz

'Look after Ollu.' Buzz muttered to Ratter, once the flames had died down. If he was going to be of any use, it was in these brief hours of the night. The smoke from the burning barrels made it hard to see the starlight, and Buzz reckoned that the enemy would be at his mercy in the dark.

He jumped onto the trail barge with a heavy thud which startled the hens. His weight made the barge rock violently. He narrowly avoided landing on the dead man, spread eagled on his back, staring at the sky. Buzz carefully closed the corpse's eyes. Partly through respect and partly so that he did not have to see their blankness. They reminded him too much of Pa.

Once Buzz had regained his balance, he began to tear at the plastic sheeting that had protected Ollu's crops from the brackish water of the River and the indiscriminate appetite of Lalo. It was thick, heavy duty stuff, and he made little headway.

'Ratter, throw me a knife!' he yelled towards the deck.

'Where are you?' Ratter responded, throwing one of the blood stained shankers in the general direction of Buzz's voice. Buzz only just dodged in time and he counted himself lucky that the glass was not shattered by the impact of its hard landing: Ratter had a surprisingly powerful throw.

The makeshift knife cut through the material easily enough and in a moment Buzz had carved out a large enough section to construct a rough, water proof bag in which to carry the revolver. Using the lethal blade, he was also able to sever the old plasticised cord that Ollu had used to tie up Lalo and fashion a kind of a belt to secure the bag firmly around his middle. He was ready.

Pyke and the others were still shouting encouragement at Ollu, and only Ratter was looking Buzz's way. He did not know how much Ratter could see, but he raised a hand in farewell and then lowered himself into the water, trying to make the minimum of noise.

Buzz dived beneath the surface, into the sudden cold and silence. He kicked strongly with bare feet, heading for the shore. His modified eyes took in every scrap of light. He could see at least two bodies in the water, though he tried not to look. One of them was a woman. Her boot lace had somehow tangled in the chain of the trail barge and trapped her where she'd fallen. She lay just under the surface of the water, facing towards the river bottom. She had long dark hair which moved in the currents with strange grace, like the tendrils of some exotic sea creature. He got away from her as quickly as he could, making it to landside in just one breath.

He pulled his bulk from the water as noiselessly as possible, trying to make his deep gulping breaths quiet too. He untied the revolver from his middle and unwrapped it. It was still dry and it had a couple of shots left – at least he hoped it had. He stayed low, hiding behind the scrubby, stunted bushes that grew near the polluted river. The rank stench of the water filled his nostrils, so that he could smell nothing else. Fortunately, his other senses were still working.

He dropped to his knees, gun in hand, and began to move forward in a kind of three legged crawl. It was neither elegant nor efficient but it did the job well enough. He strained his ears to hear his enemy and was rewarded by the low murmuring of conversation off to his right and other, subtler sounds away to his left.

As far as he could tell there were four of them – all men. One was isolated just ahead of Buzz and some distance from the others. He made an obvious target.

As Buzz crept closer he could see him lying on his belly, gun in hand, watching the river and the barge, which was still engulfed by a pall of grey smoke. Buzz could see Pyke and the others on deck clearly enough; they were in range. He had to hope that the enemy's eyesight was less sharp. Buzz inched forward, breathing only when his target moved. He was almost upon the man when his knee caught the end of a stick which knocked a stone and sent it rattling against another. It was a small noise, nothing of note, ignorable in the bright day, but here in the dark the enemy was attentive, alert for any hint of danger. The man turned to bring up his K4 but Buzz already had his own weapon out and ready.

'Drop your weapon and don't make a sound!' Buzz hissed. Surprised, the man relinquished his weapon. It skittered over the rocky ground and came to rest under a low bush. 'Get up and put your hands where I can see them!'

The man stumbled forward and extended his hands above his head. 'No. Put your hands in front of you.' As he complied, Buzz swiftly bound his hands with Lalo's cord, using one of the many knots Pa had taught him. His captive made no attempt to fight back.

'If you make a sound I will kill you.' Buzz made his voice as menacing as he could. His own heart was thumping so loudly, he was surprised it did not drown out his whispered speech. He picked up the weapon lying on the ground and slung it over his shoulder. That was easier than he'd any right to expect.

'Let's go!' Buzz pulled his prisoner in the direction of the man's companions. The two of them made so much more noise than Buzz had alone, and the prisoner kept losing his footing on the uneven ground. It might have been deliberate, though there was so much scrubby vegetation disguising the rubble, it was easy to be wrong footed by the ruined walls of buildings long decayed. That's all these Isles were, crumbling concrete islands of nothing-very-useful.

Buzz did not think his captive would alert his companions, but he could not be sure. He was calculating moves, making plans almost as if he were connected to the data stream of a comp. It was good to be taking the initiative at last.

'What's your name?' he asked the man. He had to repeat the question twice before he got a reply. His captive seemed to find Buzz's accent hard to follow. 'Dekker,' the prisoner answered at last.

'Are these men here friends of yours?'

'Cousin-brothers,' Dekker answered reluctantly.

'Who is in charge?'

The man shrugged bowed shoulders. 'Hard to say. Could be that the Mainman's hit, could be that he is tracking us now.'

'Trust me, he isn't.' Buzz said tersely and prodded his victim with the K4, to remind him who was boss.

'OK. OK.' Dekker said, conceding at once. 'There's no need to shoot. I think Josh, one of his henches, is still alive and likely to take control.'

'All right. This is what is going to happen. If anyone shoots at me, I'll kill you. Tell your cousin-brothers to drop their weapons and come out of the bushes.' The prisoner looked stricken, but didn't argue. 'Will they let me kill you?' asked Buzz as an afterthought.

'They might, if they think they can kill you,' Dekker said grimly. Buzz didn't think he was bluffing.

'Tell them I've got night vision and that they don't stand a chance.'

Dekker didn't bother challenging that claim. As he felt the barrel of his own gun pressed firmly between his shoulder blades, he started to shout.

'Hey! Josh! I'm a prisoner. Come out with your hands up or this guy'll bin me.' When Buzz nudged him further he added, 'He says not to try anything. He can see in the dark.'

There was a movement in the bushes and Buzz saw three men

coming towards him. None of them had their hands raised, and all still held their weapons ready. Buzz fired just once, in front of their feet, and they stopped.

'Drop your weapons, put your hands up or Dekker gets the next one!' Buzz was doing his best to sound adult and commanding. He walked towards them confidently, collecting each of their weapons in turn. He had no idea how he was going to tie them up while still keeping a gun trained on them. He had not thought so far ahead.

In the end, he corralled them loosely together with one great loop of cord used like a lasso. He had to tie them together tightly, as the rope was not long enough to do anything else. It was not very satisfactory, but it gave him a moment to organise himself. Fortunately, all the K4s had straps, so it was easy enough to carry them all over one shoulder.

He pulled and pushed the men until that they were held together right at the water's edge, within sight of the Ark, had anyone been looking. Four awkward, tightly packed men, bound together. Buzz performed a quick reconnaissance, just to check there were no more hidden enemies, no more weapons for Ollu. He found one other abandoned rifle on the bank-side, which he assumed belonged to one of the dead men in the water. He felt enormous relief. With luck they might have six or seven K4s now. It was possible that would be enough for Ollu? Maybe they could turn back and head upstream. Perhaps they would survive after all? He hardly dared hope.

Somehow Ollu was only just paddling back to the Ark. He could see her, face rigid with the effort of holding herself together, arms moving in piston-like rhythm, powering her way across the water. How could this whole operation have taken so little time? He called to her across the water, his voice loud in the silence She changed direction neatly and came towards him, her precise strokes cutting through the water, barely making a ripple.

It did not take long to explain what he had done. She stared at him, open mouthed.

He showed her the prisoners. 'What are we going to do with them?' She sounded weary. There was no room on the Ark and she did not want to leave enemies alive who might still harm her or Davey. He could almost see her working through her options in her mind.

'There's something else,' he said, letting the weapons fall to the ground with a dramatic flourish. His grand gesture was only slightly marred by the fact that she could not see them as they fell.

'What?' she said, bemused.

'They all had K4s. They traded slaves for weapons. We've got five K4s!'

It took her a moment to take this in. He watched as the relief hit her. He could see it in the sudden relaxation of her shoulders. She went to touch the K4s on the ground, stumbled and almost fell. He would have grabbed her, but her balance was good and she righted herself at once. 'This might be enough!' she murmured, overwhelmed. 'Ratter got one from one of the corpses. That's six. I won't need to go further down river. I don't have to go to Grennish. I can go back to the Roberts." She found his arm in the darkness and patted it. 'I don't know what to say, Buzz. The Mainman must have sold many more slaves to have bought so many weapons. Pyke and the rest are just a small group. I still want to know why they ambushed us, but this changes everything.' She grinned in the darkness,' I can't believe it. I'll bring the Ark closer so we can bring the K4s aboard without risking getting them wet.'

She sounded stunned, overwhelmed. It was almost as if she'd never had any hope of fulfilling her mission. 'Thank you, Buzz,' she said with such feeling that something peculiar happened to his insides. He never expected to have anyone look at him that way. As if somehow he had saved them.

CHAPTER
THIRTY-SEVEN

BUZZ

OLLU'S LOOK WARMED him from the inside out, which was lucky because it took some time for her to get back on board, stow the kayak, restart the engine and steer the Ark towards the bank, avoiding the all-but-invisible barrels and the submerged tree trunk that still clogged the river. He was still wet from his swim in the Great River, and he could not stop shivering.

He winced as the underside of the barge scraped against the river bottom. He could hear Ollu shouting at Pyke on deck.

'Piss and Pus, but you have to disembark here. I have the Ark to purify. I'll not have blood on its decks. Anyway, I thought you'd want to see Buzz's prisoners.'

Pyke's response was indistinct, but somehow Ollu's will prevailed. In moments Pyke and his crew were climbing off the barge.

'Where are they?' Pyke asked. Buzz could not trust himself to speak as his teeth had started to chatter, so he just jerked his thumb in the direction of the captured men.

'You did well to capture Minster men alone,' Pyke said as he passed him. 'I could use someone like you...'

'So can Ollu!' Jana laughed, a soft, unexpected noise. 'That girl will rule the Isles by the time she's grown. No woman has ever told Pyke what to do before.'

The second Jana had gone, Ratter was by Buzz's side, Lalo clutched awkwardly in his arms. 'Quick, stick the salvage in this bag. Ollu doesn't want Pyke to know about the weapons.' Ratter put Lalo down and opened a large leather holdall. Buzz did as he was asked at once. It made sense: *he* didn't want Pyke to know about the weapons.

'You OK? You're shaking.' Ratter peered at him with concern.

'Cold' was all he could say, before Ratter dragged him to the barge.

Buzz was shocked by the strength of his response to the Ark. Whatever had been wrong was getting worse. His awareness of it made his head hurt.

Ollu took the guns for him with a murmur of thanks. She disappeared below with the haul and emerged a short time later with a couple of blankets and some hot Brit-tea.

'You need to get dry, or you'll get sick,' she said. 'Can you keep an eye out for Pyke at the same time? It's not light enough for me to see him and I'm worried about what he could do if he persuades the other men to join him.'

'You really don't trust him, do you?'

She shook her head. 'The Ark is too valuable. We can't build boats this well anymore. It's his for the taking. He sees us as kids – well, maybe not you, but Ratter and me. And even with you we're outnumbered if not outgunned.' She wasn't wrong, and he didn't try to reassure her. He didn't trust Pyke either. She disappeared to the cabin a second time.

'Who is the dead guy on the trail barge?' Buzz asked, when she had gone. He didn't want to mention the corpse in front of Ollu.

'I couldn't see properly.' Ratter admitted, 'though I could guess.' He took one of the Ark's lanterns from its hook outside the cabin and lifted it high over his head so that he could examine the trail barge in its artificial glow. Lalo had eaten everything that could have been digested – all Ollu's carefully cultivated herbs, even the remains of her tether, but she had left the corpse well alone.

'That's him; the Mainman. Ollu, the angel of my vision, killed him! I dreamed it right.' He sounded very matter of fact, not at all triumphant as Buzz might have expected. 'So I am a prophet of truth.' In fact, he sounded sad.

'What does it all mean?' Buzz asked.

'I'm not sure,' Ratter answered thoughtfully. 'I think Pyke's in charge now. The Mainman sold him to Davey because he was the biggest threat to his power. You captured all the Mainman's chief lackeys and henches, all the ones that Pyke and his gang didn't kill.' He lowered the lantern and set it back on the deck. 'I think all the dead were part of the Mainman's inner circle too. He probably only brought his most trusted men to take a Barger. He traded with Davey and this ambush would make him an oath breaker. He wouldn't want that to get around.'

Ratter raised the lantern to look at the corpse again, peering at him with a kind of horrified fascination. 'I can't believe he's dead. When I was little my sisters would scare me by saying the Minster's Mainman would come to get me and cut out my throat with a poor man's shanker.' He shivered. 'He was only a man after all, killed by a girl less than half his age and half his size. Makes you think.'

'Maybe we should leave them to it, get the barge underway and head back to the Roberts' place.' He could not imagine what would happen after that. Ollu would have to leave them somewhere, he supposed. He was so busy thinking about that, he failed to notice Ratter's anger.

'We've got to go into the Minster to save my sister!' Ratter said fervently, stamping his foot against the deck in his passion. 'That's my mission! I thought you were going to help me?'

Buzz had forgotten about Ratter's sister. His promise to help the boy seemed so long ago. Besides, if she were unwillingly married to a man like Pyke, or like the dead Mainman, it would need a full-on military coup to save her. He did not think the two of them were up to that, and Ollu's interest in travelling further into Bad Water ended the moment she had acquired the trade stuff that she needed. Buzz did not say anything, and he was stunned when Ratter pulled a shanker from his pocket.

'You *will* help me,' he said, desperation in his voice. Buzz readied himself to grab the weapon from Ratter's hand. It should have been easy, but instead of attacking Buzz as he had expected, Ratter turned the lethal edge of the knife on himself. 'I have pledged myself to save her, I would rather die than fail.'

'OK!' Buzz said quickly, too taken aback to do more. 'Don't worry, we'll do it. Put the knife away, Ratter. We'll sort it out.' He had thought he'd worked Ratter out – child prophet and ally. He had not thought him likely to pull this kind of stunt. Ratter was quivering, shaking with the intensity of emotion. He no longer seemed like a child at all.

'We'll talk to Ollu and if she won't take us there, we'll walk. Don't worry, Ratter, I'm on your side,' Buzz said as calmly and reassuringly as possible. He had no idea what side that was.

CHAPTER
THIRTY-EIGHT

OLLU

OLLU HID THE cache of weapons in the wall safe in the cabin. She wondered if Davey's baby had made an appearance yet. There would be a price to be paid for the taking of the slaves, and most likely it would be Flo who would take it, though whether she would take it from Davey or the Ark, Ollu could not say. She locked away that thought along with the weapons.

She wondered briefly about taking the aye-eye off emergency measures. Pyke was off the Ark. She was free.

Her hand was almost on the panel release, but she was afraid Buzz or Ratter might come looking for her. Perhaps it was safer to leave things as they were, at least until she was out of Bad Water. She was overwhelmed with exhaustion, but she dared not give into it.

She washed her face, retied her scarf and brushed down her Captain's coat as best she could. It was very grubby and spattered with blood. She saw again the dead man falling, his face lit by the wild, flickering light of the flames. She would not think of that.

She had done what she had to do, that was all.

Back on deck she sensed at once there was some tension between Buzz and Ratter.

'What are you going to do about Pyke's lot?' Buzz asked her with slightly more intensity than the question merited. She shook her head. She could hear Pyke's voice giving orders, shouting his demands. They were still close to the bank and sound carried a long way in the silence of the night. He was making quite a lot of noise.

'I helped Pyke, Pyke helped me. I think we could call it quits.' Ratter's eyes were wide with a kind of fever. She wondered if he were ill. He'd been in Bad Water. Oh, God and The Great River, what if he had the water fever?

'I thought you were going to take him back to the Minster so that he would not take it out on Davey?'

'I don't know. We've got rid of the man who got rid of him. He seemed pretty happy to me.'

'But you said you'd go back to the Minster,' Ratter insisted.

'It's dangerous, Ratter. The Ark could be ambushed again. I have got what I need and now I have to save my Ma.'

'What about my sister?' He was more agitated than she'd ever seen him. His small face contorted with a kind of fury.

'I never agreed to help your sister, Ratter. You can get out landside and head to the Minster off your own bat. I'm not going to stop you.'

He nodded angrily. 'So the blood stuff was only about the Ark. I told you! We are a braid, us three, we are meant to be together. You have to help me or I will die – I've seen it. And I tell you something, I'd rather die right now than live through what is to come if you're not with me.'

Ollu glanced at Buzz. What was Ratter talking about? Buzz looked worried.

'Ratter, I have to get back to save Ma. That is what I came to do.' She swallowed hard, knowing that she would regret saying the words that had to be said. 'I can't come with you, but maybe Buzz can?' She looked at him appealingly, hoping that he would agree. Buzz picked up her thought where she'd left off. He did not seem surprised.

'I would rather stay with the Ark, Ollu, but I get that you can't have me on board. I'm not going back to the Roberts' compound either. I'm not keen to be a slave again.' He paused. 'I'll go with Ratter. I've already promised.' He sounded bleak, and although he'd said and done exactly what she'd wanted him too, she felt somehow emptied, hollowed out at the thought of his going. It would be hard doing everything all by herself again.

She made herself nod, brusquely. 'That's settled then.'

'Are you just going to go then? Are you just going to leave Pyke and the rest?' Ratter still sounded angry and she did not understand why. Her mouth was open ready to respond, when she heard Pyke's own voice from the bank.

'Of course she's not. We had a deal and Bargers are honourable, remember?'

There was a quick burst of mocking laughter from landside. Pyke had one of the big guns trained on her, which meant that there were at least six of those guns, not five. The part of her mind which did not seem to register her danger made a mental note of that. Buzz was standing next to her. He stretched out his arm and turned off the light, plunging the Ark into sudden darkness.

Pyke swore volubly. 'Quick get the weapons!' Buzz hissed at her, pushing her bodily towards the cabin door. She sensed rather than saw him retrieve the spear gun. Oh God, she thought as she flung herself below and started punching in the code for the hidden safe. She was trembling all over, nervous energy born of fear coursed through her body so powerfully that she couldn't think properly. She got the combination wrong the first time she tried it, her fingers stumbling on the keypad. She took a deep breath to steady herself. It was not over after all.

She got out three of the big guns. She had to do it by touch alone as she did not want to risk putting on the light. It was no longer fully dark outside, but it was black as pitch in the cabin. She breathed in loud panting gasps, which would not do at all. She was still Captain. She must not let Pyke and Buzz know she was afraid. If she had got the Ark moving sooner, she could have been well on her way by now. She had been foolish to stand around arguing with Ratter, when she should have been heading back upstream.

She secured the safe, slung the weapons over her shoulder and all but ran to the deck. Buzz's hand on her elbow steadied her. She gave Ratter and Buzz a weapon each and then got her own into position. She felt clumsy and out of control.

'I can see you, Pyke.' Buzz shouted into the blackness. 'Put up your hands or I'll shoot.'

'It's too late, Buzz.' Ollu heard them scramble aboard, dark figures pooling filthy water on the Ark's deck. Ollu should have safetied-up the boat, put out the hedgehog spikes to prevent a boarding. She'd messed up. Someone turned on the light. Buzz lowered his K4 when he saw that they were surrounded, though he did not relinquish it. Pyke climbed aboard unchallenged. His eyes were bright, triumphant.

'I'm sorry, Ollu. You've done all you could, but I'm in charge now and we need the Ark.'

'You wouldn't be in charge of anything but for me. Who do you think killed your Mainman?'

'I know, and you saved us from the polluting slaver too. We've a lot to thank you for and I'm proper sorry that I have to do this. You're a good kid – the best. I know you deserve better, but all's not fair in war, Ollu, and we are at war with the C-Crew Code. We'll do the best that we can. We'll drop you anywhere you like, but the Ark is ours now. Call it the spoils of war.'

It was the moment she had dreaded. Her mouth was so dry she could barely find enough saliva to speak, but she managed. 'You get off my barge now or I will blow it up, with you and all your men on it.'

Pyke's smile faltered. 'Don't be silly, Ollu. I'm not going to fall for that.'

'She's not lying,' Buzz said firmly. 'I couldn't work out what was wrong before, but this barge is ready to blow.'

'Sorry. I admire your wits – well tried. We're not going anywhere. The Ark is mine.'

'Don't make her blow it up! There's tekk on board, you stupid man. Can't you feel it?' Buzz sounded desperate and Ollu wondered how he could know what she'd done. He hadn't seen her and she knew no one had access to the aye-eye.

'Thanks for trying, Buzz,' she said in an undertone. 'I'm sorry we couldn't save your sister, Ratter.' She found his skinny arm and squeezed it. 'Try and get landside, Ratter, and then run as fast as you can because there's going to be a very big bang.'

She raised her voice and shouted clearly, before anyone could stop her with a bullet. 'Civilisation! Civilisation! Civilisation!'

'Get off the boat!' Buzz screamed. He acted fast, picking Ratter up bodily, throwing him towards the shore.

The whole barge began to ring with a strange electronic whine, barely within the upper range of Ollu's hearing. The aye-eye's voice responded coolly.

'Hello, Ollu. Following your instructions, the self destruct programme has been activated. This unit will self destruct in ... four minutes and fifty eight seconds. Commencing countdown. Haveaniceday!'

'You heard it! Get off the barge!' Buzz yelled. Ollu couldn't speak. The enormity of what she'd done overwhelmed her.

'Who was that?' Pyke sounded scared.

'The barge has a computer aboard – it is... it doesn't matter what it is. It's going to explode like the biggest bomb you've ever seen. I'd get off it now if I were you.'

The rest of Pyke's men had not waited for his command, but were already scrabbling overboard, their combined weight all heading for the bank side threatened to tip the whole barge over. Pyke seemed stunned.

'How – ?' he began.

'It doesn't matter.' Buzz said, 'Just get out of here!' With one last confused look Pyke followed his crew and jumped for the shore, landing with a splash in the water. Only Buzz and Ollu remained on deck.

'Go!' Ollu said, unable to stop the tears streaming down her face. She was the Captain and had to go down with Ark, but Buzz did not. She would never see Ma or the twins again; they would never know how close she had come to saving them, how desperately she'd tried. She thought of the hard-won weapons in the safe. Ma would never know that she'd met her list, she'd done what she'd promised and in that, at least, she had not let her down.

'Where is it?' Buzz said. He had not leapt for the shore. His large, strong hand was on her arm. The computer countdown continued, but she could not process what it was saying.

'What?' Ollu was finding it hard to think. Why was he still on board?

'Where is the computer?' he said carefully. She did not know why it mattered. Nothing mattered anymore, but she pointed anyway at the cabin. When he flung himself through the door she followed him. It might be better to die there than on deck. The cabin was the heart of it. Lalo was still landside. With luck she might be all right. She was not sure about the hens.

'How do I get in?'

Ollu looked at Buzz blankly.

'Let me see the computer!' he demanded. It did not matter anymore. She did not understand why he should want to see it, but she opened it up anyway. A light she had never seen before was flashing red. Buzz let out a huge sigh when he saw it. 'Two minutes and thirty seconds,' the aye-eye said conversationally.

So long? She had thought that there would only be seconds left.

'It's OK, Ollu,' Buzz said, 'Leave this to me.'

CHAPTER THIRTY-NINE

BUZZ

BUZZ WAS IRRITATED the he hadn't realised it was a self-destruct mechanism. He should have known. The wrongness he had sensed had to be something like that.

Whoever had designed and made the Ark had done a real good job. The whole of the floor was dark-shielded with some material that had been lost over time. The moment Ollu lifted the flooring his brain started to sense data. The computer was badly damaged, barely functional and it was very old – even older than the General back home. Old enough to have been made in the last days before the Holy Purge. Old enough to be exceptionally sophisticated.

He had only ever heard of one working system that ancient. It couldn't be, could it? His hand was trembling with excitement and a kind of reverence when he touched the keypad. First, he had to stop the self-destruct. He sent the all-important, urgent message that needed to be sent through the electrical impulses he generated in his own skin. Then when the connection was made his mind flooded with knowledge, with data and he felt complete.

Of course he recognised it in the first fraction of an instant of contact, as soon as he got the data. He knew this machine!

He was instantly aware of a log of shared conversations from way back, from when he was a little boy and still learning the language of the network. He almost laughed out loud with pleasure and with recognition. This was it. The General's lost contact computer, the one they'd called the 'Queen B', the reason for his long journey across the ocean. Pa had not made a mistake with the coordinates – they'd landed right where they should have. Buzz hadn't failed. His place had been on the Ark with the Queen B all along.

Christ in Gaia, but she was in a poor way. No wonder the General had lost contact. All her functions were way below optimum, riddled with software errors and her hardware was badly damaged. She was no longer webbed into the old networks and was showing no errors so the machine was unaware of her own terminal decline. She did not know she was lost: she was deluded by her own senility. He could deal with all that later. He felt a thrill of pleasure at the thought. But for now, he just had to make it safe.

'Hello, *Queen B*, this is Buzz.' He spoke in a friendly voice, for Ollu's benefit. He'd already sent the override command pulsing through his fingers before he'd opened his mouth, but Ollu needed to hear it in ordinary human time.

'Hello, Buzz!' Beside him Ollu started with surprise that the machine recognised him.

'We're going to stop the self-destruct protocol now.' Buzz said firmly.

'Self-destruct terminated,' the *Queen B* said. 'Powering down. Entering safe mode. Haveaniceday!'

'You can't do that!' Ollu said, shocked. 'There are codes and all kinds of things to make it secure. No one can stop it once the self-destruct sequence has started. Ma said.'

Buzz gently unravelled some of the chaos in the *Queen B's* processing and instructed the machine to arm the Ark, as he had first seen it, what seemed like months ago. He felt the Queen's data intersecting with his mind, ribbons of silk in his thoughts.

He'd missed this. He closed his eyes and forced out the human words for Ollu. 'I've put the spikes out, which should give Pyke a bit of trouble if he tries to get back on board.'

'I don't understand.' Ollu insisted weakly. 'How did you do that?'

He opened his eyes. Ollu looked aghast. He wanted to explain about Pa and the mission and civilisation, but when he saw her face he knew that she didn't want to know. Not now. She was in shock. She had been ready to die with the Ark and now she didn't know what to think.

It took enormous discipline but he forced himself to disentangle his awareness from the Queen B and give Ollu his full attention. She was staring at him with a kind of blind, uncomprehending wonder.

'It doesn't matter, Ollu. We're safe for now. Do you want to hide her again?'

She nodded and hit some lever behind the panelled wall so that the floor once more moved to keep its powerful secret. The design was brilliant. When the floor closed over the Queen, he could hear nothing but that low hum which alerted him to tech. Only someone with his gifts would know there was a comp there at all.

'I don't understand,' Ollu kept repeating. 'You should not have been able to do that. It is only supposed to respond to me and Ma. Even Davey can't get to it anymore.'

'Later, Ollu. I'm not sure we're out of danger yet. I think we need to go back on deck.'

Ollu pulled herself together quickly – he had to give her that. He could almost see her pushing the whole issue from her mind and focusing on the next problem. She was on her feet in a moment and gathering her discarded weapon from the deck. Ratter and Pyke had both taken theirs with them. Luckily, Buzz still had the spear gun with him.

'OK. What can you see?' Ollu said. In command again, as if she had never been anything else.

'I can't see Ratter but everyone else is waiting for the Ark to blow. They are hiding in the trees.' Buzz shook himself mentally. Part of him was back with the Queen, remembering his childhood, the General, Pa. His nerves were all on edge, jangling from contact. He was desperate to return to the comp. In its memory Pa was still alive.

Ollu's concerns were more immediate. He needed to focus on what she was saying:

'I can't leave Ratter or Lalo landside. I'll have to go and find them.'

Of course, everyone had jumped ship when they thought it was going to blow and Ratter was landside with his enemies. Buzz wasn't sure he'd fully understood, but he thought Pyke had tried to have Ratter killed back in his old life. Ratter would need rescuing. He shook his head to rid himself of the lingering touch of the Queen B.

'No. I'll do it. Wait here,' he said.

He had forgotten about the spikes. That is, he remembered extending them as he and the Queen B had shared data, but he had forgotten their practical implications. The spikes extended about a half a metre out from the barge's side. Leaping over them was going to be tricky.

'Stop!' Ollu shouted at him, just as he was readying himself to dive headlong over the vicious metal spikes. 'I forgot you'd safetied-up the Ark. I can't sacrifice you for Lalo and I doubt you'd find Ratter if he doesn't want to be found.'

Buzz nodded, relieved. 'I could do it...' he said, though he was far from sure. He still felt dazed.

'I'll not be the cause of another death,' Ollu said tightly. He had been right then. She was every bit as disturbed by the Mainman's grisly end as he had expected.

Buzz was peering out across the water when he heard high familiar voice. 'Hey, Buzz!' It was Ratter calling. 'I thought the Ark was going to blow up? Why did you lie?'

'It was going to blow up but Buzz stopped it,' Ollu yelled

back. 'Where are you?'

'Here!'

Buzz followed the sound and found Ratter balancing on one of the spikes, with Lalo tucked under his arm.

'That lot will eat her if you leave her here,' he said by way of explanation. 'Can you lift her over the spikes?'

Between the three of them they managed to get both Lalo and Ratter aboard without injury. The younger boy was covered in scratches, cuts and bruises, though he was as cheerful as Buzz had ever seen him.

'What happened to you?' Buzz asked.

'Pyke thought that you might be bluffing about the bomb – explosion thing. He reckoned that if he had me, you might let him back on board, especially if he threatened to kill me.' He grinned, his carnivore's teeth stained by blood.

'I had to fight my way out and I didn't fight very clean. Reckon I saved the boat again because I know you wouldn't have let me die.' His look was a challenge to Ollu.

'You're right. I wouldn't have let you die,' Ollu said firmly and Buzz knew she was thinking about the Mainman's corpse again

'Then you owe me,' Ratter said brightly.

Ollu sighed. 'That makes no sense, Ratter, but I do owe you both. And I will take you wherever you want to go, once Ma and the twins are safe.' She yawned and Buzz had to fight a responding yawn.

'You should maybe get some sleep,' Buzz said wearily.

'I'm not sleeping till I'm out of Bad Water. Ratter, make us some tea and see if there is any rabbit left. It's going to be a long night.'

CHAPTER FORTY

OLLU

OLLU ANCHORED THE barge in the middle of the river. She wanted to give them all some recovery time before they headed back to the Roberts' land. The three of them slumped on deck, sipping weak Brit-tea.

She might even have slept – maybe they all dozed off – because dawn seemed to come very quickly.

The dawn was every bit as beautiful as the sunset and Ollu was overwhelmed to see the whole world remade with the new day. The day she hadn't thought she'd see.

It was a new world, too. She had never been so far downstream into true dreg water. They were much closer to the Minster than she had imagined. Everywhere she looked she could see the vertical farms, the buildings that had once been the heart of the ancient city. They rose from the brown water, green and slime-stained, growth trays emerging from what had once been windows, trailing vines and fruit bearing creepers. They were connected to one another by a complex network of rope and metal walkways in the sky. From this distance the figures on the bridges were little more than moving dots, like ants marching across a leaf. So many ants; so many people. Ratter's whole face shone with joy at the sight.

'Isn't it kronk!' he said.

Whatever that meant. It was disturbing, that's what it was: a strange alien place that made Ollu nervous. She didn't have to go through there any more, did she? She didn't have to risk such dangerous waters to go to Grennish and Davey's weapon's cache? She had what she needed. With all that had happened, it was hard to keep track.

Ollu went down below to check. Buzz had collected six K4s when he went ashore, but Ratter had lost one when he leapt overboard. Would five be enough? Ollu thought about the babes. Nada had said six K4s – could she risk returning with only five? It was probably five more than Nada had expected, but by their agreement five was still not enough. Ollu chewed her sore lip. Pyke had his own weapon, and Ratter's too. Maybe she could negotiate.

An idea was beginning to grow in Ollu's desperate, sleep deprived mind. Thoughtfully, she dragged herself back on deck.

'Ratter, didn't you say that Pyke wanted to end the war with your Boss and the Mainman was against it?'

Ratter nodded, his expression indicating that he was not sure where this was going, but he was probably not going to like it.

Ollu carried on, thinking on her feet. 'Well, the Mainman was kind of his rival – that's why he sold him to Davey. yeah? Now that he is dead, and we have the proof that puts Pyke in a strong position to negotiate with your Boss. Do you think he would trade me his K4s if I took him to the Minster with the Mainman's body?'

'No way is he going to give up K4s. He'll shoot with them first.'

'Not even for proof of the mainman's death?'

'You killed him. If you take his body into the City, you're a target. The Minster Men would finish you off and then Pyke could claim the K4s and the Ark. So yes, he might go for that.'

'Have you had no helpful dreams?' Ollu asked, ruefully.

'I've had no helpful sleep,' Ratter said, flashing a grin.

'I thought you wanted me to go into the Minster?'

Ratter pulled a face. 'I want to rescue Bel, not get all of us killed. I think you should drop me and I'll make my own way there.'

'What happened to the braid?'

'I still believe in the braid, but I've never seen what happens next. You killed the MainMan like I've always dreamed. You've done enough.'

'I'm a K4 short,' Ollu said, her voice shaky. She couldn't hide her disappointment. 'Either I get Pyke's weapon or I have to go to Grennish.'

'You're missing the one I dropped landside?'

'Yes. Did Pyke take that?'

Ratter nodded. 'I'm sorry, Ollu. I didn't think.'

'It's not your fault.' She paused, still thinking aloud. 'Don't you think it would be worth something to Pyke – to come into Bad Water on a craft like the Ark? I mean, it still has Preeker tekk?'

'If the Ark looks good someone will take it from you, Ollu. You've been lucky.'

It wasn't like Ratter to be so negative. Ollu tried again. 'If Pyke was with us, his men would not attack us and neither would the C-Crew Code – at least not if it was known that we had the Mainman's body and had come to negotiate with your Boss. Once we were there, as Pyke's escort, his backing if you like, we might be able to do something for your sister.' Maybe it was just because Ollu was tired that it sounded like a plan to her.

Buzz had appeared silently next to her. 'But even if Pyke came with us,' he said, 'we don't trust Pyke further than my Pa could spit a cherrystone, do we?'

'We don't, but this is in his interest too. If he agrees a deal with Ratter's man, Riki, surely the rest of the Minster men will be happy? War is bad for everyone. Ratter said people are killed all the time, that everyone dies young. If I could help deliver Pyke to the Minister with the Mainman's body, maybe he could give me the last K4 I need, if it helps get him peace?' She could tell by the look both boys were giving her that they thought she'd lost her wits.

'Well, I can fix the Ark, restore the shields – all the tekk that has broken over the years. I could make it lock out anyone but you, Ollu – if I can get the DNA sensors to work. There's no point in anyone stealing tekk they can't use. That might help?'

Ollu smiled at Buzz. At least he was trying to be positive. She turned her attention to the smaller boy. 'Ratter? Would it help Pyke if I showed everyone the Mainman's body? Would it help him to have the Ark as a trading partner? For proper trade, not just slaves?'

Ratter shrugged, but he sounded thoughtful. 'I don't know. I'm a peeper and prophet. I don't know anything about trade. I've no vision of what comes next. I've never seen anything past the death of the Mainman. But, you're the angel of my dreams, and everyone knows the story of the C crew angel. I don't think anyone would hurt my angel.'

Ollu took a deep breath. She had made her decision. 'Buzz, how long will it take you to fix the Ark? I have no tekk parts anymore. I lost them in the storm, the night Ma got sick.'

Buzz considered for a moment. 'I can reroute some of the functions without any parts. I can get the shields up and working with just my talent. An hour? Maybe less.' He looked uncomfortable mentioning his talent and Ollu did not have the time or the energy to bombard him with the many questions she would have liked answered.

'OK. Ratter you stay on deck, keep watch, guard us as best you can. I'm going to find Pyke. I can't risk turning up at the Robert's with anything less than I've promised. I'm too close to give up now.' Ollu wasn't sure if she was trying to persuade herself, or Ratter and Buzz. Both boys looked as though they would like to try to change her mind, but neither said anything.

'I'll get the Ark to retract the spikes until you have got the kayak out,' Buzz said.

'I know Pyke – maybe I could…' Ratter began, but Ollu interrupted him.

'Ratter, I don't know what you did to him to get away from

him earlier, but I'm guessing that he won't be pleased to see you.'

'I did kick him hard,' Ratter agreed, 'Ollu I don't think...

'I'm the Captain. It's my decision,' Ollu said, with more certainty than she felt.

Buzz disappeared into the cabin to deal with the Ark's defences and Ollu got out the kayak. As she thought about trying to explain her plan to Pyke, both her enthusiasm and her confidence melted away. If this went wrong she could lose everything, and Ma might die.

'Nothing venture, nothing gain,' she muttered to herself as she settled herself into the kayak.

She threw her revolver in Ratter's direction. There was value in going to a negotiation unarmed. Besides, she did not want it to fall into Pyke's hands. Ratter took it with a grim expression on his face.

'Be careful!' he said and passed her the paddle for the kayak, a singed and blood-stained reminder of what they'd been through. She was probably making a mistake.

'Pyke!' she called, so that her voice rang shrilly through the early morning mist. Then she set out for landside.

CHAPTER
FORTY-ONE

OLLU

SHE SAW PYKE watching her from the shore.

'I want to talk!' she called out, her voice sounding thin and lost, snatched from her mouth by the breeze.

He nodded and in a short while he joined her on a much patched, clinker-built skiff. He came alone.

'You can't have the Ark,' she began.

'It was a good bluff,' he said, a hint of admiration in his tone. He looked dreadful. Someone, maybe Ratter, had broken his nose. His right eye was almost closed and the skin around it was swollen purple as a ripe plum, and he badly needed a shave.

'It wasn't a bluff. Buzz managed to stop the self-destruct. The Ark has more tricks where that came from. She is most use to you in my hands. We can be useful to one another.' She swallowed down her fear of him, and found that he was listening as she quickly outlined her plan.

'How do you know I'm interested in peace with the C-Crew Code? Ratter?' He sighed at her nod. 'He's well named, that peeper.' But she could tell he had a grudging respect for the boy. 'A K4 is worth more than a lift on a funeral barge, however fancy.'

'There's the chance of trade with the rest of the Isles.'

'We could trade with other Bargers. There are enough around.'

'But I'm no slaver and you owe me for saving you…'

He nodded slowly. 'It's not enough…'

'I'll bring you Angela – if she wants to come.'

'And why should I care about her?' He looked taken aback.

Ollu shrugged, 'I thought she was kin, however distant, and a good commander cares for all of his crew,' she said smoothly, keeping her face bland.

'You don't miss much, do you?' he said. 'All right, I'll take Jana with me as my hench and you have a deal.' They spat on the handshake and Ollu returned to the Ark, dizzy with success.

In a very short space of time, Pyke returned with an unarmed oarsman and Jana and they got the Ark underway. Ollu checked the K4 Pyke handed over to her and stowed it with the others. He wore his own weapon slung across his back.

Jana grinned when she saw Ollu, gave her a mock military salute and a flag. The flag was a sign that they were Minster men and entitled to pass unhindered; a useful thing to have. The Ark had no flag pole so they had to improvise, but next time Ollu came that way she would be certain to have both flag pole and flag.

There was a moment's tension when Ratter had to face Pyke again. Pyke broke the silence first. 'Shouldn't have tried to hostage you.' he said, without meeting the boy's eyes.

'Probably shouldn't have kicked you so hard,' Ratter replied and that seemed to be all that was necessary because both then carried on as if nothing bad had happened between them.

What happened next took Ollu completely by surprise. Ratter, Jana and Pyke clambered onto the trail barge and arranged themselves around the body. Ratter crossed the Mainman's hands over his chest so that the trail barge became a bier, as if for a dead hero. As Ollu started the engines and set course for the very Bad Water of the Minster, Pyke began to sing, a funeral dirge. He had a good voice, strong and melodic, that carried easily across the water. It echoed off the high sides of the old Preeker scrapers and the newer cobbled together fill-ins. After a while,

Jana joined him, adding simple harmony. Somehow Ollu had not expected these denizens of Bad Water to be able to sing, let alone to show such talent for it. She felt ashamed of herself for assuming that they had no culture, no civilization: Ma would not have been impressed.

Buzz had done something to increase the Ark's speed. Ollu did not know what, but she wished he hadn't. Everything was happening too quickly, and she felt out of control. She had never journeyed so far, and the Great River was suddenly busy as the Summer Fair, clogged with a mixture of craft: rafts and resiked barges, mashed-up fishing boats, skiffs, punts, dinghies, coracles, canoes and even small sailing boats unfurling rag-sails in the breeze. There was nothing to match the Ark, but most of the rigs bristled with defensive walls of Preeker wire, with water cannon, cobbled-up ballista and long shafted spears. This part of the Great River was not a peaceful place. She was glad of the Ark's own armaments, of Buzz's solid presence beside her, and the revolver, now safely back in her jacket.

Ollu tried not to show her fear, or to flinch at the scrutiny of the strangers who clustered on the bridges of timber, rope, steel, chain and placky-yarn that linked the rotting towers. Most were vertical farms with stained, decaying walls and cascading greenery. Every space that was not a walk-way or a fly-way was filled with growing things, and ivy and Russian vine even wound its way round the handrails of the swaying bridges, which creaked and groaned under the weight of too many strangers. There was too much for Ollu to take in. The whole place teemed with life of all sorts, crowds of people, herds of goats, caged birds hanging from balconies and traps full of writhing rats strung along the rotting lower floors of buildings. Wind-turbies whirred and wood-smoke rose from cook fires. Somewhere meat was cooking, and the dark River stank like a sewer. The pull of the tide was fierce here and Ollu clutched the tiller so tightly her knuckles were white. She had to forget about everything except steering a clean course through the filth of the river.

The vast audience of Minster-Men stared at her curiously. Being watched by so many unknown people brought her out in a sticky sweat. At least most of their attention was on the trail barge, on the body of the Mainman and on Pyke as he sang his funeral lament. When the people on the bridges heard him, they bowed their heads and grew silent. Pyke looked strangely heroic with his face all battered and his clothing torn, standing over the fallen body of the Mainman. The words of his song, which he seemed to be making up or adapting on the spot, were all about the Mainman's achievements and his untimely death 'fighting for the men of the Minster.' Pyke could have made a decent living in the Isles upriver, as a song peddler.

One by one the river craft pulled aside to let the Ark through. Ollu nodded her acknowledgement and hid her surprise as each craft then followed in her wake, so that they became a kind of river-borne funeral cortege. Someone in one of the boats beat a drum and somewhere else a horn played a soulful accompaniment. There was a chorus to Pyke's lament that was taken up by the people on the bridges and walkways, so that Ollu and the Ark were surrounded by a chorus of harmonising voices. She had never expected such beauty in Bad Water. She had got the impression that life was so cheap here that death would not be marked by ceremony. That too was a mistake.

'Take the flag down now,' Ratter hissed as the passed the carved stone spires of the Old Parley. 'We're in C-Crew waters.' She did as she was told. Their escort of boats did not follow them across the invisible barrier that marked the transition between territories. Instead the small vessels formed a line of boats like a necklace of pearls strung from one bank of the wide river to the next. They waited, watching as the Ark alone carried on into hostile waters. The singing ceased, and its absence made the silence more marked and strangely sinister.

'Send word that Pyke the new Mainman on the Minster wants parley with Riki of the C-Crew Code. At the usual place. No weapons. Good faith.' Pyke bellowed at the watchers on the walkways.

No one here bowed their heads. Everywhere Ollu looked she meet aggressive stares and there were people everywhere: on the walkways, swinging on the flyways, hanging on the nets which hung down the sides of the farms to allow the crops to be tended. Ollu had expected the death of the rival Mainman to be better received here. She was not sure if it were Pyke or the Ark that aroused suspicion. Bargers had captured C-Crew Code men, after all. There was the low hum of whispering and Ollu was sure Pyke's message would get through. Whether it would make any difference she didn't know.

Most of the C-Crew Coders she could see clutched shankers or some other weapon. Buzz put out his hand to cover hers, which was trembling on the tiller. She found his touch more reassuring than she might have expected, and did not pull her hand away. Her mouth was dry. She had a strong feeling that everything was about to go horribly wrong. She should have quit in that all too brief moment when she was still ahead.

There were as many boats on this stretch as the River as in Minster territory and these showed no sign of moving away. They made no attempt to attack either, which was good, but Ollu was not at all sure how long such luck would last.

'Will they go for us?' she asked Ratter in a low voice.

'We should haul a white flag of parley,' Ratter said. For someone on home turf he sounded very uncertain.

'You could have told us that before,' she said sharply. 'There is a bed sheet in the cabin. We can use that.'

Ratter did not need telling a second time. It would take too long to crank up the mast, so he tied the sheet to the shaft of the wind turby.

Ollu fixed her eyes on the river and steered a straight course through the throng of small craft as their grubby flag flapped behind them. She did not look round to see what Pyke and Jana were doing on the trail barge, but it must have been the right thing because no shots were fired.

'Head for the Palls – that big green dome. There's a jetty there at Cheapside. That's the place for a parley.' Ratter said.

Ollu did not have much attention to spare for Ratter. She was concentrating on steering the barge and ignoring the hard stares of the other boatmen. She could see the jetty well enough, a large circular structure ringed with machete men.

'The word will have got out to the Boss by now. This is the place he'll come, There. Can you see? That tall man is Riki, the Boss and...' Ratter swallowed hard. 'The woman beside him, in that shimmering robe, that's my sister.'

A glittering woman was just visible through the throng of black clothed machete men. She was sitting on a carved chair in the very centre of the jetty. She did not look much like a prisoner to Ollu, more like a picture book Queen from ancient Preeker times. All that was missing was her crown.

Ollu brought the Ark up to the only berth on the jetty, so that the trail barge that had become the Mainman's bier lay directly opposite the C-Crew Code Boss. The machete men parted to let a tall, spare black man through. He was wearing Preeker stash mixed with homespun, but it was his eyes that Ollu noticed most. They were a pale blue and hard and bright as sapphires. All his attention was on Pyke.

'Heard the Mainman's dead,' Riki said, bluntly.

Pyke nodded. 'This is his funeral barge.'

Riki took two long strides so that he was within spitting distance of the barge. He leaned over to stare at the body, his face expressionless.

'You want to talk?' Riki's voice was low and soft.

'I'll bring my henches.'

'If you must.'

At once Pyke set to climbing the rusted ladder that led to the pitted concrete of the jetty. His sudden movement set the trail barge rocking and Jana struggling to keep her balance. At his hand signal she climbed after him.

'Buzz, you are to come.'

Buzz looked at Ollu, as if for permission. If he left her, there was no one to defend the Ark but Ratter and herself.

'No one will attack you while you're docked at Cheapside Arena,' Ratter said in answer to her unspoken question. 'We have rules too, you know. Look at this place. Everyone can see what goes on here. It is supposed to keep the Boss honest.'

Ollu looked around. It was true that the nearby dome was crowded with people, that the boats on the river were laden with them. Their numbers frightened her. There might have been as many as a thousand watching, an army of strangers. None of the women covered their hair either and she could see many wore it cropped short or shaved. Such strange boldness shocked her and she swallowed hard. A captain did not let fear show.

'You'd better go then,' she said, brusquely. There was an excitement in Buzz's face she didn't understand.

'And me too. I have to see my sister,' Ratter said and, without waiting for her answer, he sprang after Buzz.

So, that was it then. She had risked Ma, the Ark and Bad Water only to be abandoned at the first chance her friends got. She could not leave. That was clear enough. The Great River was thronged with hostile craft and she was alone. God, Allah and The Great River, what a fool she'd been.

CHAPTER
FORTY-TWO

BUZZ

BUZZ FOLLOWED BEHIND Jana. He didn't like to leave Ollu, but there was tech here; he could smell it.

Pyke waited for them at the top of the ladder. Pa would have been horrified by his bruised and battered condition. He didn't look like any kind of civilised man, let alone a leader. What Pa would have made of his only son's involvement with thugs and neobarbs, Buzz couldn't imagine. Not to mention the fact that the Queen B was housed in an ancient barge, in the hands of a skinny, teenaged girl. But Pyke was a leader, Buzz could see that. And this was the chance he had been waiting for.

Pyke nodded at Buzz, Jana and Ratter, who looked ridiculously small and childlike in these surroundings.

'These are my henches,' he said to Riki's guard, a dark clothed machete man.

'No blood-sticks or binners allowed,' the man said roughly, indicating Buzz's spear gun with a nod of his head.

'OK. Here, Ollu!' Buzz turned and threw the spear gun down towards Ollu. The next second he had a shanker pressed hard against his stomach.

'You want binning?' The machete man's spiced breath was

in his face.

'What? You said I couldn't bring the weapon here. I've got rid of it, haven't I?'

'Shut it, Buzz.' It was Ratter's voice. He squeezed his skinny shoulders between Jana and Buzz and spoke to the machete man directly. 'Forget it, Dav. Buzz is not from round here. He's OK, though. He's with me and Pyke here. We're on a peace mission.' The machete man glanced away from Ratter towards Riki who nodded. Dav sheathed his weapon and Buzz breathed again. Jana grinned at him approvingly and Pyke scowled in Ratter's direction. It was clear to Buzz that Pyke thought he was the one to do the talking.

'Ollu should be here,' Ratter said.

'This is between Gaffers, not little girls.'

Buzz felt Jana bristle beside him.

'Without Ollu, the Mainman would be alive and you would be dead,' Buzz said softly.

'And this is not her business,' Pyke snarled. Pyke, like Pa, thought negotiating with girls beneath his dignity.

Riki watched them with an amused expression on his face. 'If you're done.' He signalled for the machete-men to let them through the cordon of bodies.

Buzz was relieved when the black-clad guards stepped away so that he could see the entire Arena. It was nothing more than open space and weathered concrete the colour of oats, scrubbed clean of the encroaching slime and weeds and in the middle of it the dark shape of a a huge amplifier and an electronic device he hadn't seen before. It wasn't working properly but by the low the thrum of it the potential was there. Buzz itched to fix it, to connect. He was so intent on the device that he barely paid attention to the woman sitting alone, next to the amplifier on a kind of throne, flanked by two more machete men.

Ratter saw her and yelled, 'Bel! It's me!' He pushed past Buzz and ran towards the woman, heedless of Riki and his guards. Dav raised a modified hand gun, aiming it at Ratter, and Buzz launched himself at his knees, bringing him down. Dav and Buzz collapsed together in a heap, knocking over Ratter as they fell in a tangle of flailing limbs. As Buzz landed hard on top of Dav, he heard the woman reply.

'Ray? Is that you?'

Buzz couldn't have let Dav shoot Ratter, but now he was afraid his actions had threatened Pyke's peace. He was aware of the shift in atmosphere, the sharp intake of breath from the machete men who ringed the arena, the levelling of weapons. Pyke stepped forward to haul Buzz to his feet, and at the same moment Riki hauled Dav and Ratter to theirs. Pyke and Riki glanced at each other, and Buzz thought they were both amused that they had acted as one to pull their henches apart. Perhaps they could work together.

'This is Bel's brother!' Riki said to Dav, his tone impatient. 'You know him – he was peeper for us for long enough.' Dav looked shame faced, and Riki turned to Ratter. 'It's good to see you again, Ray! We've turned the Roosts upside down looking for you. She hasn't stopped going on about you.'

'She' was presumably Ratter's sister. She shared Ratter's sharp features but on her they were transmuted into something delicate and lovely. She was dressed extravagantly, in fur and glistening finery, diamonds from another age and antique gold. Her dark eyes stared in Buzz's direction without focusing.

'Ray! Are you still alive! Are you really here!' The joy and surprise in her voice was unmistakable. 'Bring Ray to me,' she commanded, without raising her soft voice. If Buzz had been uncertain before, this confirmed it. She was no prisoner.

Ratter didn't need bringing, he was at her side before she had finished speaking.

'Bel!' Buzz had to blink back tears of his own at the joy in Ratter's voice. It made him think of Pa again.

Ratter's sister put her small, bejewelled hands on Ratter's face and kissed him on the forehead. He did not squirm or run away, but embraced her warmly. She touched the raw wound of his slave brand. Their conversation was too low for even Buzz to hear, but Bel kept stroking Ratter's tangled hair, more like a mother than a sister. At length, he pulled away from her.

'Bel, this is Pyke, from the Minster. He claims he wants to make peace and I need to know if he's telling it straight and...'

Riki interrupted. 'This is important Bel. I need you to listen to what he has to say and make your judgement.' He spoke to Bel with a kind of reverence.

Pyke looked taken aback. Riki helped Bel to her feet and she walked the short distance to where Pyke and Buzz stood together. She took Pyke's hand and closed her eyes.

'Tell me what is in your heart.' She spoke in a low voice. Pyke appeared uncomfortable, nervous even. He answered her in a performer's voice, loud enough to carry all the way to the ring of guards if not beyond.

'I want there to be peace between us. I would like our enmity to die with the death of the Mainman. I want us to rule jointly the combined cities of the Minster and the C CrewCode. I want us to set up a council and to join together our lackeys and our henches to keep the peace between us. I want us to make life better, not worse, for all our people.' There was a kind of a gasp from all the people who heard him. To Buzz, Pyke seemed as ruthless a man as he had ever met. He realised with a start that Pyke reminded him of Pa. It was a surprise then, when Ratter's sister smiled warmly and told Riki that Pyke spoke the truth, before returning to her throne. Buzz wondered if she were a fraud.

Riki moved his face, pock marked and puckered with knife scars, so close to Pyke's that they were eye to eye. His blue eyes were bright and sharp, his voice low. Even so, Buzz heard him.

'Can we count on you against the men of Grennish? They have more tekk than people. Peepers tell me they are building an army and taking the growing-lands up-Temz. We could find ourselves crushed between their base and their outposts.'

'They have giant boats? I saw one of their craft up-Temz, in the small Isles.'

'Yes, and they have been arming machete men and slaves from the up-Temz. Grennish is a hungry place, dreg land, still toxic poor. They'll want our farms and the wealth of the small Isles. We need to crush them now. Are you in?'

Pyke nodded. 'Yes.'

'And you have the Barger vessel?'

Buzz watched Pyke nod again and felt himself go cold. Pyke had done it. He had betrayed Ollu! He shouldn't have been surprised. The man had showed himself unreliable at every turn.

'Then we have a deal,' Riki said tersely. He gave a hand signal, and drums began to thunder.

'Listen!' he shouted when the last reverberation died away. His voice was loud, deep and reverberant, a match for Pyke's. 'There is peace with the Minster. Spread the word!' He raised Pyke's hand into the air, 'This Pyke is my cousin-brother,' he yelled. 'Tell it to the world.'

After that things moved very fast. Buzz thought that he must have sent out runners, unless they had working tech he hadn't yet detected, because within moments sounds of cheering and singing erupted from the rooftops.

Ratter beckoned to him. 'Bel wants to talk,' he said.

'No! Pyke is going to take the Ark. We need to get back to Ollu.'

'Pyke won't do that. Bel would have seen it. You have to speak to her!' Ratter sounded as forceful as he ever had. Buzz glanced around. Riki and Pyke had moved away from all their henches. Pyke had not yet given instructions to take the boat. He sidled away from the others and walked toward Bel and Ratter. Bel dismissed her guards, and the three of them were briefly alone.

Buzz looked into her blind eyes. Bel was no more a fraud than her brother. He knew that the moment she took his hand in her light, cool grip. She read him, made a connection with him, just like he did with the comp. She was as startled by that realisation as he was.

He felt her anxiety for Ratter, for Riki and her sister, for the peace. Beneath her serene façade, she was a seething mass of worry. Buzz couldn't read her thoughts in any clear way, but he sensed the data, the stream of consciousness that ran through her almost as if she were a machine. He did not know exactly what she got from him, but they both gasped as one, dropped hands and pulled away as if burned by the contact. He felt giddy, and it was a moment before he could get his breath.

'Gaia on the cross!' he muttered, as Bel let out a startled, 'Oh!'

'Bel!' Riki was watching her so closely, he noted every small change in her body language.

'I am fine, Riki,' she said smoothly, but Buzz knew she felt as he did. Astonished, afraid, excited, confused. Buzz had thought his abilities unique.

'It is a gift to see through your eyes, Buzz,' she whispered.' I have been blind for so long I had forgotten. And you see, even in the dark?'

'Yes.'

Buzz's hand hovered close to hers. He was eager for more of that strange connection, eager and terrifed too. Bel's hand twitched and he guessed she felt the same way.

'You are not from here?' she said, carefully, aware, as he was, of Ratter gazing at them both anxiously.

'No. I came with Pa from over the sea.'

'You are like me?

'Yes. No. My father designed me, like they used to design plants and animals to thrive in the Chaos. I was bred to connect with machines – especially ancient ones. The way you connect with people.'

Ratter's sister nodded. She was still breathing fast, as he was.

'We are not ignorant here, whatever we might look like to you. We tried that here in the Isles, just before the Chaos. There were riots. 'Geneticmodification' is a curse word here. Say that you are blessed, as I am. As Ratter is.' She touched Buzz's hand lightly, but he pulled away, overwhelmed.

'I have to go. Pyke is going to take the Ark.'

'Pyke does want peace. I didn't lie.'

'I saw.' Buzz hadn't seen, exactly. There wasn't a word for the understanding that had flowed from her to him, and from him to her, but he knew that Pyke, not unlike Pa, wanted to make the world a better place, and like Pa, he would justify anything in service of that goal.

'You'll find Ally and help Pyke make peace after Ollu is done with her mission?' Buzz knew all that she wanted.

'Yes.'

Ratter looked from one to the other, scowling. 'What just happened? What did I miss?'

Bel's grin made her look exactly like her brother, and much less like Riki's Queen and truth-finder. She wasn't that much older than Buzz.

'Buzz gets me, Ray. You should go with him and Ollu, then fetch Ally home. Pyke and Riki have forgotten who Ollu is.'

'The Angel of my dreams?'

'Yes. That gives her power. Riki and Pyke get the jitters around things they can't grasp. Go! I'll distract them for a bit. Oh, and take this.' She removed a silk scarf of deep red from her shoulders and gave it to Buzz, carefully avoiding touching his hand with hers.

'C-Crew Code colour.' Ratter explained as he casually picked up a bulging placky bag from behind Bel's throne and tucked it under his arm.

'Guards!' Bel called, and as the tall machete men leaped to answer her call, Buzz and Ratter slipped away from her throne, as quietly and discreetly as possible.

Buzz could here Bel suggesting in her quiet, gentle way that the agreement be sealed and honoured with a feast. Riki turned to her as if she were the sun, and everyone was so busy keeping them happy that no one paid any attention to two of Pyke's henches.

Buzz felt as though he'd been hit by lightning. Ratter's sister and he could read each other's minds.

CHAPTER FORTY-THREE

OLLU

OLLU COULD SEE nothing but the broad backs of Riki's machete men. The river and the craft on it were loud too, so that though she heard the cheers and music but she did not know what it meant. For all she knew Riki might have decided to please the crowd by killing Pyke and her friends. No one came for her though, so she hoped they were still safe.

She was not good at waiting and she could not leave her post at the tiller of the Ark so she gnawed the inside of her mouth and tried to ignore the curious stares of the other boatmen on the river. She unhitched the trail barge which bore the dead man. To her mind the crops on it were polluted now, and Barger rules on the disposal of bodies were clear.

She regretted abandoning the trail barge, but it was the smallest of her losses and she didn't dwell on it. Her audience watched her as she went about that business and she felt horribly self-conscious, as if she were suddenly a wandering-theatre-man in a play and she'd forgotten her lines. Some of them were so close, she could smell the tarry stuff with which they had caulked the boats, the spice of their food, the sweetness of the smokingweed that grew in abundance in Bad Water. No one threatened her or even called to her, but the hostile curiosity of the boatmen was enough.

She safetied-up the boat and, as the spikes sprang from the hull, the other craft pulled back shouting warnings to each other. They kept their distance after that. At some point, the onshore party spread to include the boats and the river rang with music. Every boat had some instrument and sometimes sang with one another, sometimes against. It was noisy and in other circumstances it would have been joyous and exciting but, as she did not know what was being celebrated, she was even more unnerved. Pox and Piss, what if they had killed Buzz and Ratter – for fun?

She tried to calm herself with the thought that she had got the trade goods, against the odds, without having to go to Grennish. It didn't help as much as it should have done. She was still a long way from home, and for all she knew Ma and the twins could be dead. She was beginning to regret the final trade that had brought her here.

'Let us through.' Buzz's voice, loud and commanding, Ollu was alert at once.

'Not without the code word from the Boss.' A tall machete man with a red bandana blocked the way. Buzz muttered something she didn't hear and suddenly the wall of machete men opened and the boys emerged.

Something had happened to Buzz. He looked shocked and pale. Ratter's grubby cheeks were tear stained.

'What happened?' she asked, panic mounting.

'Bel's fine. There's peace but...' Buzz gave her a meaningful look, and she guessed that she and the Ark were not safe.

Ratter began to descend the ladder that would bring him down into the boat, but the Machete man stopped him.

'Hey, what are doing? I've no orders you are leaving.'

'I gave you the code, didn't I?' Buzz said, firmly.

'Riki said this boat did not move unless he was on it.'

'Orders change,' Buzz replied, and Ollu was surprised that

the man held his ground. Her friend had a wild look in his eyes, one that scared her.

Ratter's piping voice added, 'This is the Angel of C-Crew Code. She killed the Minster Mainman for Riki.'

The machete man hesitated and Ollu remembered the story Ratter had told her about how C-Crew Code grew bolder in their war with the Minster because they had an angel on their side. Ratter gestured with his one free hand for her to remove her headscarf, and, as she did so, the sun emerged briefly from behind a cloud. She understood. She shook her head free of her scarf and let her wild, pale curls escape its confines. Ollu moved deliberately, putting the sun behind her so the light might frame her head and illuminate her halo of hair. She saw the effect in the Machete-man's eyes. He made a gesture of respect, and let the boys onto the Ark's deck.

'Make way for the Angel!' The machete-man bellowed at the throng of boats and Ratter added his high, carrying voice, 'Make way for the Angel of the Ark!'

'Here, we need to show this.' Buzz pulled out the bright scarf and secured it to the turby so it fluttered in the breeze.

Ollu had too many questions to know where to begin, so she merely nodded and concentrated on steering the Ark through the crowded river as Buzz and Ratter shouted ahead.

'Move! The Angel of the Ark coming through!'

Whether it was because of the spikes on the boat, the presence of the flag, the increasingly inebriated state of the boatmen or the sight of Ollu's bright hair she didn't know, but the river craft parted like a stream round a rock to let her through. It was almost miraculous. And this time she was grateful for whatever Buzz had done to speed the engine.

She sent Ratter below to care for the animals, relying solely on Buzz's sturdy presence as guard. She didn't speak again until they had crossed the invisible barrier into Minster water, until they changed their red flag for a blue one and had taken even that down. Only when they were out of Bad Water and alone on the broad river did she ask the questions that were worrying her.

'Tell me what happened. Why was the Ark in danger?'

Buzz still looked strange and distracted, but he answered her clearly enough. 'Pyke and Riki have made a peace agreement, but they are both going after the Grennish men. And they were going to take the Ark.' He glanced down at her but she kept her face impassive. So much for Pyke's word.

Buzz continued. 'Riki knew about the attack on Cassie's place and the big Grennish ship they used. He's afraid if Grennish controls the farmland of the Up-Temz and the arsenal, then the C Crew and the Minster could be caught in a pincer grip between the two. He wants to take out the arsenal and stop them taking over the farms.'

'He told you this, did he?' It didn't seem likely that the C-Crew Code leader would take Buzz into his confidence.

'Not exactly,' Buzz hesitated and Ollu knew that he had more to say. 'Something strange happened…' He looked abashed, awkward.

'Go on. I am used to strange now.' It was a lie, of course. She was as unsettled by the strangeness of Buzz's ability with the aye-eye as she was by Ratter's premonitions.

'Well, you know I can communicate directly with the Queen B, I mean the Ark?'

'I didn't know that was what you did, no.'

'Oh, well I can. It's hard to explain but Pa kind of fixed me to be that way. Anyway, Bel, Ratter's sister, does the same thing with people – she reads their hearts – sees if they are lying.'

Ollu frowned. She did not like to hear of more powers she didn't understand and didn't have.

'The thing is – when we touched, I sort of saw what she did. We read each other. She knew what was in Riki's mind and in Pyke's and now so do I.' Ollu did not have the time or the energy to think through the implications of this, so she focused on what that might mean for the Ark.

'Did she know Pyke would try to take the Ark?'

'No. That happened after they'd spoken. It wasn't something he was planning until Riki asked. I think that Pyke and Riki do want peace with each other. It's just that they might want to go to war with everyone else. Not just Grennish. Riki thinks the Grennish men have the right idea – taking over the farms.'

Ollu shrugged. 'That's nothing new. Cassie came from Bad Water, but she's of the Isles now. Good land is hard to find. Of course, people fight over it.' She paused and made an effort not to chew at her cheek. She could taste blood. 'What do you think they'll do when they know I've run?'

'I think they'll follow, with boats to fight the Grennish.'

'And to fight me?' It was the obvious question.

Buzz shook his head. 'Pyke respects you and likes the idea of a proper trade that isn't in slaves. Riki doesn't know you, but you saved Ratter so Bel likes you and Riki will do anything for Bel.'

Did Buzz sound jealous? Ollu wasn't sure. He carried on. 'I think they want you on their side. They'll understand you escaping with what's yours, but Pyke won't like losing face in front of Riki. He might try to take you on.'

'We spat on a handshake.'

'You're just a girl, so he doesn't think it counts. He's had no dealings with matriarch boats. He's like Pa; you have to be a man to count.'

Ollu tried to keep her temper. She could grow into a worthy captain of the Ark, but she would never be a man. If Pyke wanted trade with her, he would have to get over it and learn that she would hold him to his word.

'What is Bel like?' She asked, changing the subject abruptly. Buzz hadn't been the same since he'd met her. Was he in love?

There was a pause. 'I don't know… Strange, like me. Lonely. She misses her sisters.'

'Is she pretty?'

'She looks like Ratter, but not.'

Ollu nodded. 'So, I'm the only with no special gift?'

'But you are the Angel of the Ark,' said Ratter, emerging from the cabin with a plate piled high with potato cakes, goats cheese, boiled eggs and honey that he must have stolen from the Arena. 'And the Angel of the Ark is the Boss of everything. I've dreamed it. I'm still the prophet and we're still a braid. So, we better eat up and get ready for what is coming.'

Chapter
Forty-Four

Ollu

WHAT WAS COMING was a fight, if Ratter's dream was right. He was sure the Grennish men had already attacked the Roberts' and Ollu believed him, because that was what she was afraid of too. Ratter was much more cheerful about the prospect than she was. He hadn't seen them dead and he found that reassuring. Ollu did not. She might already be too late to save her family. The Grennish machete men would not spare a sick woman or babies still at the breast, and the band of fear tightened around her chest until she could hardly breathe.

Ratter could not help with tactics at all. He thought Pyke and Riki would be with them in the coming battle, but his dream was a warning and not much more. It was too much for Ollu. She was exhausted; the food had revived her a little, but her eyes were gritty with staring out at the Great River and she was so tired of being afraid. It was wearing her down, making her slow and stupid. She needed a plan but nothing came into her head, nothing but horrible pictures of her Ma and the twins, dead at Grennish hands.

'What are you thinking?' Buzz asked.

'Oh, you know, what happens next. If Ma is still alive. If Pyke will take the Ark. If we will have to fight the Grennish. What Ma will say about what I've done.'

He gave her a thoughtful look. 'I'll leave if you don't want a man on the Ark. Ratter, you will come with me, won't you?'

Ratter looked morose. 'I have to rescue Ally. I promised Bel.'

Ollu shrugged and rubbed her tired eyes with both hands. 'It is too late to pretend you were never with me. I wouldn't have made it this far without you. Anyway, I have done worse things than have you two on board. I had Pyke here– a fully grown man. I stole another Barger's salvage, revealed the secrets of the Ark to strangers. I let a dead man's body defile the trail barge. Oh, and I killed a man.' She ticked them off on her fingers. Pox and Piss, but she wasn't the same girl who'd set out from the Robert's land just four days before.

'But you got the trade stuff, the weapons to pay for your Ma and the twins and Riki let you go free. And you didn't blow up the Ark.'

'Only because you rescued it.' Buzz was trying to cheer her up, she knew, but there was nothing he could do to make her feel better. What if Ma were dead?

'You need to rest, Ollu. I can steer for a while. I'll call you if I see any other boats.' She didn't have the strength to argue. If they kept going they could be at the Robert's by nightfall. There was no sign of any pursuit, yet, but none of the boats she had seen in Bad Water could match the Ark for speed. It would be a while before anyone could catch them. Maybe this would be her only chance to rest.

When Buzz came to wake her, she was momentarily confused by the presence of a man on the Ark. Then she was fully awake.

'No boats yet,' he said softly, 'but I think we are almost at Cassie's.' She didn't groan out loud, but slipped from her bunk, grabbed a blanket, pushed Lalo away and followed Buzz's bulky form out onto the deck.

She wrapped herself in her blanket against the night's chill. 'I'll take the tiller,' she said. Buzz was right. They were very close to Cassie's. Maybe it was time to arm themselves.

'There was tech on that big boat. It isn't working now, though I sensed something there. The Queen B recognised the ship. It's ex-military and unless it's been stripped, it has bombs.'

Ollu tried to take that new information in. She'd worked out that Buzz called the aye-eye, 'Queen B.' It hurt her to realise he knew more about her family secret than she did, but she pushed her jealousy to one side. All that mattered was surviving and saving Ma and the twins. She'd got past the big boat three times now. She could not expect to be so lucky again.

'Ratter, did you dream anything that could help us?'

He shook his head. 'Only that there's been an attack on the Roberts.' But aren't there boats now, coming up behind us?'

Ollu could see a smudge of something against the sky.

Buzz confirmed it. Three vessels. By his description they were old-timer clinkers, powered by turbies and oars. They bore no flags, but they weren't Barger craft so she guessed they would be Bad Water craft, under orders from Pyke or Riki. She felt the tiniest prickle of a fear that might also have been hope. 'Arm yourselves and safety-up the boat, Buzz. We don't know whose side they are on.'

Now, when she strained, she could hear the splash of oars in the water. She heard no engines so maybe they were trying for stealth. 'I'll launch the kayak and parley.'

'Let me,' Ratter said. 'If it's Riki, he'll listen to me for Bel's sake. If it's Pyke, well he knows us all by now.'

'You can't swim,' Buzz said, 'and you're terrified of water.'

'I've watched Ollu in the kayak. I can do that. I won't need to swim if I don't fall in, and I won't fall in.' In the dim deck light, his face was set and determined.

'I'll drop anchor and wait for you.' Ollu said. They all of them had to take risks and Ratter's suggestion was not a bad one. He would be less use than Buzz on deck if it came to a fight, and he was too valuable as a prophet for Pyke or Riki to do him harm.

Buzz disappeared below deck and she knew, with an instinct she couldn't explain, that he was 'talking' with the aye-eye. She got out the kayak for Ratter and tried to calm down. Whatever happened, she was not giving up the Ark, or her Ma, without a fight.

'Tell them we think the Grennish are on the move. Offer an alliance against them, but the Ark is a free Barger-craft and belongs to no one but me. Got that?'

Ratter nodded and flashed her a grin. 'Well, you know how they feel about Bargers, so maybe I'll just say 'the Ark' is yours. Do I offer to arm them?'

'Not yet. We need to know what is going on first.'

As she helped Ratter into the kayak and showed him what to do, Buzz emerged from the cabin, a K4 slung over his shoulder, a gun at his hip, Ollu's gutting knife in his belt and the spear gun in his hand. He looked terrifying.

'The Queen B's heat sensors and radar aren't working,' he said, 'but one of the cameras still has a close-up scoper and I've rerouted the data. All's quiet on Cassie's farm as far as I can tell. I think we can risk going past.'

Ollu hadn't known about the camera. She thought it had broken long before she was born. She didn't understand the other things he'd said either, but there was no point in showing her ignorance.

'Right,' she said. 'We give Ratter an hour and then we go. Have you made any progress on the weapons?' She only asked to make it sound like she was still in charge. Ma had said the Ark hadn't had any fire power since Great Grandma's day.

'I need to get the Ark into some kind of dry dock. The gun ports are jammed.'

'Are you saying there are guns on the Ark that still work?' She couldn't keep the incredulity from her voice.

'Well, no. They don't work because they are jammed, but if they weren't jammed, the devices are intact and should work.'

'Where are they?'

Buzz sketched a diagram in the air and Ollu thought she understood what he meant. She'd spent so many days swimming around and under the Ark in good water and fine weather that she knew the Ark's hull better than she knew her own face.

They had an hour before they could move: she was already kicking off her shoes, and top layer of clothes. 'Bring the light to the boat's edge, I'm going down.'

'No, Ollu. Let me do it. I can see and I know where the ports are. I stand a better chance of forcing them open too.'

'You don't know the Ark like I do. I don't want you forcing things. Old tekk has to be handled right. I've been resyking and fabricking my whole life. I know what to do.' Even to her own ears she sounded petulant, like a spoiled child trying to prove her worth.

'But you are the captain, Ollu! You have to stay on deck and be ready to leave or fight. I'm not in charge. I'm not making those decisions. Let me fix the boat. I promise I'll be careful.'

He was right, of course, but she had never felt more useless.

'You have three minutes; the water is cold.'

'I'll take a knife and see if I can lever the ports open.' Buzz abandoned his weapons and most of his clothes on deck, stuck the knife between his teeth and dived neatly overboard to disappear into the blackness of deep water.

He was gone for much longer than three minutes. It felt like three months. Ollu watched downriver for Ratter and peered into the black water looking for Buzz. The boys were taking risks that should have been hers. She hated them for doing it and herself for letting them. Ma would have thought her feeble. 'There's no harm in delegation,' she used to say when she had Ollu scrubbing the decks and cleaning the waterweed from the turbies. Pus and boils what would she do if Ma were dead? What if Buzz were dead? He'd been down there far too long!

Just as she was beginning to panic, Buzz broke the surface with the smallest of splashes. A pale face in the darkness that might have been grinning. She tossed him the blanket as he hauled himself on board.

'I thought you'd drowned,' she said as he shook himself like a dog, sending freezing drops of water in her direction.

'No, I'm still here and so is Ratter.' He pointed out into the darkness, where he could presumably see the kayak in the pitch blackness of the night river. 'The gun ports will open now. I've closed them so we don't take on water. I've done what I can. I don't know if we can rely on them.'

'Thank you,' she said, though if she had fixed them herself she knew that they would have worked.

CHAPTER
FORTY-FIVE

BUZZ

BUZZ WRAPPED THE blanket round him and tried to stop shivering so obviously. He'd almost run out of air down below, but he was determined to fix the boat. He had to prove he was made of the right stuff.

Ollu's face was pinched and anxious and he wished he could make things all right for her. Still shivering, he helped haul Ratter aboard.

'There are three boats. Pyke and Riki and about twenty machete men. Pyke said Buzz was holding his knife from the wrong end – he'd misunderstood. Pyke was never going to take the Ark. You and he were in partnership. He wants you to know, you still are.'

Buzz could see that Ollu didn't believe that was true for a minute.

'They'll back you if trouble comes. They want you to back them too.'

'They know I'm trading?'

Ratter nodded, 'I said our first job was to save your ma and the kids. And I had to get Ally.'

'What did they say to that?' Buzz asked, through chattering teeth.

'Family first. It's our way too, like the Bargers.' Buzz thought he looked embarrassed when he remembered that Ollu's family were slavers.

'I suppose it will be useful to have more men, if Ratter's dream is true.'

'I think it's true,' Ratter said. 'It feels true – like when I saw the flames and the ambush.' He sounded so certain, but Buzz knew, through his contact with Bel, that Ratter was never sure which of his dreams to trust. Bel's insights made Buzz look at everyone differently. He only wished that Bel had read Ollu. But she remained an engima. Sometimes Buzz thought she hated him.

'Right,' Ollu said, 'then we keep moving. Buzz, get warm and dry in the cabin and make us some Brit tea. Ratter, you take the weapons and keep a look out.'

It was on the tip of Buzz's tongue to argue. He was the only one who could see in the dark and Ratter would be useless in defence of the Ark. Then he realised Ollu was right. If he didn't get warm, he was going to be sick. He would be more use to Ollu later, when it came to a fight.

When he finally returned on deck, after a battle with the hens for control of the small hob, Ratter and Ollu were deep in conversation. They looked up as he neared them.

'The big boat has moved.' Ollu said bluntly. 'Ratter got it right. We reckon it's been part of an attack on the Roberts' place.' Buzz handed out the tea and nodded.

'What do you want to do?'

'We'll carry on to the Roberts' then cut the engines and lights and observe from the opposite bank. It would be good if you could have a look around and report back.'

Buzz recalled his humiliating time as a Roberts' slave, the dogs, the terrifying tunnelling. He could think of nothing he wanted to do less.

'Can Pyke or Riki read?' Ollu asked Ratter, unexpectedly.

'No. I don't know anyone who can.'

'Well, that's poxing helpful. You'll have to go back over there and tell them our plan then. I could have sent a note on a line otherwise – like we do with the Bargers, when we are too far away to shout.' Ollu's voice was sharp and Buzz guessed that she was afraid too. After all that they'd done to secure the trade, the deal would be off if the Roberts' were at war, or if they no longer held the farm.

It was a long half hour before Ratter crossed to Pyke's boat with carefully memorised instructions to follow Ollu's signals. He returned with a small broiled chicken and a jug of goats' milk.

'They are on the voddie, and weren't interested in the milk,' Ratter explained. 'Don't worry, they'll be all right to fight. C-Crew Code men always take a drop before a clash – apart from Riki, anyway.'

There was no reason to delay further so they set off past Cassie's place, keeping as close to the opposite bank as they could without risking damage to the hull. Ollu did not cut the engine till they were almost at the Robert's. It ran much more quietly, since Buzz' repairs.

Buzz spotted the great ship first. It was at anchor, close to the waterside entrance of the Robert's place.

Ollu signalled once with her lamp to the following craft, then turned off the lights, plunging them all into darkness. There was no visible light in the Robert's fortress. All was dark and silent.

'What has happened?' Ollu whispered. 'There are no guards. The place must have been overrun.'

'No. There's no fires.' Buzz whispered back. 'After they took Cassie's place there were bone-fires. I could smell them. You wait here. I'll go and see what I can.'

'Watch out for the dogs,' Ratter said, sounding shaky at the memory. 'Do you want me to come? I know the layout.'

'I'll be fine. Get ready to defend the Ark.'

'Before you go, show me how to arm the guns,' Ollu said, then signalled that there was to be no more talking. She was probably right about that too. Sound carried strangely on the river, which made the silence of the Roberts' farm even more sinister. Buzz strained to catch the barking of dogs, the cries of the wounded, the sounds of people cooking. Anything that might suggest that people still lived in the homestead.

Downstairs in the cabin, Ollu closed the porthole cover and risked a small light. She opened the panel which hid the *Queen B* with practised ease.

'Show me,' she said, folding her arms across her chest.

Buzz placed his finger on the *Queen B*'s keypad. He felt a surge of pleasure as he connected with the old computer. Already she was beginning to repair herself, now that he'd helped her recognise her damage. These ancient machines had been designed to last a thousand years or more, and the *Queen B* was the first and perhaps the most robust of them.

This time the comp recognised Ollu's presence. 'Welcome, Buzz, General's friend, and Ollu, daughter of the Ark. How may I…'

'We need to arm the gunports and for you to fire on command from the steering tiller.' Buzz said, for Ollu's benefit. He had already given complete instructions in the first moment of contact. 'Ollu will say, '*Queen B*, fire on my command, then at 'fire' you will fire.'

'Understood. There is sufficient power for ten rounds of fire only.'

Ollu's surprise was clear to seee. 'That many?'

'Good luck in your venture, Buzz and Ollu,' the *Queen B* said, in a voice that already sounded more human and alive. Ollu was too overwhelmed to speak, but secured the boards back over the Queen as efficiently as before.

'The aye-eye can hear me all over the Ark?' she said when she was done.

'Yes. As she was designed to do. She's taken a battering over the years – not through any fault of yours or your families…' he added quickly as Ollu looked angry.

'Right.' Ollu said, 'Ma will be amazed. If she's still…'

He cut her short. 'I should go.'

'Take the kayak. Don't take any risks and report back within one hour.'

'Two. It will take me two hours at least to find anything. If I'm not back, then assume I'm dead or captured.'

'Don't get dead or captured. That's a captain's order,' she said, gruffly and did not bother to ask how he would time the hour. Maybe she assumed he had a clock in his head, which was more or less the truth.

He followed Ollu back on deck, where Ratter was waiting.

'Any prophecies?' Buzz asked, hopefully. It would be useful to have any advance warnings of danger. Ratter shook his head.

'Stay away from them dogs though. If they get you, you won't last long.'

Buzz slipped into the waiting kayak and waited for Ollu to push him off.

'Don't die,' she said.

He didn't reply. There was no point and he was already focusing on what lay ahead.

He lacked Ollu's skill in the water; her effortless strokes were almost silent, but he had to battle not to splash noisily as he powered towards the opposite bank, the giant ship and, he hoped, his own abandoned rucksack, which by chance he'd left right by the huge ship's current mooring.

He managed to get out of the kayak without falling in the water, then pulled the lightweight craft out after him and hid it under the tree. By some miracle or gift of Gaia, the rucksack was still there. He pressed it to his face. It still smelled of home. He felt dizzy with the sudden sense of what he'd lost. Then he took out his knife and the automatic from the bag and pulled himself together. The tech on the boat called to him, like off key fragments of an old song, just below the range of normal hearing. There were no visible guards.

It would help Ollu to know what threat the big ship posed. He climbed the ladder that led to the deck with one hand, keeping the other free to hold his automatic. He saw the first body on the deck, what Pa would call a neobarb, a tall white man dressed in homespun. He'd been shot and was lying in a pool of dark blood. There was no point in checking for a pulse.

Buzz's feet were noisy on the metal of the deck. Stealth was not his gift. There were other signs of gunfire, ricochet marks on the walls and, just inside the painted metal door that led below, a second body, also male. Buzz looked away from the messy impact of a bullet made of scrap metal and kept going, down into the eerie silence below deck. He stood still, waited for the echo of his boots to die down, and listened harder. No, it wasn't silent. There was someone alive down there. He could hear them. He clutched his automatic tightly and kept going.

He found two other bodies on his way; bodies still warm and not long dead. His sharp ears picked up the sound of breathing and another sound. Could it be a baby's cry? It was a high, hungry sound, like the bleating of a lamb, silenced immediately.

He found them in the largest cabin. A woman clutching a baby to her breast and a man asleep on the floor beside them.

'Who's there?' The woman whispered and the man was instantly awake, pointing his K4 in the general direction of Buzz's chest. The man was injured, Buzz could see that now, and weak from blood loss.

'Get away from us or I'll shoot.' Something about the way he spoke reminded Buzz of Ollu.

It was pitch black down there, so Buzz knew he was unlikely to be seen. He held his breath so as not to give away his position and stepped through the door as quietly as he could. It was not quietly enough. The man shot at the spot Buzz had left moments before, the burst of fire deafening in the confined space of the metal hold. Buzz's ears rang. The baby started to wail.

'Drop your gun. I can see you and I have a clean shot,' Buzz said calmly. The man swung his weapon in Buzz's direction, but the woman cried out. 'No, Davey, you might hit the baby!'

So this was the slaver. Ollu's brother.

'Drop your weapon,' Buzz repeated and this time Davey let

the gun fall. 'Kick it away,' he added. 'I won't hurt you. I'm a friend of Ollu's. I want to know the situation on the farm.'

'Well, I'm no friend of Ollu's since she stole my trade,' Davey said sullenly. 'Why should I help you?'

'She's trying to save your Ma, and the twins. Are they still alive?'

Davey shrugged. 'We came downstream yesterday, in our barge. The Grennish men were attacking the Robert's defences. We waited and when the odds looked good I tried to take the boat.'

'On your own?'

'Stell left the babe on 'The Good Hope'. Between us we took down a few. It's what we always wanted, a ship to take us far away from pissing dreg waters, and dirty business. We wanted a new start.' He lay back against the bulkhead, exhausted from such a long speech. He was still bleeding.

'Where is your mother?' Buzz asked.

Davey shook his head. 'Don't know. The Grennish broke down the shard-wall and headed up to the house. There was gunfire most of today, but it stopped when it got dark.'

'How bad is your wound?'

Davey touched his wife's arm briefly, with his good hand. 'Bad enough. Shrap wounds don't heal well.'

Buzz wasn't sure if he believed Davey or not. There was a lot of blood in the cabin, but he didn't know if all of it was Davey's own. Either way he didn't trust Ollu's brother not to fire on him again. However, he was no immediate threat to Ollu. Buzz should check for bombs, disable the boat, so it couldn't be retaken by Ollu's enemies, and move on.

'Tie something tightly around the wound to stop the bleeding. I'll tell Ollu you are here,' Buzz said and left them. He could offer no other help.

This boat was not as sophisticated as the Ark, and it was the work of moments to find the control panel that shut down the engines. The comp that had once run it had been so damaged and partially disabled that if there were any bombs left on board they could never be launched by such broken tech. Buzz did not have time to fix it, though it was hard to pull himself away. There was not much time before dawn, and he still needed to know what was going on at the Robert's farm.

Reluctantly, he left the ship behind. The Grennish had punched a hole through the wall – enough for two people to walk through it side by side. He shuddered when he saw it and remember how he was nearly stuck beneath it only a few days before. He wondered about repeating Ratter's trick of covering himself in cow dung, but decided against it. If armed men had attacked the farm, they would have shot the dogs first.

The ground was churned under foot and he followed the muddy tracks the invaders had made through the cow fields. He forced himself to check inside the slave barracks; the stench of it seemed to seep through the closed door and almost overwhelmed him when he kicked it open, weapon at the ready and heart thudding against his chest. But there was no one there, dead or alive.

He could see the bulk of the main house with its gun tower and outbuildings, a looming mass against the skyline. As Buzz peered at the old concrete structure he thought he saw the faintest flicker of firelight in one of the windows. Of course, the invaders had taken the main building and were holed up inside it. That's why he had seen no fires. Perhaps the Robert's clan and their slaves and prisoners were already dead? He wasn't keen to take that news to Ollu.

He moved closer to the building. He was expecting guards, but they were so well camouflaged, that he almost missed them. One was virtually asleep just outside the main door of the homestead, two more were marching up and down the long wall of the main building. Three guards was not many. Did that suggest that the Grennish had little to fear, or that they had few spare men?

He kept his distance from the guards as he skirted the outside perimeter of the building, looking for another way in. It was a big complex, and not all of it was in good repair. He moved to the poorest part of the building, with the boarded windows and crumbling walls. There could be other guards there, but he saw no one. There was a door too, painted to resemble the stained concrete of the building. If he could get inside, this could be his chance to prove to Ollu, once and for all, that he was a useful man to have around. He took several cautious steps closer and pulled at the door handle.

He did not expect the gun pressed hard against the back of his skull, or the low threatening voice.

'Grennish scum. You'll not get past me.'

Chapter
Forty-Six

Ollu

Ollu peered into the darkness until her eyes burned. Buzz had been gone for more than two hours and dawn was breaking. Without the darkness to hide them, the Ark was vulnerable, and she wished she knew what to do.

'What do you think?' she asked Ratter.

'If the Roberts' were still in charge, Buzz would have spoken to them. Wouldn't someone have come to get the weapons by now?'

'That boat says the Roberts' have been attacked,' Ollu said. 'Pox and Piss, I wish I could see beyond the wall. You don't think Buzz is...' She couldn't even say the word.

'I don't know. I've dreamed none of this. I've not seen him dead, Ollu, but I haven't seen him alive either. Maybe my gift is gone.'

Ollu patted the skinny boy's shoulder. The loss of his gift was the least of her worries right now, but she couldn't help responding to his distress.

'I think Pyke and his men should land shoreside,' she said

Ratter pulled a face. 'He won't risk his men without a plan.'

'The plan is to save Buzz and Ma!'

'He'll need more than that.'

Her mouth tasted of blood. Ratter was right.

'I'm going to see what is happening on the big boat. If we can stop that being a threat then we can focus on a land fight. If I can climb the mast, I'll have a better view.'

'You don't know who's on it.'

'I don't think anyone is on it. There's been no movement, no sound.'

'Nobody would leave a ship like that undefended.'

'You're right – so where are the men?' Ratter's frightened face told her he'd had the same thought. 'If it's plague – it's probably too late for us anyway.'

Ratter shook his head. 'I've never seen plague. Not in any of my visions.'

'Good,' she said. 'You have the tiller. I won't be long. Take the K4 and if you think I'm in danger, fire.' Ratter nodded gravely and Ollu went below for the waterproof resiked bag and filled it with a change of clothes, her boots and gun.

'Queen B?' It felt strange to speak into the empty room, without first revealing the aye-eye.

'Ollu.'

'I am going ashore. Ratter has the tiller. Can you sense him?'

'I can.'

'He is my friend. Will you accept his order to fire?'

'Of course, Ollu.'

The old aye-eye sounded different since Buzz had touched it. It's voice was alert, almost alive and that made Ollu afraid. Everything that made the Ark more valuable put it at risk. Pyke would likely try to take it from her, given any opportunity. 'You are not to speak out loud to anyone but me. I am going to investigate the big boat,' she said. 'Once I am off the deck, safety-up the Ark.'

'Understood. Be careful, Ollu of the Ark.'

She nodded, fighting back tears. She had a horrible feeling that everyone she loved might be dead. Ma, the twins, Buzz.

Once on deck she told Ratter the words that would turn

the Ark into a weapon, strapped the bag around her chest and, without giving herself any time to change her mind, muttered, 'With you permission, River,' and dived into the freezing water.

The chill shocked her whole body, but she had to swim across the Great River before the cold shut her down. She swam as fast as she ever had, and hauled her shaking, shivering limbs onto the same jetty that had seen Ma brought to the Roberts' homestead just days ago. Ma! What if Ollu was too late to save Ma and the twins? What if the Robert's hadn't kept their word, or if the invaders had killed everyone in the homestead?

There was no use in worrying about that. She had to act to save them, not worry that they could not be saved.

She dried herself quickly and put on warm clothes with clumsy trembling fingers. Her teeth chattered, but she ignored all her physical discomfort. She had to see what was going on.

Her numb legs barely obeyed her but she forced them to support her up the ladder to the deck of the boat. She had her weapon tucked into the waistband of her shorts and she thought she was alert to danger.

'Stop right there.' It was a woman's voice, a voice she recognised. Perhaps she was not as alert for danger as she thought. Ollu looked up, to see her brother's wife pointing a K4 at her head.

'Stell?'

'Ollu? What are you doing?'

'Trying to rescue Ma. What are you doing?'

Stell lowered her weapon, though she still eyed Ollu warily.

'This boat is mine, but Davey's dead and your friend has scuppered the workings.'

Ollu sprang up the last few rungs of the ladder, her cold and exhaustion forgotten.

'What? Davey's dead?'

Ollu could hear Stella's baby wailing from the bowels of the boat.

'He took a hit and I couldn't stop the blood.' Stell sat down heavily on the deck. 'What am I going to do, Ollu? It's your fault. Ma disowned us when you stole our trade. We had to run away with the baby and the Good Hope. Ma will come for us. No question. This boat was our way out.' She didn't sound angry, just worn out. The baby's cries were more and more insistent.

'Maybe feed the baby?' Ollu said, still unable to make sense of Stell's words. Her big brother, her childhood hero, was dead. She watched as Stell opened the door that led below deck and returned a moment later with a newborn at her breast.

'Where is he? Where is Davey?'

'He's below. But he's definitely dead, Ollu. He's not breathing and I can't hear his heart. I'm on my own.'

Ollu could spare the slaver's daughter no sympathy. She forced herself to do what she had come to the boat to do.

'Right. I'll say my goodbyes later. I have to climb the mast. Shout if you see anyone coming.'

'I won't shout, I'll shoot,' Stell said, lifting the weapon she held in her right hand, the hand not supporting her suckling child.

Ollu forced herself to concentrate on climbing. She wouldn't think about Davey. The thought of telling Ma that her only son was dead was too much for Ollu to deal with. Grief would have to wait.

Her teeth were chattering and her legs shaking now, as much with shock as cold, and she had to focus on the task ahead or she would lose her footing and Ma would have no daughter either.

It was hard to see much, even though she was so high up. She could not make out anything of the churned and muddy landscape on the other side of the shard-wall. It was only then that she realised she was crying.

CHAPTER
FORTY-SEVEN

BUZZ

BUZZ HELD HIMSELF very still as the man pushed him through the open door and into a dimly lit corridor. He was shorter than Buzz, and struggling with an injury; something was wrong with the way he was moving. Buzz knew he was stronger than the man who'd ambushed him, but he dared not ignore the gun at his head.

'I'm not one of the Grennish,' Buzz said, finding his voice. At least he'd learned that the Grennish did not control all of the Robert's homestead. Not that such information would help if he got himself killed. He made himself speak slowly and carefully. He did not know who he was dealing with and he knew his accent and manner of speech was strange to the people of these watery Isles. 'I was a slave here. I was held in the shed in the cow field. I've come to help.'

'What? A slave wanting to fight for his old master! The Roberts' never treated their slaves so well. Show me your brand.'

Buzz shook his head. 'I escaped before I was branded. I'm here to find out what happened to a sick Barger woman who was brought here with her twins.' The pressure on Buzz's neck eased a little.

'Toxic, poxing, pus and plague! 'Buzz was aware of a change

in the pressure of the gun on his neck as his attacker awkwardly shifted his weight. 'What's the Barger woman to you?'

'I am a friend of Ollu, her daughter.'

'I know who Ollu is. Who are you, and where is she?'

'I'm called Buzz, but I can't tell you where she is until I know who you are.'

The man laughed. 'I have a gun against your head, boy. Aghh!' At that moment Buzz turned fast, using the unanticipated motion against his captor. He'd worked out the man's weakness. Using his own explosive strength, he knocked the man's good leg out from under him. The man's gun skittered across the plasticised floor covering as he fell heavily. 'Putrid pus! What did you do that for?'

Buzz's own automatic was already in his hand. 'Who are you and where is Ollu's Ma?'

'I'm here.' a female voice answered. 'Who wants to know? What is going on, Joe?' The woman's tone was mild, but as she stepped out of a doorway and into the corridor, it was clear she meant business. Buzz saw a heavily built woman propel herself towards him, carrying an old sawn-off, modified to take shrap weapons.

'Drop the gun and put your hands in the air or I'll shoot him!' Buzz cried. 'If you really are Ollu's Ma, prove it.'

The woman leant against the wall for balance, breathing heavily. She was pale and her face was beaded with sweat in spite of the cold.

'Where is she? Is she safe?' She peered into Buzz's face anxiously, as if she could read his answers there.

'How do I know you are her Ma?'

'Don't be so toxic stupid, boy. Of course I'm her mother. She has a scar on her knee, and a problem with knowing her own limits. Is she all right?'

Buzz nodded and the woman relaxed fractionally.

'Where is she and what have you done with her?'

There was something of Ollu about this older woman, though she was about three times Ollu's size, fair skinned, and clearly unwell. She too had wild, curly hair escaping from a dark headscarf and eyes that flashed with impatience.

'She's on the Ark. We saw the big boat had moved and we guessed the Grennish might have tried to take over this farm too. She sent me to see what was going on.'

'And exactly how do you know my daughter?'

Buzz opened his mouth and shut it again. He couldn't tell this woman he had been on board the Ark, polluting a matriarch boat. Ollu would never forgive him. 'I helped her...'

'And where are you from?' the man on the floor said, pulling himself to a seating position then hauling himself upright. It was an impressive feat of strength for a one-legged man. 'That accent is not from here.'

'That doesn't matter,' Buzz said. 'Are the twins safe?'

The woman nodded. 'And the Missis Roberts too, though Nada didn't make it and the Mister took an arrow to his eye.'

'Ollu has fixed some of the tech on the Ark. We have fire power if it would help.'

The woman's eyes narrowed. 'That was clever of her.' She looked sceptical but didn't ask him to explain. 'We are holding this section of the Robert's homestead. The slaves that survived the first battle are with us and we have reinforcements from Cassie's farm. The Grennish have better weapons, but we have more fighters.'

'Ollu has six K4s and a couple of hand guns.'

'How by all the polluting devils of chaos, did she get those?'

'It's a long story. Do you want me to bring them?'

'Is she alone?'

'We have three support boats with twenty machete men from Bad Water with her, standing by,' Ollu's Ma's eyes widened. Buzz felt he had to be honest in the face of this forceful woman. 'You can only trust them so far. They might try to take over the farm themselves.'

'You are truly her friend?'

Buzz nodded.

'Then I want you with her.' She turned away from him. 'Ally!' She called out and a slender girl emerged from one of the rooms. She was young, and armed with a thick stick, studded with glass shards.

'My girl got her trade! In spite of everything! I knew she would! Take five of the best of Cassie's lot and head riverwards to bring back weapons. Stay out of sight and don't engage unless you have to. I mean it. I can't afford to lose you or the weapons...'

'Did you say Ally? Are you Ratter's sister?' Buzz interrupted, stunned by another coincidence.

'Yeah. What do you know of Ratter?' Ally said, ignoring Buzz's gun and raising her bodge of a club threateningly.

'He's my friend. Bel sent him to find you.'

'Bel? She's alive?' Ally raised the club still higher and took a menacing step forward, which was ridiculous because Buzz had the gun and all the odds in his favour. 'If you are fooling with me, I'll decorate these walls with your brains.'

'Bel is alive and bossing around Riki, the head of the C-Crew Code!'

'That can't be right.'

'Come with me and you can talk to Ratter, I mean, Ray, yourself.'

Perhaps the use of Ratter's real name convinced her, because she lowered her club.

'Did he make it onto the boat with the girl? With Ollu?' She asked. Buzz glanced anxiously at Ollu's mother and shrugged.

'If my daughter is safe and you helped her, I don't need to know how. I love the Ark but I love Ollu more,' Ollu's Ma said. 'Promise me you'll keep her out of any battle to come. Keep her safe.'

Buzz was already working out how to do that.

'If Ollu moves the Ark upriver, this side of the big boat, you could maybe drive the Grennish out of the homestead towards the water and they would be caught between you and the Ark.'

'They have their huge boat, who knows what in the way of weaponry and they will have guards, protecting it.'

'There are no working weapons on the boat and all the guards are all dead,' Buzz said quickly, careful not to mention Davey. He was dying on that boat and Buzz didn't want to be the one to break that news to his mother.

'You are sure?'

'Yes.'

'Good, then that is a plan. We will attack by the time the sun has risen above the tree.'

'What's that? Two hours?' Ollu's mother looked taken aback, and Buzz realised he hadn't heard anyone but Ollu talk in terms of hours and minutes. Her eyes were full of questions, but she kept focused on the issue at hand.

'About that, yes. It will take time to get everyone ready and at least an hour for Ally to get to the river and back if she has to crawl most of the way in the mud.'

'I'm a fast crawler,' Ally said with a Ratter-like grin.

'We'll be ready whenever you come,' Buzz said. 'Ollu will be glad you are safe.'

'What she did – taking on that trade, was the bravest thing I ever heard. Tell her for me, will you? Just in case things don't work out.'

'I'm sure you will tell her yourself,' Buzz said politely, though if he were honest both she and one legged Joe looked too old and sick for battling.

'Go, then,' she said, 'And let's hope for victory! Tell Ollu...' her voice died away. 'You are right,' she said, standing taller. 'I will tell her myself.'

CHAPTER
FORTY-EIGHT

OLLU

OLLU WIPED HER tears with the back of her hand and squinted out across the Robert's homestead. Her eyes were tired, but worry sharpened her up. She didn't want to see bodies littering the fields. She didn't want to see signs of a battle, but she looked for them anyway.

If she hadn't been concentrating so hard, she probably wouldn't have noticed the small troop of figures at the very edge of her vision, keeping to the cover of trees and outbuildings, heading her way. It was too far away to tell if it were Buzz, but either way, she needed to be on the Ark, to take control.

She hurried down from the mast, steadied by duty and by hope. Maybe Buzz wasn't dead. Maybe the homestead wasn't overrun. Maybe things might still turn out to be all right.

Stell was still nursing the baby in her arms. The cool, dawn light revealed her bloodstained clothing and her desperate state. Stell was nursing her brother's child.

'Do you want to come to the Ark? I can protect you there,' Ollu said, softly. Stell's grey gaze was cooler than the Great River.

'I want nothing from you. If you hadn't stolen our trade, we would not have run from Ma and come here. Davey died because of you.' Stell's voice was flat.

'This boat is still a target. The Grennish will want to take it back. The men from Bad Water will want it too.'

'It's mine and no one else is going to take it.'

'What about the baby? You can't keep him safe on your own.'

'Better to die with his mother than live with his aunt who betrayed him.'

Ollu bit back her angry response. Now was not the moment to remind Stell that she and Davey had betrayed Bargers everywhere by trading in slaves.

'The offer stands, if you change your mind. When this is over, I will be back to honour Davey.'

Stell did not answer, but swapped her baby onto her other breast and scowled. Ollu retreated to the ladder, stripped down to her underwear and swam back the way she'd come, to Ratter and the Ark.

He was waiting for her with a towel and a blanket.

'Queen B, disarm the Ark,' she called out so that the aye-eye withdrew the protective spikes and Ratter could help her out of the water.

'My talent's not gone! I saw us all on that boat on the ocean and I saw Ally writing down the agreement between C-Crew Code and the Minister–Ally writing! It's going to be all right!'

'My brother is dead, Ratter. There are people heading our way too, from the homestead. We need to be ready.'

'I'm sorry, Ollu. I was just worried that...'

She cut him short. 'I know, Ratter but let's just get through the next few hours. You may have dreamed of Ally but we haven't saved her yet.' That had the desired effect. Ollu changed into her last set of clean dry clothes, wrung out her hair and readied herself for whatever was to come.

By the time she was back on deck, the figures she had seen skirting the Robert's homestead were emerging through the shard wall. One of them was Buzz. He was still alive. Ratter gave a whoop of joy as a slim black woman followed close behind him.

'Ally, it's my Ally!' he said leaping around the deck like the child he was. Buzz still had the kayak so it was a matter of minutes before he was with them on the boat and making his report.

'Are you sure it was Ma?' Ollu was struggling not to lose all her hard-won self-restraint.

'I think so. She is much bigger than you with fair skin and curly hair. She is terrifying. Does that sound like your Ma?'

She nodded, overwhelmed with relief. Ma was still alive! 'And the babes?'

'I didn't see them, but she said they were safe. She is very proud of you, Ollu.'

'She won't be when she knows what I have done,' Ollu said, suddenly sick with shame. Buzz didn't bother to answer her.

'I said we'd take the Ark past the big boat and they will drive the Grennish towards us,' he said instead. 'We should get Pyke as back up. I'll kayak past him and give the message.'

'Do you think the Ark's gun might blast a hole in the wall?'

Buzz shrugged. 'The gunports are below the water. It would be tricky to redirect them landside. I didn't check the missiles themselves but it's worth a try.'

'Then Pyke's men should be prepared to fight landside?'

'I'll put it to him. I promised to arm Ally and the others,' Buzz pointed back to the small group of fighters, waiting by the big boat.'

'I went on the boat,' Ollu said. She could tell by the way Buzz tensed that he knew what she was going to say.

'There wasn't anything I could do, Ollu. He was losing too much blood. Pa might have saved him, but I couldn't.'

She nodded. 'I know. I'm not blaming you, but Stell blames me.' She was struggling to keep herself under control.

'Davey made his own choices, Ollu. None of them were your fault. I'll get the K4s.'

After that everything happened very quickly. Buzz took the message to Pyke and delivered the hard-won weapons to Ratter's sister, who waved cheerfully at her brother from the jetty. It was as well that Ratter couldn't swim or he would have abandoned the Ark to greet her.

Ollu steered the Ark a few hundred metres up river, past the Roberts' moored fleet of patched up skiffs, canoes and rafts and instructed the Queen B to get ready to fire. She wanted the Ark to reveal her newly discovered power before Pyke and Riki could catch up with her.

'What is the target?' The Queen B's voice sounded curious and strangely human. It was pitched so only Ollu could hear it.

'The shard-wall landside.'

'This will take a moment. Programming missiles. Ready to fire.'

'Fire!'

Ollu felt the missile leave the Ark with a jolt. She thought she saw something egg-shaped shoot through the water and out, flying through the air. There was a huge resonant thud as the missile punched through the shard wall, leaving Ollu coughing as a dust cloud enveloped the Ark.

'Missile launch successful,' the Queen B said, and Ollu thought the aye-eye sounded almost smug.

When the dust cleared Ollu could see a hole in the shard wall, three times the size of the Ark herself.

'Thank you, Queen B,' Ollu said in awe. 'That will do very well.'

There was no way she could keep an explosion that powerful a secret. The whole river bank was rimed with dust.

Pkye and Riki gave her a look of horrified and awed approval as they moored beside her and allowed the dark clothed C-Crew machete men to take up their position on the riverside of the wall, ready to engage the Grennish men once they left the safety of the homestead. That was the bit of the operation that Ollu was least sure of. How was Ma going to get the enemy to abandon the stronghold?

When she saw the pall of smoke above around the homestead, she understood. Something toxic was burning. The wind blew the smoke riverwards, making her eyes stream. It was hard to breathe. What was Ma burning? It smelled like ancient agi-chem. Had Davey been foolish enough to trade in that toxic stuff too?

It was a gamblers desperate tactic, but it worked.

The Grennish men ran out like smoked out rats, doubled up and coughing. Several staggered out of the homestead and lay on the floor, others were vomiting. Whatever Ma was burning was powerful stuff.

It was hard to see through the pall of noxious black smoke, but Ollu could make out enough to know that Ma and the others were ready for them.

From her position on deck she could see a small army of scrawny, raggedly dressed people, their faces swathed in scarves. They were an unimpressive sight, armed with shankers and clubs, bill hooks, rifles and bows and arrows. She saw Cassie, her whole face wrapped in a bandage, waving a machete and then through the smoke she saw, the tall, muscled form of Buzz, his K4 in his hand, running next to Ally's slim silhouette. Another gust of wind sent the black smoke billowing in her direction, so she was temporarily blinded as her eyes streamed. She heard the distinctive sound of a K4 firing, and then the kind of cheering that could only come with victory. There had been no need for the Ark's fire power or for Riki's machete men after all. The K4s, and whatever toxic evil Ma had set fire to, had been enough.

When the smoke cleared she could see the Grennish men had surrendered. There were no bodies on the field and all the fighters were busily extinguishing the toxic fire. Ma had won.

Ollu's knees went then. and she crumpled onto the Ark's deck, gasping for breath and sobbing. They hadn't died. None of them had died.

'What was that smoke?' Ratter said, his eyes red-rimmed and his face filthy.

'Something bad.' Ollu coughed. Ratter helped her to her feet. She safetied-up the boat and the two of them staggered off the Ark to join Pyke and Riki, who were coughing and spluttering by the remains of the shard wall. Both men were filthy with soot from the fire.

'If that's your Ma, she fights dirty,' Pyke said approvingly. 'I see where you get it from.'

'No one has died, have they? Surrender is a good thing,' Ollu said sharply.

'True. No one risks men if there's a peaceful way out,' he said. 'Toxic smoke though...' He glanced at her and had the grace to look uncomfortable, 'I wasn't going to betray you, Ollu, whatever Buzz thought. I was just making out that you were under my control rather than an ally. We still have a trade deal if you want it.'

'Yes,' she said. 'We have a trade deal, but you are never setting a foot anywhere near the Ark again.'

And then she saw what she had never thought to see again, Ma, staggering towards her, her face black and her eyes streaming. She was half supporting a grinning Joe G. Ollu forgot all her dignity as Captain of the Ark and ran, throwing herself into her mother's waiting arms. 'Ma! You're OK! I'm so sorry, Ma. I had to leave you to trade and the Missis' sister said...' She was sobbing as she spoke, so that it was a wonder that Ma understood a word. Perhaps she did not need too. She just kissed her brow and held her tightly, as if she would never let her go again.

Epilogue

Buzz

Buzz thought Pa would have been happy with his funeral in the end.

It took place a full six months after his death. By then they were in the depths of the savage British winter, but Pa was not forgotten and neither was his achievement in crossing the great ocean to renew lost ties of friendship in the spirit of science and civilisation, for the love of Christ crucified for the purification of Gaia.

Ollu, now officially Captain of the Ark following her mother's retirement, had made sure all the veterans of the Grennish war were invited to a celebration hosted jointly by Cassie and her ally, Missis Roberts, to celebrate victory and to mourn the dead. It was the biggest, most elaborate feast that Buzz had seen in all his time in the Isles and it rivalled anything the compound had to offer.

Ollu's new trade partners, Riki and Bel, Pyke and Angela, were there, dressed in the finest salvage anyone had ever seen. Lumpy Lil, and Ally, all the once enslaved, Ollu's Ma, Joe G, the twins and Davey's son were all there too. When Ollu had gone to inspect the big ship after the battle of the Robert's Homestead, Stell had disappeared and the child was lying in the crook of his father's dead arms.

It was hard to forgive them, but Davey's note to his Ma,

which included his own misspelled explanation, made it easier to understand what they had done. It would take a long time to restore the reputation of the Bargers, but Ollu, the Angel of the Ark, was already working on it and not doing badly. Ma had settled landside with Joe and set herself up as a teacher on Cassie's estate. Angela and Ally could both read now and Pyke was even talking of learning. Buzz was helping too, fixing up the tech they found. Flo had been disowned and Davey's barge given to Buzz and Ratter, to use on their trips between the City and the up-Temz. Sometimes he met with Bel and they shared their strange talents, though never when Riki was around.

Civilisation was about more than tech. Buzz could see that now. It wasn't about what you had, but what you did with it, how you shared it.

After the feasting and Pa's burial, Ratter spoke about his vision of a future in which he and Buzz and Ollu were a braid that would help unite Bad Water with good, and the old City with the up-Temz. He spoke like a prophet, and everyone was swept along with him.

Buzz was no prophet, no leader either, and he spoke more haltingly of his dream to reconnect the Isles of Britain with the mountain compound of his home. It was a dream as yet, but perhaps not an impossible one. He had got the *Queen B* working again and he had hopes that someday she would make contact with the *General* of his old home so that he could tell them of Pa's triumph, and of the civilisation Buzz had found in the Isles of Briton.

Pa would perhaps have been surprised at how many ordinary, human people were made of the right stuff, and how thoroughly Buzz had proved himself to be one of them.

Acknowledgements

WITH THANKS, AS always, for my family for their continued support of my compulsive writing habit, to Dr Farah Mendlesohn for her helpful comments on an early draft of this novel, to Kings Cross Critterati (Annie, Az, Cam, Sarah, Sue and Zena) whose enthusiasm for this project encouraged me to rework it, and to Jo Hall for her commitment to this story for which I am extremely grateful.

ABOUT THE AUTHOR

N M BROWNE has published nine YA novels with Bloomsbury here and in the US as 'N M Browne.' She has been twice nominated for the Carnegie medal and translated into Italian, Spanish, Dutch,and German.

She has published eight books for young children as 'Nicola Matthews' and has had poetry published in a number of literary magazines as 'Nick Browne' and is working on a debut collection.

She acts as a manuscript doctor and writing mentor and is currently teaching for Oxford University continuing education department as 'Dr Nicky Browne.'

Apart from these multiple identity issues, she lives an unremarkable life in SW London with her husband and whichever of her four children needs a bed.

A Selection of Other Titles From Kristell Ink

Spark and Carousel by Joanne Hall

Spark is a wanted man. On the run after causing the death of his mentor and wild with untamed magic, he arrives in Cape Carey where his latent talents make him the target of rival gangs. It is there that Carousel, a wire-walker and thief, takes him under her wing to guide him through the intrigues of the criminal underworld. But when Spark's magic cracks the world and releases demons from the hells beneath, two mages of his former order make it their mission to prevent his magic from spiralling out of control. They must find him before he falls into the clutches of those who would exploit his raw talent for their own gain, forcing Spark to confront a power he is not ready to handle. Meanwhile, a wealthy debutante learning magic in secret has her own plans for Spark and Carousel. But the sudden arrival of the mages throws her carefully laid plans into disarray and she unleashes a terrible evil onto the streets of the unsuspecting city—an evil only Spark's magic can control. Everyone wants a piece of Spark, but all Spark wants is to rid himself of his talents forever.

The Heir to the North by Steven Poore

"Caenthell will stay buried, and the North will not rise again until I freely offer my sword to a true descendant of the High Kings—or until one takes it from my dying hands!" With this curse, the Warlock Malessar destroyed Caenthell. The bloodline of the High Kings disappeared and the kingdom faded into dark legend until even stories of the deed lost their power.

But now there is an Heir to the North. Cassia hopes to make her reputation as a storyteller by witnessing a hardened soldier and a heroic princeling defeat Malessar and his foul curse. But neither of her companions are exactly as they appear, and the truth lies deep within stories that have been buried for centuries. As Cassia learns secrets both soldier and warlock have kept hidden since the fall of Caenthell, she discovers she can no longer merely bear witness. Cassia must become part of the story; she must choose a side and join the battle. The North will rise again.

kristell-ink.com

Printed in Great Britain
by Amazon